KALYPSO : 'TRITAGONIST'

by Emma Walker

Emma Walker

Copyright © Emma Walker 2006

This paperback edition first published in 2009

The right of Emma Walker to be identified as the Author of the Work has been asserted by her in accordance with the Copyright, Designs and Patents Act 1988.

All rights reserved. No part of this publication may be reproduced, stored in a retrieval system, or transmitted, in any form or by any means without the prior written permission of the author, nor be otherwise circulated in any form of binding or cover other than that in which it is published and without similar condition being imposed on the subsequent purchaser.

All characters in this publication are fictitious and any resemblance to real persons, living or dead, is purely coincidental.

ISBN: 978-0-9559788-2-1

Printed and bound by Lulu. Published by M Publications.

For Digory

Emma Walker

PROLOGUE

"Sing to me, O Muse, of the man,

that man of cunning and wiles,

forced to travel so far off course,

since conquering Troy's great walls."

"So, that's what happened to Odysseus, is it?"

Her face seemed worn and stony-grey, despite her proximity to the fire. We thought she might cry at our tale, but no tears fell from her eyes. Instead, Kalypso, the once beautiful and celebrated mistress of Odysseus, crouching there before us, stared longingly through the twitching flames. The wide cavern in which we sat was consumed with melancholy, as if her very emotions were feeding the air. We watched the crackling embers for a glimpse of that which entranced her so, deep within the blaze before us...

Kalypso : 'Tritagonist'

Why would you stay here alone, fair Kalypso?

Why would you not let Odysseus go?

How could that man of superior skill

be hindered against his own will?

Emma Walker

ONE

Kalypso : 'Tritagonist'

KALYPSO : MONODY

This is how it is for the mistress.

After he left me, I would walk the island.

Alone.

In my head, from behind that melancholic scenery of my thoughts, would appear Hermes. They call him the god of boundaries, of imagination and invention. The bridge between the worlds of gods and men. *Lord of the daydreamers.*

He would acquaint me with all that had passed, in versions of stories I would sometimes doubt and sometimes despise. Stories of how Odysseus had reached his homeland, how he had returned to his longed-for wife and child. Yes, perhaps he did think of me now and then, wondering at the horizon, memories slowly fading to fantasy.

But never enough for my liking.

"Why did you ever think to disrespect the marriage vows?"

incredulous Hermes would ask me.

Incredulous! *Thee or me?* Hermes the cheater; Hermes the thief. Dear to me though he is...

Such hypocrites, the gods. Zeus himself lay with countless women, behind the back of his 'perfect' wife Hera. Impregnating, fornicating lord of all gods. His many conquests sung by the bards. Hermes - that very same questioning Hermes - was the product of such an illicit affair, with Maia. My own eldest sister, Maia. *If you believe her stories.*

Not to mention the true reason Odysseus found himself washed upon my island – the infidelities of Helen and her rogue of a lover, Paris. Unfaithful, adulterous - and yet sanctioned by the goddess Aphrodite! Goddess of Love? *So they call her.* Yet what torment she wrought in the hearts of many with her vanity and preference!

"Why would you encourage a man to break his sacred vow?" insists Hermes.

As if I held him captive for all those years against his will!

As if I dragged Odysseus to me by force or witchcraft! Never once did I stir a charm or chant a spell for that man.

As if he hadn't *chosen* to keep sailing, rather than return straight home.

Oh yes. I mean what I say.

Kalypso : 'Tritagonist'

He *chose* to stay.

He needed me then.

As for the sanctity of the marriage vow - all those processions, animal sacrifices, and the passing of gifts and promises; the copious drinking and ritual eating; then that physical union... *Expected copulation.* All a public show for the sake of relatives and neighbours. *What a joyous way to celebrate a life-long bondage.*

Oh, I'm sure it meant a great deal at the time, to all involved. Then it served as an excuse, until finally it became a prison cell, outside of which everything enjoyable is thought to be a sin. All the hopes of the happy couple dashed as soon as they realise it isn't possible to love just one person forever; to never again be touched by the outside world, never long for more than that disappointingly small sphere they've found themselves in...

Don't look...

Don't touch...

Never desire...

Ah, the mistress. Wicked seductress; decadent temptress; a mischievous spirit in disguise. Too many people believe she holds an axe over the marriage. They tell of how, as nothing more than an enchanting thief, she takes all the best parts of the husband, leaving the guilt-ridden scraps for the poor suffering wife back home...

I say she holds a mirror to the dismay.

Yes, this is how it is for the mistress.

Ask after her and she is worthy of only a few indifferent comments, most of those mere speculation:

Kalypso... daughter of Atlas... prevented Odysseus from reaching his beloved wife and child in Ithaka for several years until (they say) the gods intervened and forced her hand...

Now look up the wife. *Perfect Penelope.* An entire collection of eloquently recited stories. An extensive list of suitors too! While here stands the mistress, lover of only one man, accused of the wrongdoing.

Penelope is entirely too indulged.

Kalypso : 'Tritagonist'

CHORUS : PARODOS

We want to hear your story, we said, and she closed her eyes, looked upward into the violet light of her mind...

We saw before her a raging sea, its black jaws yawning and foam-flecked. Waves crashed and clawed and spat at each other, competing to be the more ferocious. Dark waves grasped at a darker sky; bullying winds pushed and shoved from all bearings. The once opulent long boat, its oars, its towering mast, all its occupants were slowly battered, smashed and broken. Tossed aside like scraps. The noise of the storm, the destructive rain, those punishing waves would drown out the creaking timbers, the screams and shouts of dying men...

Only one sailor survived. Clinging weakly to a plank from the ship's side, a final piece of the mast clutched in his fist. Thrown in all directions, he gave up the fight against Nature, letting Her decide his course...

KOMMOS

"But why were you alone on the island in the first place?" we asked.

"Ah," she replied, drawing out the sound like a sigh. "An obvious question." A sad smile flickered across her mouth, the gentle creases bisecting her aged lips. Her hair, once a burnished mahogany, was now slashed with cords of silver-grey that hung down heavily beside her face and about her shoulders, framing her ancient, inscrutable beauty. Her eyes lightened with memories and the energy needed to tell them.

"You know, of course, my family background?"

We assented in a way that caused her to mumble, as older people do, at our polite acquiescence.

She must enlighten us none the less.

"Kalypso, Daughter of Atlas, King of Atlantis City, as well as countless colonies about the known world," she began her story grandly. But the pride in her words slowly gave way to scorn...

Kalypso : 'Tritagonist'

KALYPSO'S FIRST EPISODE

As with most men, one woman would never be enough for my father, and he held a particular fondness for women with too much water in their signs. Independent, unstoppable women who would envelope him with their love and then, just as easily, seem to slip away from him, like the clouds from the early morning sun. He would never learn...

I grew up with countless brothers and sisters, most of whom I barely knew, just as I never truly knew my father - was he this man, was he that? That's the beauty of court life - so many bards, so many gossips. Too many conflicting stories told. The little I knew of the real man was gathered by stealth. He could be attentive enough in the right moods, but he was a busy man, always preparing and plotting, disappearing for months or years, returning with a victory that would take as many months to celebrate amongst his countless allies as it had to win in the first place. I would admire him as a man, for he always looked grand and courageous. He was an imposing sort. As tall and as solid to me as a mountain, peaked in white, his voice the rumble of an avalanche. I could see the envy in the eyes of many who visited him. But for his role as a father, I had no opinion. Indeed, I had no comparison, and for a long time I assumed his behaviour was identical to that of any father. Only when I saw how some children of other families of the Court - especially slave children - were treated did I understand what I lacked.

Most of my sisters had an abundance of my father's spirit in them. If they were not following after hunters and warriors, helping to fight their battles, or singing and crying over the losses they doubtless caused themselves, they were chasing philandering "gods" and returning with illegitimate children. One after another, they spawned them. My father could hardly chastise them, since they were only following his virulent example; it was he, in his neglect, who allowed them more freedom than they should ever have had as young women. While he was barely around to watch over us, those left in charge were too busy fostering their own wealth and titles.

Yet, after my sister Asterope admitted to her second illegitimate pregnancy, my father decided enough was enough. He'd been missing out on too many allegiances, which in themselves might bring him additional wealth and ancestral land. After all, why have daughters if you cannot gain any benefit from them?

So it was that *I* paid the price for my sisters' indiscretions. My father arranged a marriage for me. Well, it was said to be for me, though I recall he paraded a couple of my other sisters out as well, just in case the groom's father might consider me unsuitable. Menelaus was the man named to be my husband. Menelaus. Son of Atreus, King of Mycenae - a family and land I knew nothing of. I call him a man now, yet we were both children, barely into puberty, at the time of our contract. I understood even then that the dowry paid for me was minimal and far easier to part with than most. It was the political possibilities of our union that interested my new father-in-law. Promises of military protection and guaranteed allegiances. Promises that, in the end, came to nothing.

Nevertheless, with my dowry agreed, I climbed aboard a great ship, with three maidservants and a few carefully selected bards, whose songs dealt solely and exhaustively with my father's unimpeachable honour. All of us bound for the Kingdom of Mycenae. Wherever that was.

I never did find out...

Emma Walker

KALYPSO'S SECOND EPISODE

I was told that the interminable sea journey to Mycenae would take an additional fortnight, as my new father-in-law had other errands to run (I being but one such errand, and nothing more). Ever since that journey, I've never wished to return to the sea. Aside from losing my home and all those places I had come to love and think on as my own (my favourite being that pretty corner of the garden my elder sisters liked to keep), I was being banished to another man's world for a crime I had yet to commit! Pre-emptive punishment. For my sake at least, my father should have welcomed my new husband into his house, not sent *me* away. But now, through me, he had sealed the allegiance he craved, and that was enough. I will never forgive him, nor my wanton sisters, for their treachery toward me; my father, abandoning me for his own gain, making me pay for the sins of my sisters...

I suffered seasickness for the first few days. You would think a woman with water in her bloodline and adventure in her ancestry would cope better with such a journey, but I never took to sailing. It didn't help that Atlantis City was to be found in one of the roughest stretches of the known ocean. The waves rolled and spun us like dropped discs. Out on deck, the air, though fresh, was heavy with damp and salt, and the spaces below suffered from the smells of humans and animals crammed in together.

 I very quickly learnt that life at sea bears little comparison to the careful structures of our life on land. Women were sparse on board; separate cabin space was in fact the scant protection offered by a simple linen curtain. I was reliably informed that a war ship would have been even less pleasant an experience for a female traveller than this mercantile vessel, but that did little to cure my resentment. We were told to stay as often as not in these linen 'cabins', for our own safety, but such rules lasted only for as long as land was in sight.

 My maidservants, sent as attendants and chaperones, soon grew bored of indulging my foul mood and sickness, and began to enjoy the new freedoms this voyage provided them. There were sailors, servants and passengers enough to keep them occupied and entertained; I, by stubborn choice, enjoyed precisely none of it. In their absence, I found that I was lodged next to a rather unruly group of bards, busy composing their doggerels for my upcoming wedding feast and any other events at which they might have a chance to perform. Most of these earnest individuals would leave the lower decks for large parts of the day - no doubt to practice out of earshot of one another, or to indulge in whatever they could find to do on board, which to my mind was very little but eat, sleep or reluctantly assist the crew in the more unsavoury elements of maritime routine. But one musician plucked and strummed and warbled for so long that, after one long day of it, I could stand no more.

Perhaps, were it not for his tuneless noise, I would never have left my safe isolation. At the time my only reason for leaving was so that I might regain to a more peaceful state of solitude. In an angry flurry of cloth and stamping feet, I prepared to vent my frustration on this unsuspecting man. I pictured myself demanding silence, making it plain I was of a far more important standing than he could ever be, and that I could have him thrown off this vessel at any moment I chose if he did not immediately comply with my wishes. Then (despite the possible financial ramifications it might bring upon my betrothed's household, which, in my anger, barely crossed my mind) I might even break his lyre, should I detect even a hint of insolence. That, I thought, would teach them all a good lesson. In my mind I was impetuous and authoritative, having more in common with my father than I could have realised. In reality, thanks to the unsettling voyage and my languid demeanour, I was slow and weak.

He was carefully balanced atop an amphora. I can still summon every detail of that moment. He appeared almost naked, but for the rumpled cloth around his midriff. And he held not a lyre, but a pandouris. Of all things! An old, battered, three-string pandouris.

Nearby candlelight danced on his skin; his shadow rocked casually behind him. I stood and watched as his one hand moved deftly along the instrument's neck, while the other plucked ferociously at its strings, and my mind began to wander inexplicably from its angry focus...

KOMMOS

"There is a magic to music," she said, her focus shifting suddenly from the flames, back to us, her startled audience. We felt as though we had been caught daydreaming during an important instruction. "Even the simplest of notes, played with an overflowing heart, can set the soul free to feel; an irresistible joy perhaps, or even a mysterious sadness. I felt that the first time I saw him, but I learnt to enjoy it much later.

"I was concentrating so hard on the movements of his fingers, sounds teased out with caresses and gentle plucking, that I neglected to take into account the pitch and yaw of the vessel, and fell straight onto my backside as it climbed a particularly violent swell. I sat there before him, his attention finally diverted from the cacophony he was making."

We tried not to look too amused by her misfortune, wanting to retain a respectful air of interest in her story, but she smiled briefly to herself.

"I cannot now remember which was the worse - the noise or the fall...?"

And we relaxed in the knowledge that deep in aged Kalypso there still lurked a sense of humour...

Emma Walker

KALYPSO'S THIRD EPISODE

I made quite a spectacle as I fell, pulling one of the linen sheets down with me. I wasn't sure if the ship had listed as violently as it seemed, or whether I'd exaggerated the movements in my head and weakened legs. I must have proved entertaining, for the young bard was distracted enough to put down his pandouris and laughingly extract me from the tangled heap I'd created. He propped me up, telling me to "rest easy" and "flow with the waves". Pointless, poetic-sounding words that stirred the irritation in my chest, mixing it with the anger and humiliation already trapped there. He haphazardly re-hung the fallen sheet, then fed me some wine, holding the cup with the same fingers he'd previously been using to play those discordant strings. After a couple of sips it occurred to me that his other arm was behind my neck, his hand spread wide and warm over my left shoulder. I could feel his rough skin against mine. I felt clammy, uncomfortable, and inexplicably wished to look and smell better. There was such heat flowing from his palm, only matched by the burning in my throat as the wine trickled down into my empty stomach. I lowered my eyes and, with a feeble voice, I attempted to object to this physical closeness.

"What would people say if they saw us sat like this?" I hissed.

"What do I care?" he replied blankly, in a tone that baldly contrasted his agitated movements. He continued to help me drink from his skyphos, one handle held by him, the other steadied by my own pale fingers, when suddenly, close to my ear I heard him whisper: "Besides, I will simply tell them you threw yourself at me." I heard him chuckle cruelly as I choked on my last mouthful of wine. He patted my back and withdrew his hand.

After filling a cup for himself, back to his pandouris he went. He did not, however, immediately return to his strumming, but merely placed the instrument on his lap, cradling it as a nurse would a baby. He reached into a cloth lying nearby and pulled out a pale loaf. Tearing it into two uneven pieces, he offered the smaller half to me. His movements were at once precise and utterly unselfconscious, and even as I watched, I felt my irritation dissolve in the warmth slowly climbing my neck and into my face. I did not like or respect him and yet he fascinated me somehow.

"Eat," he commanded as he began to chew. I shook my head and he gestured even more fervently that I should do as I was told.

"I don't feel hungry," I groaned. I was also a little insulted by his insistence - as if he had any power over me! But my stomach moaned so loudly that I feared my objections would not be heard over its own.

"Do you good," he persisted through another mouthful of bread, sliding the remaining portion towards me. "You should eat. It'll make you feel better."

"I doubt that," I mumbled, finally accepting his offering and reluctantly eating, piece by tiny piece, mindful of my churning stomach.

"Give you something to throw up later," he added in that same impish tone of his earlier whisper, and this time I saw the twinkle in his eye.

I could never explain why, but in that one moment, that single connecting glance, my destiny - that of the obedient, patient wife and mother I might have become - would be forever altered to what you see before you...

Kalypso : 'Tritagonist'

KALYPSO'S FOURTH EPISODE

My stomach was mildly content for a while, and as an ultimate test I even accepted a piece of bread dipped in oil, which was the most pleasant foodstuff I tasted during that whole journey. That and the wine soon restored my strength and I had at last begun to accept the unnatural balance of the sea. I even shared a sweet and sticky pomegranate, which he offered to me by hand, his fingers seeming to linger and brush keenly against mine, and I once more ached with that strange and compelling warmth.

And then he plucked a few strings and it all came flooding back.

"I left my bed to complain about *you*!" He looked up at me with brief amusement before returning to his tune. "I can't sleep with all that incessant... well, *practising*, I suppose *you'd* call it."

"It is impossible to remember a long poem without practice and repetition," he answered without ceasing his play, in such a matter-of-fact tenor that I felt quite sure the words were not his own.

"Can't you practice up on deck like the others?" I huffed. He chose to ignore me at first, and so I stared at him, hoping to make him uncomfortable.

"Of the two of us, I think it is you who should get some fresh air," he finally dismissed me. Before I had a chance to argue, or even feel disenchanted by what seemed like a snub, the lower decks began to fill with the heavy sound of passengers, pouring down from above, complaining about sea breezes and sudden rainfalls, and I was compelled to return to my restored linen cabin with the other women.

If I had thought the noise of one man to be bad, the sound of more than a dozen bards, noblemen, maidservants, not to mention off-duty crew, was so very disturbing, I began to think a walk outside in the rain might indeed be the best thing for me. It seemed such a long time since I had felt the sunlight on my skin - nearly a week, I inaccurately guessed. I looked over my shoulder at the gossiping maids, comparing notes and personal hilarities I had no interest in, and in which they had no intention of including me. Three silly little girls, I thought to myself, though two I knew to be far older than I. Still, they were without breeding and therefore of little consequence. Instead I could not help myself from surreptitiously peeking through a crack in the linen partitions, out through the crowd, to see if *he* was still there.

I caught sight of my future father-in-law talking earnestly with a tall, broad-shouldered man, most likely an important member of the crew, I decided. The former stood, finely and efficiently dressed, with damp spots on his clothes where the rain had caught him. He was neither flamboyant nor plain and I found it hard to tell if I would like living in that man's house. His stance seemed much more rigid than my father's. He had barely spoken directly to me since we met, but by the same token he had not been unkind. My sister Maia had already warned me that it would be my mother-in-law I would need to take more notice of. Especially since my husband had yet to do his military service, which would leave me, she laughed, "in effect, a war widow" for at least two years. In my head I planned to create a cosy little garden sanctuary, like the one I had been forced to leave behind, though my mind was racked with horrific images of being forced to do hateful things by this new family. What those hateful things might be were still an uncertain fantasy...

Suddenly I noticed my bard, sat very close by and looking straight at me through his dark curly fringe. I pulled the linen back around my face so that he would know I had spotted him looking, waiting for him to blush at his brazenness, but I confess I was not altogether surprised when he did not react so. He raised his eyebrows mischievously, and I responded with a disapproving scowl though I'm not sure how well I concealed the sudden and unfamiliar rush of excitement flowing through me.

"What?" I mouthed at him when I thought no one else could see. He intonated upwards with his eyes and chin and then winked. I hastily pulled the linen back across me to hide my blush and the smirk I could not hold back. My heart beat so fast I thought the whole ship could hear. Once I had regained control of my face, I pulled the linen back again, just a small way, to see if he was still there. He was, looking down at his pandouris, tenderly rubbing its shell with a piece of cloth. He looked up instantly, catching my eye. I exchanged a bashful smile for his impish one, and again he signalled towards the upper deck.

"But it's raining?" I whispered, and in case he couldn't hear me (which doubtless was the case), I emphasised my point with a ripple of my fingers. His response was simply to shrug coolly. Without any further reference to me, he placed the musical instrument on the floor, indicating to a fellow passenger to watch over it for him, who assented with aloof politeness. My bard stood up, slipped on his footwear, wrapped himself loosely in a cloak, and then slowly began to make his way through chattering and resting bodies, over boxes and other scattered objects, all the while making strange but discrete movements with his hands that only I would interpret.

I smiled, buzzing with curious excitement. Two of my accompanying maids were chatting over their small tapestries of flowers and deities; the third was curled up and resting. I pulled a long woollen cloak over my head and shoulders, then, carefully as I could, I departed the linen cage and followed the path of the young bard, making sure my face could not be easily seen by anyone who might recognise me. Only as I reached the steps leading to the upper deck did I realise my feet were bare. My sandals sat inside the linen cell and I could not risk a second walk through the crowded lower deck and the inquisitive eyes of those girls. A gale was blowing in intermittent flurries, and I gripped tightly at my cloak lest it blow away and completely reveal me.

He appeared above me, a temporary barrier against the wind, looking down at my hesitant attempts to climb the sodden steps.

"Is it very bad?" I asked as I took his hand and let him steady me, deliberately squeezing a little more tightly than necessary, wondering if he too could feel that warm flutter deep inside.

"Can't be, the sails are still up," he replied, though the thin veil of rain was already seeping through the wool of my cloak. Indeed, the two large, square sails flapped about noisily in the strong air above us. "Must be blowing us in the right direction at least," he added with some satisfaction. I screwed up my dampened face with obvious disappointment, and he laughed as if I had told some great joke.

After some amusement, we finally found a place to stand and avoid the confused looks of those sailors working on deck, positioning ourselves so that we could hold on to the ship without gusts of sea spray beating into our faces.

"So, who are you being sold to?" he asked, as a comment on my look of displeasure.

"I'm not being sold!" I protested, even though I realised that was probably the most accurate description of my circumstance I had heard for some time.

"Well then you must be a rarity," he quipped. "Anything with any value on this ship will be sold to someone."

"To whom are you being sold then, assuming you have some value?" I returned his mockery, though his response was more serious than I had anticipated.

"The highest bidder. Though it's not me they want, but the songs."

"You're too young to be a bard," I dismissed him.

"And you're too young to be a wife," was his quick retort. "But if it's what we are meant to be..."

Kalypso : 'Tritagonist'

KALYPSO'S FIFTH EPISODE

It was the first time we would stand together on deck, watching the sun arc over us and dip into a molten sea, the sky slipping a dark cloak onto gilded shoulders. I already knew it would not be the last, even before I knew his name. I had been surprised at how well informed he seemed regarding my predicament, but, as he assured me, ships' gossip is more expeditious in movement than that on land, he assured me.

He introduced himself as Damon. "Damon of Athens," he said, though even then it seemed unlikely that he truly called Athens home. From time to time I had seen and met Athenians at my father's house, and his accent seemed strangely at odds with theirs. When I pointed this out, he claimed his parents had moved to the City before his birth, and that he had picked up their Eleusian inflections as a youth. Looking back I suspect he carefully mixed everything he said with lies and half-truths. But if he had told me the sky was nothing but empty space, and the blue we see merely a silk cloth, put there by Zeus to stop the clouds floating away, I would have happily believed his theory and, furthermore, helped him to assure the world of it. I took everything he told me as truth, since he seemed to know so much more than I. The way he slipped easily between moods and tones - from wise to impish and back again to an earnest seriousness; it was frustrating, yet somehow alluring. And there was that look in his eyes, that playful flash that made my body vibrate like one of his plucked strings. No sooner had I basked in its warmth than it disappeared, like those same imprisoned clouds blown free of the sun. A cruel coldness would follow, yet my innocence and confusion would urge me closer to him.

We call it love, don't we? When someone has the power – proffered power - to make us happy and carefree, open to anything one moment, the next more miserable than we ever thought it possible to feel while still alive. We, in our ignorance, call that love. If it truly is love, to crave the attention and despair at the absence, then I felt sure Damon of Athens was my first love.

At least, he was the first man I'd ever known in this way. We would talk and confide together, until the seasickness and my anger at the betrayal and rejection by my own family drained away. Most often, we talked about him. Men, I already knew, have a propensity for talking about themselves, and I was not at all unhappy with this arrangement, since I hoped to learn a great deal from this wanderer. Here was I, on my first - and most likely last - real adventure from home, with so little knowledge of the world beyond my father's walls.

Damon of Athens, I hoped, would fill my head with stories of great lands I would never see, peopled by fascinating cultures I would never meet, feasting on foods I would never taste. Despite his being a bard, therefore naturally prone to exaggeration and fancy, I still had some faith in his honesty then.

I thrilled at the impropriety of our behaviour during those weeks on board. A closeted princess, a child and daughter, who had only ever seen life through the crack in the door that separated her father's court antics from the women's quarter. Suddenly I understood the allure of the freedom my maidservants felt. Ships were not States, and they had their own unspoken rules of decorum. Damon and I spent the next three days creeping about the ship, trying to find a quiet crook in which to talk. This was incredibly hard to do and frankly reckless, yet somehow we were often alone together. Who knows what might have happened had anyone uncovered this immoral behaviour of mine? I am still amazed we did not get caught and thoroughly reprimanded for it. Had my future father-in-law not been so distracted, and my maidservants been less self-indulgent, everything might have ended very differently. But the gods, it seemed, were on the side of love.

Damon wasn't tall; he was barely five-finger-widths taller than me. He might not even be considered striking in appearance by conventional standards. He had broad shoulders tapering softly to an almost feminine waist, a thicket of dark curly hair on his head, but barely a wisp anywhere on his torso. And short legs, I recall. But it was not his outward appearance, more his artistry; a voice that pulled me to him like an enchantment. There was mystery and heartbreak and no little amount of darkness to be found in that voice, and it made him as beautiful and unfathomable as the sea upon which we were borne.

His singing voice had in the past, he told me, attracted the attention of an uncle. This uncle, with his parents' consent, had become his mentor, instructing his apprentice as best he could in the lyra, the chitara - and his precious pandouris, of course - as well as familiarising him with the great myths and stories popular at feasts and celebrations. Damon claimed to have an inspired gift for translating news (and rumour too, I have no doubt) into poetic narrative, which had - at first - made his uncle very proud; a pride that gradually curdled into an insidious jealousy as he watched Damon grow beyond his own talents. His uncle would encourage patrons to hear Damon play only in accompaniment, or leave him over-familiar tales to recount to an indifferent crowd, while he would charm audiences alone with new compositions – some of which Damon had created, and for which he was rarely, if ever, publicly credited. "A bard's song," his uncle had told him, "is not his own once it leaves his lips, just as you cannot possess the muse - the muse possesses you."

One day, whilst in Scheria, his uncle met a woman. "Without doubt as beautiful as she was wily," Damon declared. She had fallen so in love with the music, the voice of his uncle, and the beautiful string melodies he played, that she had no choice but to make him fall in love with her too, so that he might never leave her. She spent many hours introducing his uncle to all the best households and patrons, until his name and his songs were upon the tongues of the wisest and worthiest in the land. But she had misjudged the receptacle in which she carefully placed her affections, for no matter how deeply he might have felt for her, he could never promise to remain in one place for very long. The bard is nomadic, both by trade and by nature, travelling wherever wind and tide might carry him, spreading tales and collecting stories. She could never be more important to him than his music. This woman, Damon recalled, had taken them both into her home as beloved guests, with all the warmth and hospitality the careworn traveller might wish for. But, a while later, as they made to leave, a great violence overcame her.

Damon did not reveal exactly how it had happened, but, in this lovesick woman's ensuing rage, his uncle had suffered a terrible blow to the head from which his vision had never fully recovered. Fortunately, thanks to her, he was by then such a respected entertainer that many patrons took pity on him. His name continued to flourish with popularity until it was virtually synonymous in their land with the bardic act. No respected festival was ever held at which he did not attend.

Damon chose instead to go his own way, make his own fame. With his uncle's intervention and his constant travelling, he had avoided the call to military duty so far, but he knew a return to Athens might put an end to that. It wasn't that he was afraid of fighting for his homeland, he said. His only fear was the loss of the time he would otherwise have had to spend composing and playing music. The thought of recounting an heroic tale in the first person, the chance to feel the weight of shield and spear in the hands, to tug upon the chariot reins, to hear the cries of wounded and dying men... It was seductive, he admitted. But it was nothing next to word and melody teased from the ether with knowing hands and a plaintive voice.

So Damon told it.

His stories wound such curious, unpredictable paths that to reciprocate with my own was often somewhat daunting. I would awkwardly relate tales from my childhood and from the darker corners of my father's house; tales I had heard of my father's adventures and which, alas, he had steadfastly refused to share with me himself ("A young girl's ears were too soft for such things," he had pronounced with a gentle lion's roar, kissing my forehead and sending me quickly away). I was almost relieved to see flickers of amusement at the corner's of Damon's mouth as I told of my sisters, and which of the unfortunate gods would take the blame for each pregnancy. But I could never tell these things as well as he might to me. Women, I supposed, were not great storytellers.

After four more days of snatched, clandestine meetings, a good deal of talking and sharing between us, and those anxious moments (for me, at least) in between, he declared proudly that he had composed me a song. My delight was palpable and even now my heart swells at the thought that I could inspire any man to words and music. Even a man like Damon. That star-lit night, as our fellow passengers reluctantly tackled another fish supper, Damon and I crouched on deck in relative seclusion behind a large crate, where he drew out his pandouris and began to tune the uppermost string.

"Why a pandouris?" I asked him, with an air of derision. "Surely all the best bards play lyres? Or chitaras? Are three strings really enough to touch a lady's heart?" I goaded. Yet despite my teasing, I already knew the answer to my question. I could never help but admire the sounds he managed to create.

"Why only three strings?" He shook his head as though this question were the very sign of ignorance in me. "Because those three strings can be plucked and strummed just as well as the great lyra can. But," he laughed as he told me, "the Muse leaves them alone."

"I do not wish to be blind before my time," Damon intoned half-seriously. "And is so simple," he explained, "that even a young woman might be able to master it with ease."

I found it easy to see why the muse might discard it on sight, as I did, next to other, more beautiful instruments. It is hard to imagine anyone could have preferred such an instrument over the visually beautiful, complex lyra - despite his insistent and, to my mind, absurd belief that one day every one would prefer it.

"My uncle thought it the lesser instrument when he made me play it to the crowds. He would predictably choose the chitara with which to dazzle and leave me the humble pandouris for simple accompaniment. But I learnt to play it so well that the audience could not contain their admiration. Now it is my life and my livelihood; indeed my first and greatest love. Besides, the muse may not favour the instrument anymore, but she does not abandon the player. She sends me plenty of inspiration. Did she not send me you, Kalypso?"

It is strange how a name bestowed on you by indifferent parents, and worn like an ill-fitting pair of sandals ever since, sounds almost poetic from the tongue of a true love. I thought it too awkward and consonant to be graceful, yet my heart bloomed in my chest as the word formed in his mouth and fell from his lips, and I craved hearing it again and again. As if sensing my delight, like a true performer seizing his moment, he began to strum:

"The stars are ashen grey next to my Kalypso's beauty,
Her voice is soft and sweeter than the god's ambrosia,
Fair Aphrodite could not stand to be compared to her,
Such beauty will be envied thus across our many seas..."

(Which is as much as I, in age, now remember.)

When he'd finished, I could not move. Should I have applauded or congratulated? The entertainer craves both, yet I was incapable of either. My whole being tingled with tiny dots of warmth I could not explain. Such a sensation as I never wanted to end. To think that he could admire me so very much as to compose a verse just for me! I would be immortal through the ages in the words of his love...

"I'll work on it every day - make it as wonderful as you, my goddess," he promised. In my dumb elation I must still have appeared pleased because I barely noticed him lower the pandouris to the ground and move closer to me. It was all a strange and wonderful dream. As his hand brushed my cheek, an infuriating voice in my head suddenly asked if this was right. Had not my sisters (whose bodies were so often used - as they told it - by Zeus, Poseidon, Ares...) also felt uncontrollably overcome, even paralysed by this perplexing ecstasy, before disasters befell them and great Atlas' household swelled a little larger? What if Damon was a god himself, disguised to seduce me? I imagined the furious look on my father's face if that were to be true...

Who cares? I thought as I succumbed to the fingers moving over my skin.

"I wish I could kiss you, Kalypso," he whispered so close to my face, I could feel the warm caress of his breath.

"Why can't you?" My question - an invitation - seemed unnaturally breathy. I was not myself - I did not sound like myself.

There are no such things as seducing gods, a rational voice inside my head tried to argue away my fears. *Who cares?* The same impious reply, like a chorus of my sisters. Dark and sinister in its reasoning, and yet exactly what I wanted to hear...

He did kiss me - or perhaps I kissed him? I remember it as very mutual and passionate. It lasted an eternity, as, I am led to understand, the best first kisses do, during which time I allowed his hands to tug at and smooth over my cloak, then my tunic, until finally he reached beneath.

"Are you sure about this?" he asked in a tone of sincerity, tenderly kissing my neck and cheeks to show that he was still eager. I held my mouth against his shoulder to stop myself crying out.

"No," I answered when I was finally able to speak. "But I want to anyway."

As our kisses grew in fervour and our bodies began to mould together, he suddenly stopped. As quickly as it had begun, he ended the moment and recovered himself. I lay where he left me, dishevelled and confused once again by his sudden change of heart. Had I said something wrong? He was not looking at me unkindly. Damon knew of my impending marriage. I had confessed it that first time we talked. Now, as he pulled away, seeming to protest my urgent need for him, I wondered if he did so because he was respecting me as another man's property? My mind flooded with the reality of our situation - crouched in a corner of a passenger ship, with my future father-in-law no doubt pacing about below us. I wondered if Damon had heard someone approaching nearby, or perhaps he was worried I might unwittingly make a noise and alert someone to our presence? With no answer forthcoming, I began to self-consciously rearrange my clothes as he watched. I raised myself up and he smiled warmly, but with a hint of cruel amusement I felt, at my insecurity. Gently, reassuringly, he stroked my hair.

"I think you should give this some thought," he at last explained. "If you are sure you want to do this, we can meet again tomorrow. There is a way... But I want you to think on this for now."

By "this" of course I knew what he meant. *Expected copulation...* For all that he might later have done to offend me, that withdrawal, that strange offer to let me retain my virginity until my dreaded wedding night with a stranger, was something I have curiously admired ever since. He certainly did not respect my future husband's place in all this, or he would never have made the offer at all. But to this day I have no idea if his respect for me was genuine, or just a well-worked game plan.

KALYPSO'S SIXTH EPISODE

Either way, it certainly worked in his favour. I could think of nothing else all night. I heard my maidservants chattering together, but caught none of the substance of their conversations. Having been given the choice, I found myself struggling with an impossible decision. Finally, my mind swimming in arguments, I took a desperate chance.

"Eudokia," I called to one of my maidservants, causing all three to fall uncomfortably silent.

"Yes, my lady?" she answered, turning reluctantly toward my direction, so that I felt like a small child walking in on a secret meeting, about to be berated for the intrusion. Remembering my place - and theirs - I sat up accordingly to face them.

"What would you think of a woman who chose to be intimate with one man, even though she was committed to another?" My cheeks burnt fiercely with each word. I fought to hold a steady gaze toward Eudokia, though I could not look at any of them directly, fearing they might sense some personal reason for my asking. Perhaps they already could? I felt sure my own behaviour had altered since my meetings with Damon and though it was not their place to judge me, they would certainly do so behind my back.

They said nothing at first, though some muffled clucking and scoffing was heard. Eudokia herself remained steadfastly silent.

"I'd think her a whore," was Melaina's eventual cold response. I was strangely taken aback. For all their own flirting and gossiping, I at least expected something of a debate on the subject. Instead, they all muttered in agreement and, when I in my surprise did not pursue the conversation further, each turned back to their own activities. Perhaps my strange mood swings during the trip had sufficiently alienated me from their interest? Or maybe they had instructions from my father not to encourage any kind of behaviour that might jeopardise the marital union? While I tried to understand their reaction without giving too much away, Ligys, the younger of the three, spoke up.

"Do you know such a questionable woman, my lady?" Her shrill voice cut through my speculation. I looked up to see the three young women, their eyes sparkling with accusation and malicious curiosity, watching my every flinch. My cheeks, which had only just cooled from their earlier embarrassment, tingled with renewed apprehension. What if all my sneaking about with Damon was not so secret after all?

"No," I laughed uneasily at their silent accusations. "Of course not."

I thought of creating an excuse for my question. I could try and pretend it was an attempt to join in with their gossiping conversations, and I made my tone imply as such. But since I doubted they would include me anyhow, I simply renewed my status over them. I did not have to explain myself to servants, I remembered. Nevertheless, I decided to avoid them as much as I could for the rest of the night. In fact, their attitude towards me had the worst possible outcome. I felt deflated and alone. I convinced myself that on this journey my only true companion had been Damon. I needed him more than ever. I *was* in love with him. But it was as much spite as love that, in the end, forced my decision. I had every intention of meeting Damon tomorrow and committing to what we had started.

Kalypso : 'Tritagonist'

KALYPSO : MONODY

Damon had said it so: if it is who we are meant to be, if the Fates have so chosen, then we cannot avoid our destiny. Damon's true destiny I could never fathom. Would he end up like his Uncle? Would the love of a woman only capture him by force and ill circumstance? Would he never stay still for fear of finally falling victim to life? He was so hard to read, I wondered that the Fates themselves were not constantly struggling to entangle him in one of their schemes.

Still. Poor Menelaus. I am sure he was never a bad man, as men go. He might well have been a good and loyal husband. But the Fates, it seemed, had destined him for a less than faithful wife. While he escaped my betrayal with barely a mark on his adolescent ego, so Klotho, spinner of life's great shroud, decreed a bigger misery would later come - for all of us - in his eventual wife; that beautiful, golden-haired Helen the Whore.

KOMMOS

"I was no stranger to the concept of sex, you understand."

Kalypso did not look at us for signs of shock or surprise at her admission. Instead, she tended gently to the fire, bidding the glowing embers to form their flame and burn brightly again, wafting the sweet-wood smells about us.

"It is true," she continued in our silence. "As a young girl, it was one of my own brothers who first taught me what to expect. We did not (I should point out to your now amusingly serious faces) perform the act for real. But I do recall, and have in fact never really forgotten, how he one day, while we were at play, suddenly mounted me and began to rock back and forth on top of me, his explanation being, "This is what mothers and fathers do"."

"Incest!" we cried in alarm. "The gods would punish you severely!"

She chuckled at us then; a throaty old woman's laugh, as if she had only teased us into this arousal.

"The gods?! Why, the gods themselves were the most incestuous beings to ever inhabit this world! They might tell you it was once necessary, but I've seen animals with better morals.

"Now, now; don't be so concerned at my blasphemy. At my age, I am quite sure they know how I feel. Besides, I do sincerely doubt my brother had any real notion of what he was doing to me than I did. Children are well known for innocently copying the behaviour of adults, while adults have a tendency to blindly follow the conduct of gods..."

KALYPSO'S SEVENTH EPISODE

The next day came soon enough. As I made to leave the linen chamber and learn what I supposed to be the true secrets of desire, Eudokia surprised me by taking my elbow in her hand, pleading me for a moment of time with her eyes. I knew I had arranged to meet Damon very soon and this unwanted interest caused an impatient reaction in me. But her eyes, at just that moment, seemed so sincere, as if her life depended on her passing this advice to me.

"What is it you want, Eudokia? I am in dire need of air," I snapped, retrieving my arm. She looked back over her shoulder but, unusually, not for her fellow conspirators' support, but quite the reverse it seemed.

"You asked what I might think of a woman who betrays the man to whom she is promised?" she whispered.

"Last night I did, yes," I answered, making it understood by my tone that this question was now irrelevant to me.

"Well," she paused, "I think it *is* a choice. An important one. In this life, my lady, you can either take what is on offer as it's offered, and live with the consequences; or you can wait for the *right* offer to come along..." She trailed off at the sound of stirring behind us, and began slowly to edge back to her fellow maids. I stood for a moment, watching the floor space she had presently vacated, thinking over her enigmatic words. What was she supposed to mean by waiting for the 'right' offer? In my reality, my choices were very few. I could be with Damon, the man I felt certain I loved and could love me, or Menelaus, the man to whom I was sold. I did not see how either fitted into her odd recommendations. And ultimately I did not have time to consider it further.

Damon had made an arrangement with one of the sailors. Apparently this was not the first of such deals made by passengers on this journey, so he explained to me as if that would alleviate any potential shame I might feel. (It did not.) It was an odd feeling to learn that we were not the only two people in need of such a peculiar privacy, considering the short length of the journey so far, and I understood that good money was made or promised for discretion. It was a very different world at sea, I decided. He told me he had lied about who I was, claiming I was instead one of my own maids; both our lives would depend on my identity not being known, thereby dispelling any gossipers who might spread the word to my future father-in-law. Nevertheless, there was still the awkward matter of reaching the small trapdoor that led to the very lowest storage deck. Time began to move so fast. My whole body pounded with anxiety. I did not know what I might be expected to do or what would be done to me, just as I still do not know how we got there without being noticed.

The cargo hold was low roofed and cramped, as well as cold and damp, though previous inhabitants had obviously made an effort to create the required space. I was anxious at how far down into the sea we now were. But Damon soon bolstered my spirits with wine and compliments, kisses and gentle touches, warming me with his own body heat, and by the time he entered me I had completely forgotten where we were.

Damon knew only too well what he was doing, but I don't suppose I had ever doubted that wouldn't be so. He moved my body about into positions that suited him, and I merely allowed him to arrange me any way he wished, often without words. There were moments when I wondered if I was doing what was expected of me. Half my mind tried to stay focused on the event, while the other half recalled the overheard stories of gossiping servant women. Damon had warned me not to make too much noise, but I heard myself moaning now and again, breathing as if in panic. Despite his earlier caution, I noticed this seemed to please him anyway, so I continued even when I was not sure if it fitted the moment.

I do still remember the movements, though it is so long ago now that I barely remember how it felt. Despite what I had been led to believe by my sisters, I cannot recall that it hurt me in any great way. There was some discomfort, but I put that down to the peculiarity of the experience. Mostly I remember the creaks of the wood as it arced and lurched below us; I recall the confusion in my mind, and his seeming entirely oblivious to that; and finally, after he was finished, I cannot forget the sudden emptiness and the strong need I had to be held in his arms and kissed as he had done so beforehand.

I was to be disappointed. I learnt no life-changing secrets and felt strangely empty. There was no surge of joy or affection. His intention, when all was done, was only to tidy himself and extricate us both from the scene as quickly as possible. Practical expedience. We parted company without so much as a brush of our fingers, and I returned to my bed, demanding a basin of water to wash myself. I had expected to feel elation, loved in abundance after such an act. Instead, just as I had the night before, I felt very alone. I washed and dressed myself in clean clothes, all the while trying not to give in to the tears that begged to fall from my eyes. Melaina and Ligys saw nothing but the same temperamental girl they'd had the misfortune to serve from the start of this journey. Eudokia's eyes, however, were filled with some form of pity when she looked on me that day. I dismissed her angrily then, but I often wonder about her now, and how it was that she knew. I think, in other circumstances, she might have had a story or two of her own to tell me, perhaps a heart in need of as much attention as mine. In another world, I might have enjoyed her friendship.

Later, when Damon and I met, sat on deck in one of our usual hiding places, everything between us seemed well enough. Damon was as calm as if nothing had happened; nothing had changed. I was disturbed by this. There was no increase in his affection for me, no suggestion of a repeat performance. Just Damon and I, and a pandouris between us. Even his choice of conversation was of the usual tone and now a little disappointing.

"Tell me your favourite tale, Kalypso, and I shall sing you a rhapsody."

I did not like to confess I was not in the mood for songs, since it was clear his attention had already returned to music. After some meagre thought, I dispassionately sighed: "Echo and Narcissus."

"Echo and Narcissus?" he scoffed. "Children's stories!"

I had no real favour for the choice, yet still I argued. "I happen to think it a very moving story." It had changed my whole consideration of echoes. I now felt a sadness whenever my voice came back to me in an empty room. Poor, unrequited Echo; forced to love a man who could only ever love himself.

Damon decided to indulge me in mockery. "Hmm... How about:

"Educated echo was a talker to the core.
She chattered, nattered, prattled 'til her friends found her a bore,
And she was such a virgin that all touch she did abhor,

So Pan would have her torn apart until she was no more."

"That's not the story at all!" I protested angrily, and he laughed at my temper. I had snapped childishly and felt a mixture of shame and hostility. "I said Echo and *Narcissus*, not Echo and Pan."

"I prefer that one," he dismissed me.

"Why? Because it's bloody and gory and makes Echo out to be inferior, just because she enjoys talking and doesn't like to be touched by men? Isn't that her choice? What right did he have to force her otherwise?" Damon was obviously disinterested by my outburst, but I continued regardless. "That's the real nonsense! Why should a male god feel so threatened by her desire to remain a virgin?" Damon let out a half-laugh.

"That's an ironic question coming from you, madam," he snorted. I felt my spine bristle. I was vulnerable and I realised he was enjoying that. So I changed tact.

"Why did you want to do *that* with *me*?" I asked him innocently. My meaning did not escape him and he too appeared to change his manner in an instant.

"Because, my Kalypso, you are beautiful. More beautiful than any other woman. With your beautiful eyes, beautiful skin, beautiful brown wavy hair..." His eyes and hands echoed each statement, stroking my skin, following the line of my tresses from the crown to the tips. His fingers followed the route back down my spine and he played gently with the ends of my windswept mane. "Your husband Menelaus will be a very lucky man," he added dreamily.

"Husband?" I scoffed, waking sharply from his soothing attention. "How could I possibly marry anyone but you now? I love you and you..." Something quavered behind his eyes. If I had been a little more experienced, more perceptive, I would have recognised the sudden chill I felt as stronger than a sea breeze.

"You cannot marry me," he spoke bluntly, letting go of my hair. "I told you. I'm a bard; a musician. I have to keep moving."

"Then so will I!" I interrupted him excitedly, a wonderful plan forming in my head of travels to new countries, the two of us meeting grand and interesting people... A plan he clearly second-guessed before I'd even spoken.

"It's just not possible, Kalypso."

"But of course it is! I could-"

"No!" He had raised his voice and the sound knocked me backward into a great dark hole. "I travel alone."

He made to leave, but I grasped his neck and shoulders desperately from behind, held him tight to me, whispered softly in his ear.

"I won't hurt you, Damon. I promise. I am not like your uncle's woman. You can love your music *and* me, as much as I love everything about you."

He was still for a moment. I could not see his face, so I believed him to be thinking and in my head I prayed fervently to the gods that he would make the right decision. Eventually, he relaxed his stiffened body. Half turning towards me, but not looking my way, he said, "Let me think about it." Then he unloosed my grip on him, picked up the pandouris and bid me goodnight with a brief kiss on the hand.

I had no idea what to make of all this, having never experienced such a complicated person before. I swung violently from positive hope - belief that the gods would put it right - to grave despair and fear of impending rejection. But how could he reject me, I reasoned, after what we had done together? We barely knew each other, and yet already we were in love. We had been so close I could not imagine us parting again.

I crept back to my bedding and sobbed the night through, feeling every rise and fall of the boat, every dip taking me lower into a state of self-made depression.

We did not speak the next day. It was the first day since we had met that this was the case. I made sure he saw me walk by on a number of occasions, despite being modestly covered by my shawl, yet he just as deliberately ignored me. Later that afternoon, with the shouts of "Land!" hailing from above, the upper decks slowly filled with clamouring, land-starved passengers, murmuring with excited relief, and causing no end of grief to the sailors at this most critical of moments. As the captain calmly but forcefully ushered them out of harms way, I saw a sight that caused me no end of anguish. Damon was stood talking quite intimately with Melaina, my third maidservant.

I had always found something distrustful about her, ever since she had been placed in my service. She was of foreign descent, with black, wiry hair and tanned, glowing skin that stood out strongly against the fairer-skinned people of my father's lands. Were she not dressed in the elegant clothes of a noblewoman's servant I suspect she could look quite frightening. Yet it was always her manner, more than her looks, which unsettled me; the way she relented to orders with a disdainful glint in her eye. I had nightmares of her one-day making me the servant, while she punished and admonished us all with nefarious glee.

Damon looked toward me while he addressed her, even smiled my way. I felt my blood boil, and chose to turn my back on them, secreting myself within the linen prison quarters I wished I'd never left. Melaina might have seemed the quietest of the three of my maids, but I'd long suspected she was also the most intelligent (Ligys being too easily coerced and Eudokia too compliant). I fought back angry tears as my brain replayed images of the previous day over and over. I could still feel where he had been, still smell him on my skin. Yet there he was behaving like I was just another passenger, just a fellow traveller, of no great importance. How could a love behave so cruelly?

I did not choose to validate my disappointed, unhappy thoughts straight away. I waited patiently after Melaina's return, for an appropriate moment to reproach her. As the excited conversation between the girls seemed to dim, I made my move.

"Melaina, who was that man you were speaking with earlier?"

"Which one?" she asked in a tone that cut through my soul. Eudokia blushed a little and looked away while Ligys chuckled under her breath.

"The one with that ridiculous instrument on his lap," I clarified. Melaina turned to me with an ugly smile.

"Why, that's Damon of Athens," she answered very coolly, the other two echoing her smile with matching grins that made me feel quite uneasy. "Everyone knows Damon, my lady. He was at our lordship - your father's - court just before we left. Played at one of the smaller parties in celebration of your impending marriage. Isn't that so, Eudokia?" The latter agreed coyly, again turning her face away, I thought to hide some private amusement.

"Perhaps we should ask him to come and play for us? Our own little private show?" Ligys suggested in her moronic, shrill voice. The other two stayed quiet, not yet wishing to echo the air of enthusiasm Ligys had given to this ridiculous comment, waiting instead on my response. I stood still too, pleased to have the chance to make them squirm for a moment - Ligys, most of all, feeling singled out in the discomforting silence, abandoned by her co-conspirators. I took a deep breath, pulled myself up tall, and looked all three straight in the eye, with particular emphasis on that perfidious Melaina.

"I think it quite unseemly of you - all of you - to be so openly standing about and talking with grown men as you have been. You have set a disgraceful example of my father's household," (I ignored the scoffs of irony at this comment - as much those in my own head as from my audience) "and I do not wish to see this behaviour repeated at any further point during this journey, nor at the house of my husband. Do you understand?" The three nodded coldly at the end of my reprimand. I made to go about my usual business, waiting for each of them to do the same, but caught Melaina by the arm as she left to fetch my food.

"If I ever see you talking to that man again, at any time, I will beat you myself, and you will leave my service thereafter." Melaina looked at me with some curious horror. I suspected this threat may have gone to far, but my anger had to be soothed. Something about the sudden fear I finally evoked in this sinister girl managed to do just that. I did not want to become a cruel mistress and had often felt hampered by my youth over my own social standing. But it was too rare that I chastised these girls, I realised. No wonder they had run riot throughout this entire trip. I knew my alienation from these girls - my slaves - was now complete.

Kalypso : 'Tritagonist'

KALYPSO'S EIGHTH EPISODE

Our ship docked at the port of Sulcis that evening, and I was informed that my future father-in-law had arranged lodgings for myself and my maidservants at the house of an acquaintance. I left the boat even more reluctantly than I had joined it, supported on the arms of Ligys and Eudokia, while Melaina followed behind with the small selection of my belongings needed for the brief sojourn. My stomach, having grown used to the jolts of the waves, now felt queasy at the stillness of the hard, dry ground. My feet tottered, and my accompaniment, suffering the same ills, were only just supportive enough. In fact, the girls were surprisingly sedate and competent, their conduct on land remarkably different and a great improvement from that they had displayed at sea. I wondered how much of this change in attitude was down to my earlier reprimand and would not have been surprised if Melaina had gossiped about my private conversation with her. As I looked over my shoulder, I certainly noticed a more sullen air to my third maidservant. Or so I thought.

I caught sight of Damon, through the bustle of sailors, passengers and locals, talking with a small group of men, laughing gaily at something. More of my repressed anger swelled up inside me. It may have been this additional tension, but more likely it was my poor sense of balance and disorientation. Either way, I vomited.

Most of the rest of the short journey to my overnight lodgings was a blur. My future father-in-law had shown enough concern to send someone to examine my health, and to make sure I had a comfortable and private room. He personally appointed a household servant for my general food and toilet needs. But beyond that, I heard nothing further from him as he immediately disappeared to a symposium or some such elsewhere. The women of the household seemed all too disinterested in their visitors - perhaps put out by the necessary changes in their accommodation. Left alone, I pondered on what Menelaus' father now thought of this weak young girl he had chosen as his son's wife and mother of his progeny. But there would be no way of telling from his stoic demeanour if he was disappointed. Lolling about in bed, awash with misery, I convinced myself that he was. If only he truly knew how disappointed he *should* be. But at that point in time, the disappointment was all mine.

I fantasised about Damon, creeping through the courtyard of this stranger's house, paying off my servant to allow him close to the women's quarters and to tell him which room was mine. Then he would crouch below it, trusty pandouris on his lap, and sing my song to me again. I strained my ears for any noise of that kind, but there was no music to be heard. Just the distant breath of the sea, the occasional sound of human and animal life, and water trickling in the courtyard.

For the first time on this trip I had a comfortable, anchored bed in my own private room, without the intrusive sounds of men snoring or instruments being plucked just beyond thin, makeshift walls. No waves beating against groaning wood, no tittle-tattle whispers of my maids from right next to me. This comparative new silence was deafening. I sat myself up in bed and reached down for some wine. With each sip, I visualised Damon's hand, holding the second handle of my cup, now more like a distant memory than a recent event. My eyes welled up again. What I would have given for a good friend at that moment. I even envied my maidservants, housed in the very next room to mine, always sharing secrets and stories between themselves. I leaned my head back against the wooden partition and at that moment discovered, although not as thin as linen, that these walls were still not quite thick enough to hide neighbouring voices.

Doubtless my maidservants, faced with their own version of privacy, had not reckoned so. For, with my ear pressed against the cold panel, I began to overhear almost every word spoken between them. It took me a few moments to differentiate the voices - shrill Ligys being easy enough, but Eudokia and Melaina both having softer voices that caused me to strain closer to hear more of what they said.

Ligys was rapid with excitement. "Oh do tell us what he said," she was insisting. "Tell us everything! What were the words he sang?" One of the other two was attempting to hush her, but continued her own encouragement for the story. The third then began to speak.

"He has asked me to meet him tonight! At the Harbour Meeting House, at ten of the hour."

"A meeting house? After dark? You can't possibly! If you're caught, you'd never survive the scandal! And she'd have you beaten black and blue for it!" the second more sensible voice was protesting, and I began to suspect this was Eudokia.

"Oh, it's worth the risk." The three girls giggled with nervous excitement.

"Now tell us about the song," came shrill Ligys' voice again.

"OK, but you mustn't laugh - even at the silly bits - and you must not tell a soul. I'm not sure if I remember it exactly, but it went something like this:

"The stars are ashen grey next to my pure Melaina's beauty,
her voice is soft and sweeter than the gods' ambrosia,
before this raven-haired, heavenly maid's story is over,
she will outdo her mistress's wealth for all the world to see."

There were protests at more laughter, and then the treacherous Melaina added, "He's promised to work on it every day - as he does our love, he said."

I could bear no more of this. With a scream of fury, I hurled my cup and contents across the room, where it smashed and splattered my host's tidy decor. Seconds later, my bedroom door knocked, opened swiftly, and there stood the house servant, candles in hand, quickly moving to light my oil lamp, and turning back to me with a worried look on her face.

"Lady Kalypso, you are unwell again?" She hovered nervously, keeping some distance lest, I supposed she thought, I might turn this sudden madness on her. I was so white hot with rage, I could not at first answer her. Without further fuss, she moved to the mess I had made and began to clear it up. As she worked silently and cautiously before me, keeping sideward watch of me, my three disloyal maidservants - those scurrilous snakes - slid through the doorway, saying nothing, assessing the situation for themselves.

"We heard you scream, my lady," Eudokia broke the silence. "We heard a crash. Is everything...?" Her voice trailed off as I turned to look at them. Ligys, as usual, shuffled uncomfortably behind the other two.

"Is there something we can do for you?" Melaina's cool voice cut through the moment like ice dropped onto fire. The steam rose through my body.

"Get out!" I screamed in their general direction. "Get out! Get back to your room and do not leave it again - not one of you - without my say so!" They stood stunned for a moment by my outburst. But as I began to swing my legs round to leave the bed, all three pushed their way swiftly through my door and back to their room. I heard their door close with a deliberate thud. The house servant had also paused in her work, unsure if my outburst was as much directed at her, and not wishing to draw any attention to her continued presence. I slumped on the edge of the bed and waved to her to carry on, before burying my shaking head in my hands. No tears came. I was beyond that now. I heard the scraping and clunking of the clean-up, the muffled voices behind the wall to my right. I could guess what they would be saying about mad Lady Kalypso, but I didn't care. I looked up just as the servant was making to leave, tiptoeing past with the shards of cup.

"Come back, I require your assistance," I ordered her. Warily she turned to face me, keeping her head bowed as I spoke. "Is there some way to lock that door?" I asked, motioning in the general direction of my maidservants' room.

"To lock the room next door?" the servant clarified tentatively. "Well, yes my lady."

"I wish you to do so. Immediately. I also wish you to find me a chaperone. *Discretely*." I added with a significant resonance to this last word.

"A chaperone, my lady?"

"Yes, a chaperone!" I echoed impatiently. "I wish to go out. Check the clepsydra on the way for the time - I did see one in the courtyard, did I not? I need to be at the Harbour Meeting House before ten of the hour."

"But a chaperone, at this time of night? Well, I'm not sure-"

"Find me one!" I yelled, before reminding her, "Discretely. No one must know of this but you, me and the chosen chaperone, or I shall make it my business to see you severely punished any way I can. I expect you to choose the chaperone with great care - a boy of honour. Understood?" I waved her out without a reply, not wishing to argue the point further, and watched her bow and depart in bewildered obedience.

Emma Walker

KALYPSO'S NINTH EPISODE

By the time my chaperone - a short, balding, stocky man with a kind enough look in his eye - appeared to collect me, it was past ten of the hour. At my command, he took me as quickly as he could to the meetinghouse and, perhaps under guarded warnings from my house servant, asked no questions along the way. Our destination itself was bustling with noise. A party of men, varied in ages, stood talking around tables outside the entrance. Beautiful youths sat on benches while their admiring elders looked on. Such things did not occur so much in my father's world, but I had heard plenty of stories about pederastic relations in foreign parts and was always filled with a lascivious curiosity on how and why. That night, however, I pulled my cloak tightly around me, hiding as much of my face as I could, while my chaperone looked up expectantly at me.

"Excuse me?" I began, catching the attention of a couple of the group, but my small companion motioned emphatically at me to stop.

"It is not seemly," he whispered close, "and we want no trouble, do we, your ladyship?" I did not like to tell him that was exactly what I wanted. "Why does your ladyship not tell me what it is we want from these men, and I shall attempt to approach them on your behalf?" He did have a kind and trusting voice. So I told him whom I was looking for, and he approached some of the men with great obeisance to make my request. Many of them looked on him like a dog that had just rolled in dung and I formed an instant dislike of those unnatural fellows. My chaperone, unaffected by their rudeness, returned presently with no news.

"None claim to know him, and as I cannot describe him to them, they are not being of much help, your ladyship," he apologised.

"Then we shall go in and speak with the proprietor," I replied. I saw his face flash with alarm, but under orders he led me inside the small establishment and speaking with another servant, attracted the attention of the owner toward me.

"Can I help you?" he asked in a rough and ungracious way.

"I'm looking for a man named Damon of Athens. We have an arrangement to meet here this evening." His face, during my speech changed from furtive to roguishly amused. I knew at once the conclusion he had drawn, but I ignored it.

"I'm not sure I know anyone by that name staying here," he said through a sickly smile, looking at me with expectant eyes. I motioned to my chaperone to hand me my purse, which he had concealed on himself at my request.

"Might I suggest," said I, handing him a suitable token, "that you check your rooms and courtyard to be sure?" He turned the ingot over in his fingers, only mildly impressed, then shuffled away through a back door. In his absence I busied myself with the view outside, listening without any real interest to the philosophising on the stars and the sea by the strange men's drinking party. An argument grew over what constituted real beauty - the face, the fingers...? Some guffawing arose at other suggestions...

"Melaina," came a voice from behind me, and I shuddered at its resemblance to that of a man I had thought once to know. "I'm sorry, my beauty, but when you didn't show at ten, I..."

Lowering my cloak from my head I turned to face him, and enjoyed every moment of watching the mortified expression set across his face. At first we simply stood, waiting for the other to pounce, our small audience tensing. As his face began to relax and a smug impression returned, I began my protests.

"How could you?" I demanded in as cool a voice as I could retain. "How could you use me so, discard me that coldly and then... Ugh! With one of my own maids? What have I ever done to you that I deserve such vile treatment?" He squirmed slightly in my angry gaze. "I thought you loved me as much as I do you?" I instantly realised my mistake. He shook his head, almost triumphantly.

"No, Kalypso! It is you who are at fault here and blaming me will do you no further credit. I told you who I was from the very start. I told you I was not one to settle, and I never once - never *once*, mark me - said that I loved you." I fought back angry tears, desperately trying to think of some example to argue this with, distraught that I could not. Had I really been such a fool as to believe that my feelings were the same as his? "I do adore you, Kalypso. You are still the most beautiful girl I have ever-"

"Shut up!" I yelled at him as I would a slave, half fearful of the public embarrassment his words might bring me at that moment. "Your lines are... I know now..."

As I struggled to find the right words to beat him with, another body appeared from behind. A tall, auburn-haired woman, who took hold of his shoulders as I had once done, and whispered provocatively in his ear, though loud enough for all to hear.

"When are you coming back to the room, lover? What's keeping you?" Following his gaze and catching my eye, she needed no further answers from him. "Who are you?" she asked, her tone altering rudely.

"How dare you? It is none of your business who I am, whore. I am here to speak with Damon of Athens, and I would be grateful if you would release him from your unfortunate grip and leave us immediately."

The woman did not move for a moment, but clearly found everything I said of some personal amusement. She stepped in front of Damon, looked me straight in the eye and asked, "Who? Damon of Athens? Lady, you have the wrong man. This is Aeschylus," she laughed, running her hand over his half-naked chest and kissing his cheek without a thought for her surroundings, and I felt my insides writhe. "Aeschylus of Thebes," she confirmed. "Has been so all the many years I've known him, ever since we were children together." Damon had stopped looking at me. His head hung low, his face was expressionless. When still no one in the room moved, the auburn-haired woman seemed to lose patience. "Look, lady, I don't know who you think you are, but Aeschylus and I have a good deal of catching up to do, so either leave of your own accord or I will show you the door myself!"

I pulled my cloak back over my head as if to make to leave, which seemed to satisfy her enough to escort her deceitful partner back to their private hole. As I watched them leave, an unexpected smile began to grow. First inside me, then across my face, until I could almost laugh out loud. I did not know what I had expected from this encounter, but I was to leave with far greater knowledge; the secrets of desire finally revealed themselves. Damon of Athens, or whatever his name really was, had been nothing but a coward. Fancy, a man allowing a woman to fight his battles! No wonder he was running from military service.

I called to my chaperone, who had stood surreptitiously in a corner this whole time. The housekeeper watched us both, thoroughly perplexed. Tying my cloak around my neck and leaving an extra (though smaller) ingot for his time, I turned to leave.

And there, in the doorway, stood Melaina, instantly stealing my smile.

We said nothing, holding each other's gaze like a war in itself. She let it be noted with one look that she knew everything she needed to about me now. Then she departed, and my chaperone and I followed, though we saw none of her throughout our return journey, and I was glad of that. How much had she overheard? What assumptions had she come to? I now realised all my previous threats were made fruitless. If I punished her for defying me in going to see Damon, she could raise questions on how I knew it to be so and cast doubt on my own improprieties. My power as her mistress was instantly usurped.

KALYPSO : MONODY

Of course, if I could have predicted the future, I would have happily left Melaina to Damon. They were two of a kind and most suited to each other. I would have liked to see her denigrated as I was, crying herself to sleep at the sheer folly of falling in love with such a man.

Instead, she was able to laugh off more than just a near mistake. Added to the humiliation I knew she would make me feel - whether she talked to others of this or not - I had the disappointment of realising I had never been loved or wanted. My first experience with a man was a miserable failure. I had dishonoured my father and my future husband. I had been no better than my immodest sisters in my conduct.

And I was alone.

Kalypso : 'Tritagonist'

KALYPSO'S TENTH EPISODE

The next day was the hardest of the journey. I was exhausted from a sleepless night, blighted by fears. I said not a word to my maidservants and chose instead to ask the house servant to bring my things to me while I dressed. While the men were out exercising, and my three girls attended to their own duties - returning my overnight artefacts to the ship - I was invited to the local temple by the ladies of the house to say a few prayers for my safety during the next part of my journey. It was suggested I also make an offering for a prosperous and productive marriage. I sheepishly agreed, leaving behind a large tip for my house servant with confidential instructions that she share it with my chaperone. Once at the temple, my prayers and offerings in the end were silent requests for forgiveness, retribution and escape. As much as I convinced myself that in the sanctity of the temple no one but the gods would know this, always my mind was filled with images of devious Melaina and how I might escape her guilt-ridden clutches or have my revenge. I had no idea how much of our encounter at the meetinghouse she had told the other two maids, as she well knew. Every time I caught her eye from then on I could see it. She had smelt my doom and was waiting for a chance to pronounce it. I tried to rationalise that she could have no useful purpose for injuring me, though blackmail could be her future plan. I had to find a way to stop this from happening.

Oh yes; I shall not lie. Her murder did cross my mind. But I would have struggled to get away with it on a ship. It would also not have absolved me from the terrible mistake I had made.

I spent the first day back on the ship reacquainting myself with its rocking movements and staying well behind the linen walls. I did not even check to see if Damon had rejoined the ship on its departure. I wasn't sure which I would have preferred - to never see him again, or to know where he was. My suspicions about my maidservants grew to such an extent that I forbade them do anything which brought them too close to me. They were to arrange for the ship's cooks to bring food straight to me and I would greet him - highly unorthodox, as I saw the captain think with a raised eyebrow, but my father-in-law did not seem to mind this sudden imposing spirit. I chose to tidy my own hair, even when the teeth on my comb snapped or the knots were a chore to unbind. I made sure any wine or water brought to me for drinking purposes was tried first in my presence. By Melaina. I insisted on it being her, and I could see that specious look in her eyes as she tried to match my malicious glare. Finally, and most telling of all no doubt, I insisted they arrange a second linen partition between my sleeping space and theirs. They had excluded me for long enough on this journey, and now I would do the same to them.

Towards late evening of the second day, my curiosity and loneliness got the better of me, and I found myself peeking out through the fabric walls. It seemed as though an age had passed since I'd last done so. I felt like a different woman. A woman, and not a young girl anymore. I looked across to the space where I had once seen cowardly Damon. Neither he, nor the amphora on which he had crouched were there any more. Instead, two passengers were snoozing on the bare floor. Not a pandouris in sight. I relaxed back, though I would not say I was relieved. I did feel a little stronger, with strength enough, I decided, to walk out on deck by myself. Wrapping up in a woollen shawl and remembering my sandals, undetected by those gossipy maids, I crept past bodies and marched up to a nice vantage point on the main deck. I held on to the ship's edge with one hand and quite enjoyed the feeling of the spray against my face. The sun was playing hide and seek above me, changing the temperature as it moved. Just on the horizon I saw a bulge in the sea. The dark line I assumed, even with my simple eyesight, must be land. I called out to one of the young sailors working nearby.

"Is that where we've just come from?" He walked over to see what I pointed at.

"No, my lady, that's close to where we're going *to*. Though not so close if we can help it. *That* is the island of Ogygia."

"Ogygia," I repeated, rolling the word around my mouth. "Why would you not want to go too near?" I asked curiously.

"Oh, it's a nice enough island, so they say. Uninhabited too by the likes of us. But it's the route to it, you see. It's renowned treacherous. You see all that water there?" He pointed to the stretch just between us and the ever-growing island, and I nodded, unable to avoid a glance at his bronzed muscles glinting in the sunlight. "You can't see them 'til you're close. And barely even then. But that water is filled with a type of rock that can cut a ship's hull to pieces in the wrong current. No, my lady," he added forlornly, "that's a shipwrecker's island."

I thanked him for his knowledge and he seemed quite pleased I had. "If you should need my assistance again, my lady, you just ask for Eurylokhos." To my surprise he rather cheekily winked at me and walked away.

Kalypso : 'Tritagonist'

PARABASIS

I recall much discomfited mirth as Odysseus listened to the tales of my youth, and we shared our little victories and defeats. It never ceased to surprise us how closely our lives had come to crossing on so many occasions.

"Eurylokhos!" Odysseus had shaken his head in amazement when I first told him. "He must have been a very young man when you met?"

"I *was* young myself once, you know," I said, pretending to take his words as an insult. "And that is assuming it's the same man."

"Oh, it must be, I'm sure. How that sounds like him!" he chuckled away. "Never one to shy away from the ladies. I can't believe you met Eurylokhos! He was one of my finest men, my good friend. He might have been my *best* friend were he not such an argumentative man! And not so clever at arguing me with words - for that I might have enjoyed! I met him while at Troy, you know. He was a good soldier. He was my Second as we sailed home. Impetuous man. But fun for it.

"We stopped off at Aeaea one time, and pulled lots to see who wanted to approach the locals for supplies. The moment he won, he saw it more as a privilege - a challenge even - than a chore. Off he went with a couple of other poor souls who would have been obliged to listen to his officious decision making for the whole route, no doubt. If it weren't for the fact that he never thought anything through for too long, he'd have made a great captain - so fearless and enthusiastic.

"Anyway, off he went and we heard nothing from him or the men for several hours. Then, from out of nowhere, he came bounding back, panting marvellously; he was so out of breath. He must have run for miles - he sounded like a wild animal as he reached us! When we finally got him to speak he was in a terrible rage. It seems that while trying to collect supplies, the men had stumbled on a... well, a more than welcoming house run by some particularly beautiful ladies, let's say."

"A whore house?" I interrupted, raising my eyebrows with amused consternation.

"You would not have called those ladies whores had you seen them - no, even you would not, Kalypso. And as for *house* - well, it was grander still than that. How such women came by that palace I do not know."

"Oh, so you saw it for yourself?" I questioned light-heartedly.

"I assure you, nymph," he implored, prodding me playfully, "I had no more choice in that than I did in ending up here! My men were foolish enough to accept a drink, and the next thing we knew they were offering every kind of service we could ever desire - which wasn't as much as you'd think after so long without such attention - but at a price those fools were never likely to afford! Something they'd forgotten to check before taking wine and women. It fell to me to bargain with the woman in charge for my men to be excused for their folly and, after some... wrangling, I struck a deal." He blushed a moment, refusing to make any more of his indiscretions, quelling a wistful smile.

"But Euylokhos! My word, for a ladies man, he still gave those boys a real talking to for entering that honey trap."

Odysseus laughed at his own memories. Below us, a wave crashed heavily against the shoreline, breaking the spell, and his face suddenly changed. Seeing in him a need for comfort, I hugged his arm and leaned in close. I did not need to ask what happened to Eurylokhos. Odysseus eyes could see him even then. Out in the waves; he was lost.

Emma Walker

KALYPSO'S ELEVENTH EPISODE

From my private space on deck, I stood and watched the island of Ogygia loom along the length of one side of the boat until I felt as though I could lift it up in one hand, pinching it out of the waters. As I wondered how much freedom one could feel, living alone on such a beautiful, deserted place, I heard a sound behind me that caused my heart to throb against my ribs, a sickness circling my belly. It was the unmistakable sound of the pandouris.

I turned as calmly as I could, my body shaking and fluttering uncontrollably inside. There he sat, in full profile, half a ship's length away. He seemed intent on that infernal plucking and strumming, but his head and his eyes turned to meet my gaze, looked away, then back again. His eyes seemed dejected, his body language apologetic but inviting. He smiled, that same pathetic smile of shame and remorse he had delivered at the meetinghouse. Remembering that pathetic exhibition of his was an effective boost to my nerves. I could see what he wanted - my forgiveness, my concession. My idiotic devotion. I stood still, trying to decide which of us was the real fool, remembering what a good actor he could be - already a protagonist and deuteragonist in his own little drama! The gods alone knew how many parts he played altogether, how many names he used and masks he wore...

With renewed strength, I marched past this unimpressive musician, back to my linen prison, a plan forming in my head. A plan so ridiculous I could hardly believe in it, and certainly did not expect to accomplish it. Yet it seemed, at that time, to be my only chance of freedom. I would escape the madness I had brought upon myself or die trying.

I could not now marry the man chosen to be my husband. Even if I could learn to live with my secret disgrace, Melaina would always be there to remind me. Who knew what her plans were for me? If I tried to rid myself of her, nothing but murder would obtain her silence. Despite my revulsion towards her, I did not expect to have the stomach for such a deed, and arranging for her death by other means would only increase my guilt. Besides, I still had no idea how much she had told Eudokia and Ligys, or any other person. Where would it end? One of them would be sure to speak up. Ligys, no doubt. My thoughts turned to the modest chaperone who had witnessed the entire scene only a few nights past. What if they were to question him, those hard-hearted soldiers of my father-in-law's army? How would he cope? At the very least, I decided, I should try and save the innocent from such agonies.

Finally, there was Damon. Something about the look on his face made me realise that if I stayed on the ship too much longer with him, I might destroy myself all over again. For all the hate inside me over what he had done, I could still see the man who had until now made this journey bearable, changed my life in a way I could never alter. He really had been my only companion and I was already feeling the emptiness and self-pity his betrayal had left me with. How easy it would have been to give myself away again.

Hastily, I filled a large purse with a few simple possessions - a hand mirror and my broken shell comb (the last gift from my father, so ironically damaged), some ingots of modest value and a few favoured items of jewellery. I then tied it tightly around my waist and against one hip. To the other side I added a leather flask of wine I hoped might last the tumult I was about to put it through. I wrapped myself in a cloak and strapped it tight against me with a leather belt. All the while my mind was wild with thoughts, questions, instructions... Could I really do this? If I failed, at worst I would arrive a sopping mass at Hades. Or perhaps it would be a greater calamity to be saved and have to explain my defection. I envisioned a swift return journey to my father, greeted as a dishonourable child, and treated to a lifetime locked away for madness, mocked for my failure.

I convinced myself this plan would be the only way to make everything right.

Kalypso : 'Tritagonist'

The sun was close to setting behind us. The dark, thin line of Ogygia was still plainly visible, though I knew I would have to move fast. A star-filled sky was approaching. Waves bounced us gently over elegant troughs, but the wind was good, billowing out the sails from behind. Everything seemed pleasant. Damon's pandouris was quiet for a change, and he was stood talking with another man. As he saw me approach he excused himself and waited for my greeting. I gave no direct indication that I would converse with him, but made to saunter by him as close as possible, so that I heard him speak quite clearly.

"That's an unusual look for you, my lady?" he indicated my outfit, particularly my visible belt and those hip-packages protruding beneath my cloak, which must indeed have looked quite odd. I said nothing in return, but as I passed him, I let slip a few ingots from my hand, which clattered close to his feet. I stopped, turned and looked at him, then down at the littered floor. He shook his head with something like ridicule, then resting his pandouris against the side of the deck, he tamely leant down to retrieve my valuables, foolishly succumbing to *my* trap.

Seeing my one good chance, I grabbed the pandouris from behind its distracted owner and ran as fast as I could to a point on the other side of the deck, facing the mysterious island. I climbed on to the ship's edge and sat with my legs hanging over, holding the pandouris aloft in one hand and gripping on for dear life with the other. I had no idea how long I would be able to balance myself like that. The speed at which we were travelling came as a surprise to me and the darkening water looked to be much further down than I had imagined it. Already my nerves were faltering.

"Stay back!" I yelled at the approaching sight of Damon and some other flabbergasted men, most likely sailors. I shook the pandouris for emphasis, and saw Damon motion to everyone to do as I'd said.

"What is it you want, Kalypso?" he asked in a frightened tone. "What? Whatever it is, I'm sure we can discuss it calmly." I watched the contortions cross his brow as he thought desperately. I knew he only cared for one thing in this scenario and it was not me. I let a triumphant smile spread across my dampening face, and very slowly lowered the pandouris. Just as he looked ready to relax I made some deliberate, shuffling moves toward the sea, dangling his precious instrument just above the rapacious wake below me. Again he motioned for the increasing audience to stay back, and reached out a hand in a pathetic plea. "Please," he whimpered, almost buckling at the knees, "just tell me. You really want us to marry? Just come down and I'll have the arrangements made as soon as we reach the next harbour."

"Is it just women you cheat, Damon of Athens, or are you a traitor to men as well, Aeschylus of Thebes?" I slurred. Though no one else seemed to understand our conversation in the slightest, his cheeks rouged and his temper snapped.

"What would a woman know of a man's love?" he spat.

"More than a man like you could ever know of a woman's!" I hit back. In the distance now, I saw a crowd of inquisitive onlookers forming, this being the best and most entertainment they'd seen in a long time. Among them, of course, stood my father-in-law, a man of no expression even in this humiliating moment; and my maidservants - two with a look of horror and disbelief, while treacherous Melaina watched me intently, with calm curiosity.

"Captain," I yelled to no one in particular (not being completely sure who the Captain was), "this man, who claims he heralds from both Athens and Thebes no less, has cheated Greece of a soldier in her army for the last two years by hiding from his military calling and civic duty." I waited for some background muttering to quieten, watching Damon's nostrils flare at my allegation. No one knew quite what to say, but I had not finished.

"Furthermore," I cried aloud to the over-crowded deck in the flickering torchlight, "those three women who call themselves my maids have in fact, Captain, been entertaining your sailors in private throughout this whole voyage, accepting gifts by return, like the little hetaerae they wish they could be! Look on the whores of your ship, Captain." Many eyes turned on the three girls. Ligys burst into tears on poor Eudokia's shoulder; Melaina burned with as much rage as her partner in crime before me. The man I assumed to be the Captain muttered something about not wanting women on his vessels, which caused some chortling close by him.

"Woman, desist!" Damon yelled, returning all attention to our little scene. "Stop your unwarranted insults! You have gone mad! How can you say such things about these innocent girls? You are clearly unwell... Perhaps it is the anxiety of your impending nuptials?" he added smugly, almost causing me to falter in my attack. For a moment I could not decide if he was deliberately wounding me before the man who would have been my father-in-law, or giving me a chance to excuse myself and return to my damaged life. "Get down from there now, give me back what is mine, and no one will speak of this again."

By way of response, I released my little finger from the sea-sprayed pandouris. He noted this with a quick glance but stood defiant before me. My middle fingers slowly loosened their grip, and his body shifted uncomfortably as the instrument swung like an erratic pendulum caught in the breeze, scarcely held, so it seemed, by my thumb and forefinger (though in truth I was gripping on to it almost as hard as I held the boat's side beneath me).

I fixed his nervous figure with a hard stare and through gritted teeth I spoke:

"Finally, to *you* then. You have dishonoured and deceived me, as well as my treacherous, good-for-nothing, inconsiderate maid, and who knows how many others beside. Thanks to you, I have lost *my* life, *my* future livelihood, *and* my first love. But I shall die a vengeful, happy woman yet..."

And so I let go of the wood.

PARABASIS

"But, how did you come to be *here*?" Odysseus asked. "On this island?"

"I fell from a ship," I answered, a little too nonchalantly.

"You fell?" he repeated, and I confirmed it, though I could not look at him as I did. I felt guilty to be telling him such a half-truth. Almost as much as I was ashamed of the childish reality of my past behaviour.

"Were you hurt?" he asked, showing great concern for me in his eyes and upon his brow. I found myself laughing at the irony.

"Yes," I said. "At the time I thought I had been hurt more than it might ever be possible to recover from." I looked at his troubled face, remembering the foolishness of my immature self, and added, "But now I know otherwise. They were mere scratches..."

I eventually told Odysseus about the voyage, though I did not dwell on Damon's story as much as I have with you. As I reached that same point in the story, my hand letting go of the ship, a sudden excitement came over him.

"Wait a moment," he interrupted, "I think I know this story!"

"What do you mean?" I laughed. "How can you know about this? I haven't told you before. Have I?" He was pensive a moment and, as was usual when he got that look in his eye, his attention turned to the waves. "What do you mean?" I repeated hesitantly.

"It was Eurylokhos that told me. Told *us*, I should say. I remember now. He didn't give your name, but you must be the same woman. If there are two of you, then may the gods damn us all!" He joked.

"We saw this island, in the distance, long before the storm hit. Some of the men were keen to sail in, try and find some supplies and fresh water. The sea was growing rough, and I felt inclined to agree with their logic. Eurylokhos, however, recognised the place instantly as Ogygia, the haunted isle. He ordered us to steer as far from it as possible, which had us all curious. He was usually first to jump at the chance to land and explore. Now he looked at us with serious concern. I asked him, what was his fear? He explained about the hidden rocks beneath the waves, the peril of so many ships in the past. But my crew were not to be swayed by any little rocks! We'd snuck through giant cliffs renowned for their avalanches - huge rock boulders that would fall and smash passing ships to pieces at the slightest whisper of a sound! We'd escaped so many scrapes and near misses - by the gods, we were war heroes, weren't we? We were invincible!" Odysseus paused and rubbed his sad, furrowed brow at this recount of his old self.

"Eurylokhos refused to let me change course, until we were almost at loggerheads once again. A lot of bad words were said between us - coward-calling on my part, poor leadership accusations from him, and so forth. As if all those complaints we'd withheld from each other for so long were being aired in one last confession... Finally, competing with all our concerns, he told us that, although it was *said* that the rocks would be our end, there was another story, known by all good sailors, about this lonely island.

"This strip of sea, he explained to us, is known as ship wrecker's alley. So many vessels have strayed by this route and have never been heard of again. Naturally there were rumours of sea monsters and other ungodly things, but never any proof. All that changed one day. Only one man has survived death in those waters, after his boat was overturned, by swimming as hard as he could against the winds and tide, eventually washing up on the shores of Ichnusa. Aside from the immense fatigue the man suffered after his ordeal, he was also unable to speak for months, even after he seemed to have regained his physical strength. When at last he spoke of his nightmare, he shook and shook throughout his tale until the effort made him collapse. What he told was this:

"He and his fellow shipmates had seen Ogygia, the haunted isle, in the distance, much as we had. They also made to sail towards it, but as they did so the clouds began to gather above them and the rains began to fall. The winds picked up until the boat was being tossed almost uncontrollably in the waters. These were experienced boatmen, and they worked the sails and oars as best they could. Yet the nearer they came to the island, the worse the sea's temper grew. And then the wailing sounds began. Deep hums and high-pitched squeals that seemed to come from all about them, but particularly from below. The seamen were convinced they heard names being whispered in their ears as the gales blew against them.

Growing increasingly uneasy, some of the more superstitious men decided to encourage the rest to turn back - nothing was worth losing a ship over, after all. Following a brief discussion, all agreed to change direction. Which they tried to do. But the oars were now battling against an evil tide, and as the men looked over the edge of the ship, they saw what looked to be bodies floating up toward the hull. White bodies, it seemed to them, with long wavy hair and grasping fingers stretching out towards them. The seamen, though frightened, were still brave and curious explorers, who refused to be spooked by tricks of the light - mere reflections, they agreed aloud, combined with the underwater life being stirred to the surface by a roughly churning sea, they proclaimed. And so they tried to go on, rowing as fast as they could against a strengthening tide, but still seeming to float backwards more quickly than they were pushing forward. More and more of these pale figures appeared and the great wailing increased all around them.

The ghostly beings began to strike the boat from underneath, grabbing and tugging at it. The oarsmen, those who were closest to the attack, felt their oars ripped violently from their hands. Many hardened men began to panic, desperate to find a safe part of the boat to hide within, but there was none. The white creatures ripped and pulled and split at the wood, smashing through it, pushing it in all directions with their incredible might, until the great holes forming at the base let in so much water that the boat sank more quickly than a tossed stone. How that one man managed to survive, even he could not readily explain. The last thing he heard were the petrified screams of his men from behind him as they were dragged by the white beasts, down beneath the terrifying waters.

"The wise men of Ichnusa, on listening to this man's story, explained that the beings he had seen must have been the spirits of those men and women who had drowned at that place in times past. Stuck in waters even Poseidon himself had abandoned, they could not see the way to Hades and had not yet accepted they were dead. Each ship that sailed by was seen as a means to their rescue, and in their attempts to climb onboard, the souls of the undead would rip the boat of the living apart with their supernatural strength..."

Odysseus, you might know, was a good storyteller and I shuddered at his tale.

"You don't believe in all that, do you?" I asked him, looking out at the apparently calm waves he had described as so petrifying.

Kalypso : 'Tritagonist'

"Perhaps; perhaps not," he replied. "All stories have a root of truth, do they not? Perhaps they saw seaweed and rocks, perhaps there *are* things in the water - in this entire world - that we can never hope to explain. Either way, the story spread quickly enough amongst all seafaring people, and so this island has been avoided ever since, with plenty of tales of near misses and possible sightings to add to the collection. But I did ask Eurylokhos exactly the same question you have just asked me. Why should a sensible, fearless seaman like he, be afraid of an old wives tale? He answered thus:

"During one of his father's routine passages, there was an incident close to this island. A young woman, clearly mad or spurned, perhaps both - *his* words, Kalypso, before you rebuke me - had threatened some of the passengers before jumping overboard with a stolen instrument in her hands. All a very curious show that no one could quite explain, nor ever did. Usually a sailor would gladly make an attempt to save someone if they thought it possible - no one likes to lose a fare, after all. But this time no one, except the apparent owner of the musical instrument, made any moves to jump in after her. Not even impetuous Eurylokhos, he told us. The deprived bard was desperate to get his stolen instrument back, and many of the sailors had to hold him forcefully down, telling *him* of the undead below.

Eurylokhos' own father informed the man that, true story or not, he had no intention of putting the rest of his crew or his passengers at risk. In the end, an older nobleman made the desperate man cease his demands, refusing the captain's suggestion to briefly weigh anchor, and stating that any man who tried to jump over and rescue the girl would be left behind with her. And that was an end to it. Eurylokhos said it changed that whole voyage. There were whispers that a woman's wailing was heard for two nights after the incident, and many unsettling suggestions of sea beasts, which did not stop until all the travellers on that vessel were safely docked at port. It was one of the more sombre journeys he'd ever been witness to, he said - and some of ours would have won no pleasure prize! The younger Eurylokhos, I realised, had learnt that superstition is a powerful argument against the foolhardiness of men. Even the bravest among us will weaken if he thinks that Hades is chasing him."

"So they left me?"

"I'm sorry Kalypso," he said, pausing to consider my distress. He kissed my forehead and pulled me close to him.

"I expect the nobleman was my future father-in-law," I thought aloud after a pause. "I wonder how he managed to explain my behaviour to my father?"

"I doubt he had much chance to, if it *was* Atreus," Odysseus replied, and I could feel the movement of his chin against my crown as he spoke.

"Why?" I asked dolefully. Odysseus pulled back and looked at me with some surprise, then smiled sympathetically and shook his head.

"I keep forgetting, you've been here all this time, you won't have heard any news since you arrived. Menelaus' father was murdered, not long after his return from that voyage, I should think."

I was taken aback by the horror of this. That proud unemotional man, whom I had expected out of sheer displeasure to never speak of me again, was actually silenced forever, knowing his last action was to make a terrible match for his son. I felt some considerable remorse about his death, trying to decide who might have committed the deed.

"Did my father retract his offer of protection?" I asked.

"Your father offered him protection? Well, that was unfortunate. It wasn't any army or political opponent that did for him, Kalypso. Nor, I should say, your father or anyone, to my knowledge, of your father's kin. Atreus was killed by a family member - a nephew, if I remember rightly. All your father's protection couldn't save a man from death at the unsuspected hands of his nearest and dearest. It's one of our greatest fears..."

We sat and watched the water floating energetically back and forth below us, lost in our own thoughts on mortality. The sun, as if to join in with our mood, was beginning to hide itself away.

"We should make a sacrifice," I decided. "One or two goats?" I suggested. "We can make it in the name of any god you think best - Athene, Poseidon, Zeus?" At first he did not reply, playing with some sand beside him, watching it fall between his fingers.

"What good will it do?" he eventually asked in a small, tired voice.

"Well... We can ask the god, or gods, to help lead these lost souls to Hades? Show them the way, so they're no longer trapped? Clear the path to the island?"

He looked up, adding to the list of reasons, "And make it easier for me to get home?"

I ignored his remark and melancholy silence floated down between us.

"You were to marry Menelaus?" Odysseus broke the gloom. "Hah! Just think of it: if you had married Menelaus, and I had never made that naïve oath, hundreds of good souls might now be alive, instead of frightening the halls of Hades with their battle scars!"

"It feels callous to laugh at the past," I said.

"It *is* callous to laugh," he granted, yet he too could not help but laugh with me, incredulous at this development in our stories. "What a small world," he mused, wistfully looking out across the ocean.

"Wondrous small world," I confirmed, leaning into his broad, bronzed shoulder, "that of all the people in it, it should be you and I - perhaps the most contemptible for our part in history - stranded here together!"

TWO

Emma Walker

KALYPSO : MONODY

So. Now you know why I came to be alone on this island, with nothing but a stolen pandouris and that which the Sea, in her mercy, might throw to me. A bitter mercy at that, since I realised early on that my gain was always another man's tragedy. In the end, I learnt to ignore my empathy for man, preferring to believe these wrecked offerings were gifts from my Oceanid ancestry, who had done little for me in the past. I thought myself a sea nymph for my incredible luck in the water, catching just the right tide to bring me to this place.

Meanwhile, it seemed Klotho, even then, in her infinite and unfathomable wisdom, had chosen for me a life of unrequited love.

Sometimes I would accuse my upbringing for my disastrous and negative relations with men. My father was not the greatest of role models, having had three wives by the time of my birth. Had I not just followed the examples set by my many sisters? To be stranded alone on this island, far from the disillusion of men, would at least save me from an unhappy marriage, or a miserable and disrespectful motherhood, abandoned by my child's father and shunned by polite society for my impropriety

Other times, I accused cheating Damon of Athens, that rogue of a man, for my plight. But in the end, I only had myself to blame. If I had made the better choice - whatever that may have been - when faced with temptation, I might not have been punished so. But as the scoundrel himself would say, our destinies are set long before we decide on them. I may have been abandoned for many years on this island, with no knowledge of the outside world, thinking myself safe from the miseries of the Fates. But mine was not a small role in this great tragedy of ours after all.

Emma Walker

KALYPSO'S TWELFTH EPISODE

For my part, I don't remember any clawing hands, or pale white faces. No hollow black eyes and wailing or whispering voices. If that had been the case, I doubt I would be telling this story now. My heart jumps at the mere thought, but the reality would make it stop dead I'm sure, and add me to their ranks in an instant.

The moment I entered the water and began to sink beneath it, panic struck me. I struggled against my own clothes, against the rushing tide and no doubt the wake of the ship as it pulled away as well. I had told myself as I let go of the boat that all I had to do was stay under long enough to confuse them - which in this dark water would not, thankfully, be too long - and I was wearing nothing bright enough to be spotted without a strong lamp. After that, I just had to swim backwards until I reached the island, taking care to look out for any protruding rock that might scrape or pummel me - though I predicted (and prayed) these rocks would be less of a problem to a surface swimmer than a sunken ship's hull.

Unfortunately, once in the water - which was surprisingly cold at dusk - I completely lost my bearings. By the time I surfaced, gasping for breath, flailing around in circles with one free arm and one pandouris, the sun had completely set, there was no moonlight and my eyes were blurred from the water. Added to that my tears and chokes of sheer terror at finding myself alone, and it all seemed like a recipe for disaster. I knew I was being tugged along by the tide but I had no idea if it was taking me in the right direction.

After a few attempts at some deep dry breaths, I felt sure I could see the lights from the ship just ahead of me. I looked about again, and listened as hard as I could but there were no sounds of rescuers in the vicinity. Making a guess at the direction in which the ship was travelling, I lifted myself up until I was floating as best I could on my back, and pushed myself along with quick and hard movements of my hands. My mind was filled with doubts: Was this the right direction? What if they came back for me? What if my head hits a rock before I see it? What if there *is* something else beneath the water, some sea monster that takes a fancy to me for his midnight feast?

I was certainly not a weak swimmer - I'd had a natural affinity to water throughout childhood. My father's garden had some beautiful and grand lakes and ponds in which my mother had taken me as a baby. She used to laugh at how easily I had learned to swim, happy to stay under water for minutes at a time. When I grew older, I would splash about in the hot months, sometimes playing with my nephews and nieces, trying to teach them how to float upside down. I filled me head with as many of these pleasant memories as I could. But there was no getting away from the huge differences. My father's ponds had been clear and calm - barely a ripple that wasn't made by myself as I moved through the water. But now, for every push I made, the waves seemed to shove me harder in any direction they chose.

My determination to keep hold of that irksome pandouris which had begun my whole adventure was causing my downfall. I needed a focus for my emotions and it was that instrument. More and more of my salt-drenched hair stuck to my face and clung to my neck until I wasn't sure if that, or the great gulps of unwanted saltwater filling my lungs, would be first to suffocate me. In frustration, I tried to throw the pandouris away, allowing me use of that extra arm. But, in my exhaustion, an arm's length was the best distance I could manage to hurl it, and so the damned thing began to float just beside me, mocking me with how much better it handled the waves than I. This new fact gave me an idea. I decided to put my useless neighbour to a test of its buoyancy. I experimented with it as a support, pushing the stave just beneath my chest and resting upon it, as if on the shoulders of my mother when I first learnt to swim. This wasn't terribly effective at keeping the water from my mouth, but it did give my hands and wrists a break. That was until the bowl of the stave, like my lungs, began to swell with water and I found myself gripping hold of the neck just in time to stop it slipping below me. I don't know why I wasn't ready to let it go, but clearly its link to me was not yet severed.

And so we drifted wearily onwards, until the moon's light slithered through the lessening cloud cover and I could at last see that our trajectory was not so far off after all. A renewed enthusiasm filled me and seeing the island looming almost within reach, I made one last attempt on my back, pushing the water away from my hands with all the strength I had left, using the pandouris on one side, and kicking so hard with my feet I left my own wake behind me. Like the man in Eurylokhos' superstitious story, I would be lying if I told you I knew how I eventually made it to dry land. All I remember was the sudden feel of something solid against my neck, shoulders, back... until I collapsed on a bed of shingle.

I must have lain on that less than comfortable surface for some time, resting my tired, aching muscles and gasping for an ordinary breath between waterlogged splutters. When I awoke, shivering in sunlight the following morning, I appeared to have floated some way up a shingle and sand-covered beach, wrapped tightly in my sopping cloak and hugging a pandouris to my chest. I thank the gods even now that the island - but for a few wild animals - was truly uninhabited, else what a sight I might have been, and smelt, to the natives!

Emma Walker

KALYPSO'S THIRTEENTH EPISODE

When one arrives on a deserted island, you might expect, in such tales, to hear that certain priorities are immediately attended to. Getting one's bearings, for example; finding fresh food and water, as well as establishing some form of shelter. But, although not being entirely helpless and uneducated, I had been a lady of some means all my life, accustomed to having servants and slaves for these jobs. My impetuous decision to bail from the ship had not, after all, been as well thought through as I'd imagined it. So my first action, on realising where I had awoken, was to cry. Bitter tears of relief and failure.

After indulging myself long enough in this useless behaviour, I realised I had nothing on which to wipe my face dry, since every piece of cloth upon me was still sodden and filthy. My hands were sore and smothered in sand and dirt, adding to my malaise. I was too tired from the night's attempted drowning to begin an exploratory hike. I never liked to believe in the existence of the bards' world of great lumbering beasts, with nothing but ill-will in their hearts and a taste for human flesh. Relying on the information that this island was desolate and little harm would therefore come to me, I decided my next deed was to dispense with my wet clothes and dry them - and myself - as best I could in the slowly warming sun. This was an effort. My muscles were in pain and felt heavier than freshly-cut logs. I was covered in a disturbing number of bruises, the sight of which made me sob some more. Nevertheless, I slowly managed to peel the clothes away, hanging my tunic on a branch and spreading my cloak out on ground that I assured myself could not be reached by the tide. Other items I hung or laid about the area until I was satisfied they were all within reach of the sun's rays.

It was disappointing to have nothing but the surf in which to wash, and it seemed of little use as I crawled unhappily toward it. But I still needed to clean away the sweat and damp smells as best as possible, taking further note of the bruises and wincing as the saltwater smothered the grazes I hadn't felt occur the previous night. I had been immensely cheered at the sight of my undamaged wine sack and, after cleansing enough, allowed myself a carefully rationed swig to try and perk up my strength for the tasks ahead. Not having the means to dilute the intense liquor, it hit my empty stomach with a disturbing jolt. Shortly after which, I fell straight back into a heady sleep.

KALYPSO'S FOURTEENTH EPISODE

I awoke with far more awareness than from my previous waterlogged dreams. I felt for a moment as though my instincts had been turned on and I could hear every sound and sense every danger about me like a hunted animal. My heart pounded and I breathed deeply in an attempt to still it, lest its thumping be overheard. I wiped the grains from that side of my face which had rested upon the sand, becoming acutely aware of my nakedness. I crawled about collecting unnaturally crisp and partially dried clothing, which now smelt thoroughly disagreeable. I improvised an outfit, wrapping my cloak about my body and tying two corner ends behind my neck. My skin, prickling uncomfortably from its exposure to the sun's heat, fidgeted and itched with every fibrous contact.

Meanwhile, I noticed the pandouris slowly burnishing in the glaring light. I thought once again of destroying the cursed thing, using it for firewood, grinning victoriously as it burned down to ashes. I looked out to sea, musing on the image of dastardly Damon. I imagined

Kalypso : 'Tritagonist'

him ferociously rowing a small vessel over rough waves, determined to punish me for my theft and retrieve his moronic three-strings. I laughed inside as I realised the coward would do no such thing. He was more likely to send out an army of his submissive, foolish women, each believing themselves to be Damon's favourite, each wishing to please him by my defeat, while he sat busily admiring his own cleverness to manipulate weak and silly girls. Surely there could be no one else in time, I thought, as wicked with love as he?

(I would continue to think so until Odysseus told me the tales of Helen the whore...)

I was returned to my senses by a sharp and painful reminder from my stomach. I walked toward the wildly growing orchards beside the beach, believing I recognised some of the edible berries and small fruits growing there. The trees were not of a tall variety nearest the beach, and they bent awkwardly. As I squeezed through branches, watching the undergrowth and treetops for any anomalous movement, I experimented with tasting the unfamiliar. I had nothing then but my teeth to rip open skins, but hunger outweighed disgust, and soon I was eating figs, under-ripe grapes and berries, until I felt queasy. I had remained within eyesight of the beach and my possessions during the food hunt, still harbouring a fear that I might yet not be alone, but as the sun began to dip in the heavens, I knew I must be more adventurous and find some form of shelter. Sleeping on the sands could be fatal if the island suffered heavy rains overnight. I scooped up my belongings, the stolen pandouris, and a few further fruits, then gingerly made my way along the sands, glancing through trees and shrubs to the side of me for any signs of movement or obvious shelter. Once or twice I was startled by the flight of birds or the shuffle of some small animal or vermin in the bushes, and chose not to investigate, sticking close to the shore, away from unknown dangers. Eventually the ground became hard, and stones and pebbles jabbed into my soles. The land rose up high beside me and I found I was searching the rock face.

There were cracks and fissures all about the precipice, most of which appeared too small or hollow to entertain, some of which made me shudder, as if warning me away. All the while my mind had been diverted to the wreckage I saw strewn about beneath me, resting haphazardly against rocks, causing my path to veer and zigzag, on occasion dipping into the water to avoid a collision. As much as this sight concerned me, giving the island as forbidding an aura as the seaman had described, I was also childishly excited at the prospect of a treasure hunt. I contended there must have been objects of all sorts of value tossed at this land and left to be buried by the earth and water. And just as my preoccupation came to a height, there it was.

I saw the cave from a distance. I was instantly drawn to it. I could not help but stare, pondering on what it might be like to live inside. It was outwardly decorated from above with a crown of tumbling vines and cedar branches, the origins of which were bending dramatically over the cliff's edge, adventurously stretching their way to the sea. Birds nestled comfortably amongst the leaves, squawking and chirruping to each other, all beckoning me over. The entrance did not have the same unfriendly darkness as others in the vicinity, and it was wide enough to step through with ease. It was also slightly turned away from the sea, sparing it from the full impact of a raging tide. Nevertheless, the floor inside was damp underfoot. Even with the sun at its zenith, very little light could reach what I assumed to be the main chamber. While I knew this to be the best shelter I had come across, and felt some sense of security within the cavern, I was still unnerved by the darkness. As I dropped my things to the ground, the noise bounced about the blackened walls and made my heart and stomach flutter nervously. I scampered back out into the sunlight, ashamed of my childlike fears.

It took some time to acclimatise to the island and learn the basic techniques of survival, which I had never even heard mentioned in the women's quarters of a great household like my father's, let alone been taught. Had I not been such an inquisitive girl when very young - spying on servants, eavesdropping on my father's conversations and arguments, picking up scraps of information, interrogating anyone who showed me polite interest - I might never have known that rubbing wood or certain glassy stones together can create fire; foreign waters should always be boiled, wherever possible, before being mixed with wine; grains must be ground down before they can be made into porridge or breads...

All of this I heard Hermes' guiding voice reminding me. Knowledge and practice I soon discovered to be worlds apart. My frustration and fears were only alleviated by daily treasure hunts, strumming the pandouris and singing accompaniment until late into the night when I could no longer keep my eyes open or my fingers moving. (Damon was right - even a foolish girl like me could learn to play it; and I like to think I wrote far better songs.)

I would never let the fire in the cave burn out while I had my wits about me, an irrational fear of the dark prevailing. The first time I brought torchlight into my new grotto, I discovered it to be far from small. This main chamber was still a mere entranceway, and a grander cave, with small fissures and little offshoots, nooks and caverns set about it. With the addition of light and a good brushing out of dust and lose materials, it became a warm and tranquil shelter, gradually decorated by my finds from the shore. I made mats and bedding from large strips of material, which had most likely been sails or covers of a type. I used lumps of wood as boxes and shelving, made tables from rocks and planks. I kept the best of the pottery finds - those only barely chipped yet still good enough for use - for my victuals, but filled the damaged pots with plants and other objects.

All this happened gradually, of course, as I grew accustomed to my new surroundings, my new home. In time I discovered the wild goats and herbs further inland, the fish and crustaceans of the shallow

Kalypso : 'Tritagonist'

waters. Whenever I felt alone, I would sing, moving my fingers clumsily about the pandouris, trying to emulate those sounds I had once heard it produce in that vagrant Damon's hands, smiling as Echo played and sang the notes back to me, her voice being my only company. Our men may have abandoned us unfairly, yet we remained bound together in this sanctuary of mutual disappointment.

KOMMOS

"Doubtless you do not wish to hear of *my* life on the island, though," she sighed. "Of how I slowly learnt, by trial and error and necessity, to fish and hunt , to guess at which plants might be edible by observing the animals and birds in their feeding (although sometimes I thought they conspired to trick me when I spent the night groaning from sickness). Or of how I grew used to the silence of a world without conversation. Nor are you interested in how the pandouris and I gradually became friends, allowing me some pleasant, if pensive, recreation at times; learning and composing, while never forgetting the rotting instruments origins.

"No, I can see you are all eager for stories on great Odysseus and how *he* fared on my island," she waved a tinder stick accusatorily at us all and we blushed guiltily at her perception.

"We want to hear your story, fairest Kalypso," we assured her. "Tell us all you wish."

She smiled disbelievingly. "Odysseus was always so much better at this," she sighed once more, stoking the fire. The flames licked the air, spitting and hissing, until through the heavy smoke there appeared the form of our hero...

Emma Walker

THREE

Kalypso : 'Tritagonist'

KALYPSO'S FIFTEENTH EPISODE

I had been aware of the storm that night. I had watched its fury grow on the horizon. The gusts blew sharply across my island, through my trees. They chose no single direction, but raged from all sides. Lightning cut through the blackened low clouds. Sheets of rain were illuminated, then quickly disappeared within the darkness. There were neither stars nor moon, no sky for as far as the eyes could see.

When the rains reached my island, I took shelter in the protective warmth of my cave. Its twists and turns meant the winds and water could never quite reach its belly. My fire burnt steadily, its crackling and sputtering only interrupted by the occasional distant rumble from somewhere outside.

Tomorrow, I thought, as I rested my body on the warm soft padding of my bed. Tomorrow I would have much work to do, cleaning up the shoreline of the night's rage.

I had almost forgotten this sombre image when I woke. I stirred the still spitting embers of last night's fire until a gentle warmth began to emanate again. I washed myself with a small basin of spring water, cleansed my face, letting the water trickle through my fingers. There was a sudden change in the air, as if a new wind were blowing from some hitherto unknown direction. I saw my reflection looking up at me and wondered uncomfortably at it. The fire sparked and crackled loudly and I felt myself jump back from the bowl and shiver, as if someone else were there, watching me. Something was different on my island that day.

I threw on a light robe, tied a cord around my waist and shoulders and picked up a woollen shawl in case the chill of the storm still lingered. On reaching the mouth of the cave, I was greeted by a blast of cool air and felt the freshness that only comes from a storm just passed. The sun had already begun to dry the earth and a mild wind still persisted, whipping my clothes and hair playfully about me. I breathed in the soft smell of recently fallen rain mixed with the extra saltiness of a well-churned sea. Wrapping a shawl tight around my shoulders, I tied my billowing hair back and stepped out onto the warm and damp sands, letting clumps surge between my toes and crumble away with each step, leaving deep and uneven footprints behind me. The sky paraded its morning shades of orange and pink and pale blue. Far in the distance I could still see a lingering blackness and prayed it would continue to dissolve into the horizon.

I noted only one fallen tree at the forest's edge. I was not surprised to see which - a particularly beaten, well-worn old tree. I knelt beside its split and helpless trunk, stroked its once honoured bark and promised it a good and useful return to the earth. *Firewood*, I thought to myself. Once it had dried out. The ashes would return to the earth with renewed pride.

The waves lapped hungrily at the beach. As I walked around the island's edge, surveying my lands for any further damage, I began to notice and collect up objects that appeared to be thrown at my feet by the sea. Like offerings to a goddess, I mused.

Unusually, these objects began to move me. Many were common pieces of damp and tattered wood. But in between were scraps and balls of soggy cloth that might have been anything from a sail to a cloak or tunic. There were so many items. Jewellery and armoury gleamed in the sunlight. I was used to the occasional article appearing in the sands, particularly after rough weather. I hated to linger long on the disasters that brought anything to my shore, but the flotsam and hulk about me were too great in number to be sacrificial offerings to Poseidon. I scooped out a dagger, still held in its tight sheath. The remains of the belt, which had once held it to a body, was split apart. As I turned the dagger over in my hands, realising I held a very personal piece, I knew there had been a tragic shipwreck.

I felt sure no life had been spared. As the air was already warming, I took off my shawl and used it to collect up the smaller objects. Once again I began to feel that strange sense of being watched. I quickened my pace, reaching down only to pick up those more conspicuous items thrown at me by the tide, looking uneasily about me, keeping alert for the source of my discomfort.

Just beyond the entrance to my cave, I glimpsed it; a large plank of wood, slowly drying out in the sun's heat, and on top of it the body of a man. I froze, my heart quickening at the sight. I could not bring myself to move any closer.

His skin was deeply bronzed and glistening, his dark hair straggled across his face and neck. Here and there were patches of what looked to be blood on his pale tunic and his laced, fawn-coloured boots. These were wet through and clinging tightly to his body like a second skin.

As he had not moved for some time, I called up my courage, tied my shawl together at the corners, encasing all the day's treasures within it, and walked towards the stranger. I dropped the bundle carefully and quietly to the ground, as if the slightest sound might disturb him. His eyes were tight shut and smothered by his matted locks. His right hand clasped a splintered pole, which might once have been an oar, or even a spear, but now resembled nothing more than a useless club of sorts. Up close, his skin appeared to be covered in bruises, and some minor cuts were seeping blood. I also noted some scarring here and there, and wondered at the stories behind the marks. But it was his chest that really drew my attention.

Between those broad muscular shoulders, I was alarmed to note a shallow movement...

And another...

And again!

I crept swiftly to my shawl, found the dagger, freed it from its sheath, and wiped it gently against my dress. Hesitantly, I leant next to the body, closely watching his eyes and arms for movement. My left knee rested on the edge of the drying wood, which creaked a little beneath this new weight; my left hand held the dagger, which I moved towards his nose. Meanwhile, my right hand and leg tried to retain my balance on the sand as I held the blade just beneath his nostrils. Sure enough, there was breath moving in and out of him, leaving a white vapour mark on the tarnished metal as it travelled.

The stranger was alive.

Emma Walker
_____

KALYPSO'S SIXTEENTH EPISODE

A sudden sharp pain came to my left arm. He had taken advantage of my lapse in concentration and his hand, now emptied of its wooden implement, was gripping hold of me with all its might. Luckily, his strength was no real match for me that day. Had he not been so exhausted from the previous night's adventure I expect he would have thrown me off in a flash and held *me* at the blade's edge. Instead his eyes dulled with the effort. He exhaled deeply against my throat and then let his grip loosen until it fell back to his side.

I found myself held still, watching him as he did me, though how much he could actually see through all that hair I wasn't sure. I threw the dagger back towards the shawl, out of harms way, and for pity's sake began to scrape back the mass that had congealed across his face, partially blinding him. He had, I discovered, a full beard framing his mouth and jaw line. I saw his lips tremble. They peeled apart slowly and I expect him to speak. Perhaps he meant to, but instead he coughed. First gently, then with some hacking that began to concern me. Fearing he might choke, I tried to roll him off his back and on to his side. His left arm hung limp and useless, but he attempted to use the stronger right arm to aid me in moving him. Somehow our joint efforts managed to force him so far over that he fell off the wooden plank altogether, face down into the sand, still spluttering. I found I had to stifle a cruel laugh. Why this poor man's misery should be comical to me I could not tell you, but when I hurriedly edged him back on to his side, his look of frustration softened on catching my eye. I sensed a smile on his lips. I brushed some of the sand from his face and shoulders. His eyes lazily watched every movement I made. Again we stared at each other, as if neither of us had seen another person all our lives. Then his eyes began to grow weary and I realised this would not do.

"My name is Kalypso," I told him, the old words forming in my mouth as though they had never left it. "Can you move your legs?" I asked, after considering him a moment. He did not reply, but I looked down to see his boots twitching slightly. "Only I'm not sure I can carry your weight by myself and the tide won't stay out forever. I suspect you've had enough of the sea for now?"

He was of no further help to me, and I could only be sympathetic, remembering my own arrival on Ogygia. After three attempts by me to lift him with his good arm, it became obvious his legs were simply too tired to move. He lay apologetically on his plank of wood, breathing heavily, as if he had been doing all the work. I stood facing the breeze, hands at my hips, thinking through the options. I only had one more idea. I returned quickly to my cave, pulled out a reel of the strongest cord I had, and ran back to him. There followed an elaborate charade of moving him on to the sand, wedging up the plank, threading the cord beneath it lengthways and widthways over him, appealing to him to hold the roping steady with his better hand.

The gods alone know how uncomfortable this must have been for him, but I had little compassion when comparing it to the pain and aches I felt in my arms for the next few days, after having to pull such a heavy load over sand and shingle on what seemed like an eternal journey. It was all I could do to roll him on to some softer bedding before collapsing myself.

I managed to feed him some diluted wine to clear his throat and warm his lungs, and in gratitude for all my efforts he almost instantly succumbed to sleep. While he slept, and after adequate rest of my own limbs, I began to cut away carefully at his now filthy clothes and tend to the more prominent of his wounds. It was my rather optimistic intention to somehow reassemble his clothes in a clean and better state at another time. Meanwhile, I shuffled through my stores for some cloth that could be quickly fashioned into a suitable outfit.

The day's commotion had meant that my usual routine - fetching fresh water and finding a meal - had been entirely forgotten. Every time I considered leaving the cave to complete one of these tasks I was drawn to looking at his helpless, sleeping body. I knew too little about tending to a man, let alone a wounded one. I was afraid to leave him alone.

KALYPSO'S SEVENTEENTH EPISODE

Eventually I escaped long enough to complete my collection of those remnants that had washed ashore. The smaller, useful items I carried back to the cave. The bigger pieces, mostly wood and rags, I dragged up toward the trees. If they dried out well enough, the former might be good for fire or carving, and some scraps of the material could patch old seams. Anything that appeared to be the remains of drowned animals (I could not allow myself to think they might be anything else) I returned to the water, to a departing tide. I trusted that would be an end to it. Once the stranger regained strength, none of these objects would be here to remind him of his tragedy.

I spent the time nursing him as well as I could, though I had no real experience of this role. I kept his wounds clean, and did my best to feed him.

Attempts at conversation, such as they were, sounded laconic and confusing, communication in the first few days being nothing more than barely audible grunts on his part and monosyllables on mine. When he woke, dazed and troubled, he seemed barely aware of himself or his surroundings. I would lift him up as best I could to feed him broth or diluted wine, but his actions were mechanical. I would try to wash down his back, from where sleep's sweat had collected, and I managed to cut away some of his wild growing hair and beard. He did nothing to hinder or help me. His only aid was to stay in the position he was put until I bade him, with gentle nudges, to move again. I would try to instruct him with words, but from his murmurings I had no idea if he understood my language and felt foolish speaking to a man with no obvious sense.

I began to compare this man's temperament with the very storm that had dragged him to the island, for his fever and discomfort would slowly roll in, build up to a great crescendo, then quickly dissolve away to nothing until you began to forget it ever occurred, or at least were happy to. How he disrupted my sleeping patterns! Not simply because I allowed him full use of the comfortable bedding I had gathered for myself, while I sprawled disagreeably on rolled cloth or anything else I could place between my body and the rocky ground. I slept lightly, against the opposite wall of the cave, afraid that he might wake while I slept, and then - who could know?

He muttered while he slept; sometimes I would hear words I thought I recognised, but they all too quickly faded for me to be sure. Other times I thought they might be names, and I felt a great pity for him. I wiped away the tearstains and dust that gathered about his eyes the morning after. I tried to be gentle, but more often than not my actions woke him and I would use this as an excuse to offer him refreshment, while his eyes stared at the ceiling, vacant or puzzled.

One time, I remember, I had fed him some wine in the usual way after he roused, then washed his motionless body with a damp cloth soaked in scented water - all the while his eyes seemed full of sadness. The fire was low but I had added to the flames some chips of a bark that produced a sweet smelling odour as it burnt. After I had washed his crown and moved the stray, clammy hairs out of his eye line, I sat and looked at him. Despite the odd mixture of feeling he evoked in me, I was still mesmerised by this stranger, by all that I did not yet know about him. Those sad eyes, I realised, were also watching me. I was about to move away when I noticed his lips quivering and forming shapes.

"Am I dead?" he spoke at last, the voice husky and cracked with effort. I was pleased to recognise the sounds as an Achaean dialect, though I confess I only guessed at the words. He seemed incapable of repeating his question and I was bemused. To hear his voice at all was startling. I wondered how long he had been able to speak, or had been trying to?

"No," I answered him at last. He groaned and turned his head away, closing his eyes to the world.

I spent the rest of that day in a great melancholy.

Later that night I found him quite terrifying. It seemed, along with speech, he had at last found the strength to move himself, and not long after I had laid down to sleep, I heard shuffling noises from his bed. I sat bolt upright, my back against the cave wall, watching from my distant space. First tossing and turning, he kicked out with his feet, tensed his hands and scrunched his face. This went on for some time, while I sat, hugging my knees protectively, observing but too fearful to approach; especially so when the strange cries and short impatient wails began. I knew he might be in some pain, but what could I do? I could see no blood to stop, and he did not appear fully awake, so I could not ask him to explain. I felt sure, if I went to him, I would only be injured myself.

So I waited.

Finally, he thrashed so hard, he threw himself right over, face down, half off the bedding and onto the cold, hard floor of the cavern. He stopped. There came a noise from his throat, like a swallowed sob. And then nothing.

I watched a little longer to be sure, hoping for a surge of courage, hoping I had not witnessed something awful... When it seemed he had not moved for an age, I tentatively crept to his side and rolled him as best I could back on to the softer bedding. Gentle as I tried to be, I could not push him without some force, which caused him to groan once again and my heart to flutter in panic, but I was relieved he had not died.

The moment he was returned to the bed, I noticed his panicked eyes, but before I could think or speak his hands grabbed my shoulders, and tried to use me to lever himself up, though he succeeded only in pulling me down to him. It all happened so quickly I had no time to fight or escape. I simply froze. My face became level with his. He was shaking and perhaps I was too, but I was too numb to notice my feelings.

"Hide me!" he whispered. "Hide me!" It was a plea that chilled the air between us.

"From what?" I asked, which emerged as no more than a hoarse whisper as well. His eyes drifted over my shoulder and my heart stopped. I could not turn to look because of his grip and the terror of what might be there. What demons had he brought to my island?

Without an answer, this man's demons already began to fade. His eyelids and head drooped and he pulled me haphazardly down to his bed, my face smothered by his shoulder. I listened without moving, still unable to see behind me, but I heard nothing unusual.

The soft rumble of the waves, the crackle of the dying fire, the dripping at the cavern entrance...

I took in a deep, calming breath against his skin. Slowly, I disentangled his arms from my shoulders, his fingers from my hair, placing them back down by his sides. Again he moaned, turning away from me.

The following morning, as daylight rose, I checked the coast for other caves. None, I knew, would compare to mine, but at least I would know where the others were. I knew where to go if I needed to hide.

Kalypso : 'Tritagonist'

That was the worse of his earlier episodes. He still woke me with muttering and crying, thrashing and rolling, then just as suddenly stopped, falling deathly silent into a deep sleep. But there were no more strange and terrifying supplications, so I relaxed and put that down to a bad dream.

To soothe my fragile nerves during my strange guest's alternating moods, I would sometimes hum to myself. I noted how much calmer and quieter he became as I did. One day I caught myself humming a song I could not identify, when suddenly I remembered: it was one of Damon's. I grew angry with myself and stopped mid-tune. Despite the passing of time, I still felt a heavy bitterness towards those memories and I inwardly cursed that he continued to affect me so. Yet when I stopped thinking on my own plight, I realised the stranger was stirring, making what sounded like a weak vocal protest at my abrupt silence. I became doubly intrigued when he began to fill the quiet with an attempt at a tune of his own. He was awake, though his appearance was still that of a drowsy man.

It reminded me of an episode at home with my father. I had once observed the illustrious Atlas after a long night's gathering with friends, at which a great deal of drink, food and merriment had passed. It was early the following morning, and while the rest of the household began their usual routine, my vast hulk of a father was still collapsed on cushions in the great hall, protesting at any attempts to move him, singing one of the previous evening's songs (and very badly). His eyes were bloodshot and half opened, as if the weight of his eyelashes insisted on pulling the lids together while his determination was to keep them apart. His voice faltered and changed in tempo and pitch and volume through every verse. It was both a miserable and amusing event.

My guest on the other hand, though he looked dazed, made my heart soar at his efforts. I listened for a moment or two, trying to discern a tune and when I felt I had it, I began to join in. If I went awry, and our two voices disharmonised, I even heard him chuckle. There was an odd warmth to the bond we seemed to make through this unknown song, and our humming and giggles only ceased when I realised he was no longer joining in, the tune having lulled him back to sleep. For a moment, without his voice, I felt strangely alone, but I held on to that light, happy feeling, that he and I were perhaps not so very different.

It was not long after this that my guest began to speak more fluently, requesting food and thanking me for help given. He confirmed that he was indeed Achaean, though his accent was heavy and rough. Despite all that had occurred during his convalescence, I felt strangely timid around him, and he behaved quite shyly near me. He was able to sit up by himself and politely insisted on washing (as much as he could reach without my help). I suspected it would not be long before he would be happy to leave the cave, though I couldn't picture what might happen after that.

I liked to sit on a raised rock near the beach, spinning my little makeshift spindle, dangling my legs over the edge, and letting the twine fall down between my knees, twisting and jolting as it worked. I was so doing, just beside the entrance to the cave, when he first emerged into the open air of his own accord. I wasn't too surprised by this; his strength had been steadily improving. He was wearing his original tunic, which I had repaired badly and cleaned, and he had a cloak of animal hide wrapped about his shoulders.

I flashed him a friendly smile before returning to my simple work, not wishing to seem overly keen in my interest. I saw from the corner of my eye that he was obviously still tired, straining out his limbs beneath the sun. After some attempts at exercise, he made his way over to me. For a moment he stood and watched, making me blush a little under his gaze. I'd had no direct contact with another human for so long and still knew nothing of value about this visitor. He cleared his throat and I tapped the ground just next to me to indicate he could sit of he wished. He slumped down gratefully, hanging his legs over the edge, and picking up one of my completed spindles. He turned it in his hands with mild admiration, placed it back down and returned to watching me. I smiled thinly, still a little uncomfortable at working with an audience.

"How are you feeling?" I asked.

"Good, I think," he smiled. He paused for a moment, before adding meekly, "I'm sorry, I suppose you will have told me many times, but I do not remember your name." I laughed gently, grateful for his confession.

"I've only told you once. And you were considerably delirious," I assured him. "I am Kalypso."

"It's an honour to meet you, Kalypso," he said with some genuine warmth. Our eyes and smiles met. There was a strange pause between us in which I waited for his own introduction, but instead found myself probed intensively by his steady gaze.

"And you?" I finally pushed him.

"Sorry, I... My name is Odysseus, son of Laertes." He said this with an air of pride, and I was aware that I should have known why. I smiled awkwardly.

"You are someone very important, then?"

He looked dejected. "No. I am nobody now," he sighed.

"Well, nobody is welcome on my island," I joked to cheer him up. He accepted this with a smile that changed his whole face so wonderfully that the breath caught in my chest and I blushed. "I am most glad to know you at last, Odysseus son of Laertes."

He looked away from me, down at his knees.

"I've been meaning to thank you," he said shyly, "for saving my life."

"Oh, I wouldn't go that far," I dismissed modestly. "Restoring your health, perhaps, but your life had already been spared when I found you. I only did what anyone else might have."

"Nevertheless," he insisted, "another person could simply have left me to die… or worse."

"Worse? Surely no one could really do anything worse?" I protested.

"Believe me, in my travels I have met such beings as would… Well, let me just say there are stories I could tell of sights that I've seen which still make the hairs on my neck stand on end."

"Really?" I asked excitedly. "Oh, do tell!"

Odysseus looked at my eager face and laughed kindly, "I do not think they're suitable for a gentle maid such as yourself."

"Shouldn't I be the judge of that?" I assured him, but not wanting to push unnecessarily I added, "Perhaps you can tell me after our evening meal? A scary story just before bed?" He laughed again and agreed.

"Truly though," he continued, "I am grateful for all you've done. I could have been anyone; good, evil-"

"That you still could be," I interrupted.

"-an enemy," he continued.

"An enemy? How could I, the sole inhabitant of an island, gain an enemy? Unless," it suddenly occurred to me, "you're from Athens? Or Thebes, perhaps?"

"Neither one," he said, "I'm from Ithaka." His tone was full of that pride you only hear in those who value their homeland.

"Ithaka?" I repeated. "I'm not familiar with that city."

"It is not a mere city," he explained, "it is an island..."

So my first experience of Odysseus' natural ability as a storyteller was through his descriptions of his homeland. For a man who had not spoken for a fair few days, he certainly made amends for it. His manner was quite relaxing, his voice and narration very engaging. Ithaka was low lying, he explained, like my own island, but Ogygia dipped through its centre as if the gods had shaped it like a great mixing bowl, while Ithaka, Odysseus assured me, was an elevated isle, far more rugged than mine. I knew there would be little chance of me convincing him that any other island might be better while he insisted its greatest fault made it superior.

As I was admiring his enthusiastic account of Ithaka's agriculture, he suddenly jumped up.

"Where are the rest of my men?" he demanded. I was stunned by this change in subject. Even in improving health, Odysseus' ability to alter moods was still more abrupt than the weather.

"What do you mean?" I asked with genuine confusion.

"My men - the other sailors. The others washed ashore with me. I noticed no one else in the cave. What have you done with them?" I found myself staring at this man with his sincere and hurried questions. I opened my mouth to speak but could formulate no words. It was

Kalypso : 'Tritagonist'

strange enough for me to find myself holding a conversation with another person after so long. How was I now to find the right words for such an uncomfortable moment? I felt ashamed that I could not tell him there had been no other survivors. But as I barely knew this foreigner Odysseus, nor his capabilities, and he had swung so quickly into this state of impatience, I feared what other characteristics might be within him.

My dumb silence caused him to view me suspiciously. He looked about us and then back at me, making erratic movements with his head and jerking his eyes about the scene. "Where did you find me?" he questioned, his voice not yet betraying any anger, which in itself unnerved me.

"Just over there," I waved my hand in the general direction, keeping my eyes fixed on his movements. "Beyond those trees and down is a stretch of beach. The same stretch I first arrived on myself." Odysseus allowed his eyes to follow my directions. "But I'm sorry... You were alone." His gaze dropped at this. He was silent for a moment, before asking:

"Are there other similar beaches elsewhere?"

"A couple," I admitted. "Some appear and disappear with the tides."

"And you searched those? All of them? For my men?" he persisted. My mind wandered back to a day or two after Odysseus arrival. A body - or part of one, I could not tell - had appeared, caught between two rocks. I had been too frightened to deal with it at the time and seeing it so discoloured and almost completely submerged, I knew it was beyond my help. In the end, I had used a stick and my foot to shift it free from the rocks that held it, just as I had done with the previous animal remains, letting it drift back out with the waves. I had felt terrible, wondering if I should have dealt it a more reverent end, haunted with dread that it might reappear at any moment. I cried, both for the dead and the living, as I walked briskly away. Odysseus' accusing look brought my shameful deed flooding back.

"I haven't looked today," was my eventual and feeble answer. Strangely, this seemed to snap him into action.

"Then *I* shall make a search," he declared, and began to walk towards the beach.

"No, wait!" I called after him. He stopped to let me catch up.

"The island..." I stuttered, trying to think of a good excuse to halt this impetuous man and his desperate quest, "it's quite large. In good health it might take you a whole day and night to cover it. In your current state..." I looked at his determined face and tried to think how best to deal with him, but I was at a loss.

"In which case," he interceded, "the sooner I start, the better. My men will be waiting."

"You know," I quickly interrupted, "perhaps you *should* go for a walk. I had intended to show you about the island, after all, when you were well enough. Perhaps some time to think by yourself, a little exploration and exercise, is just what you need. But might I suggest moderation? See how the morning sun is still low in the east?" I pointed and he acknowledged it. "Why not walk until it is almost above you, then turn back? For your health's sake, you do not want to be pushing beyond your capabilities yet, do you? I feel sure the more you do this, the further you will reach each day. You could take that direction one day, that the next?" I suggested, pointing either side of us in turn. He flashed a friendly smile at me.

"Nurse Kalypso, I am grateful for your concern at my well-being, and I hear your good counsel. But I must reach my men and bring them back to safety too. I will return with them presently enough, the sooner I start," he insisted, turning about once more.

"Wait!" I tried again, stretching for his arm, then pulling back as he noted the touch. "Sorry," I excused myself, "but... if you insist on..." *This madness? This obvious attempt at bringing a miserable reality to your denial?* "...this search, I have a couple of items you may want to take with you." I sprinted back inside the cave and he followed slowly behind me. By the time I reappeared with the objects, he was waiting outside the cave's mouth.

"Here," I said, handing him a small waist pouch and a sheathed dagger. "The pouch," I explained, "holds my two lucky stones. They were the first two I managed to ignite a spark from, and not, I might add, without a great deal of effort, frustration and tears! I kept that flame burning for many many days; I was so afraid I'd never get it alight again. In the end, I had to put it out. The cave was full of smoke and I could barely breathe within it." Odysseus laughed as I babbled, which was nice to hear, even if it was at my folly. I felt like a child next to him, and had to repress the urge to point out that it was quite some time ago - I was a wiser woman now.

"Also this," I said, handing him my wine pouch. "This flask is a cherished item from my past. It survived the journey to the island with me and its contents were invaluable when I first arrived - though I have refreshed them since then."

Odysseus hung the objects from his belt with thanks.

"Are you sure you wouldn't rather wait? I'll be happy to show you about-"

"I'll be back before you know it," he interrupted, patting me gratefully on the arm. And with a reassuring smile, he walked away.

Kalypso : 'Tritagonist'
_____

KALYPSO : MONODY

It was not just a friendly, icebreaking story. It really had taken time and patience to learn the art of lighting a fire. My first days on the island were horrendous and terrifying. I suffered from hunger and sleep deprivation, and began to think drowning would have been the better option. I found very little to eat, attempting to survive on grasses and leaves - raw; mashed up or dried out - and gradually learnt which shrubs were good for eating and least likely to cause discomfort soon after. When I finally managed to light a fire, I cried with exhaustion and elation. I had spent so long trying to master one element that I had yet to learn other practical talents such as fishing and hunting for something to cook on the ensuing fire.

I stumbled on a ragged piece of fishing net, which had obviously washed ashore some time ago, and used the better part of it to catch the smaller fish and crustaceans that swam closest to the shoreline. But my diet remained appalling for quite some time, and I was exhausted from all the effort to stay alive and the countless sleepless nights. Any crack or snuffle I heard after dark made me start; every noise was exaggerated in volume against the cave walls. I stayed close to the small area of land around the cave for fear I might discover the existence of an island monster after all.

Once I began to understand the nature of the island, my sleeping and eating patterns improved greatly. I uncovered which nocturnal animals and birds had been disturbing my sleep. My wanderings about the length of the island revealed a variety of wild growing crops, which enriched my dietary habits. Fruits and berries were plentiful enough, though I was sharing with an assortment of birds and small livestock.

Suffice to say, my way of life developed so much that I had made the island my home and, by the time Odysseus arrived, I was far less troubled.

Yet the day he disappeared on a quest for his lost shipmates, I felt myself return to my early discomforts. The night he was gone I did not sleep at all. I kept a fire burning outside the cave, rather than in it, and rested myself before it on the open ground, twitching at any sound that might indicate his return. My mind was racked with guilt that I may have allowed this man to walk to his death, if not physically then spiritually at least. Should I have insisted I go along with him? Should I go and look for him now? The latter I decided against. If he was moving about I might never be able to catch him up, and if he returned here to find the place abandoned, that too could have terrible consequences. I already feared the mood in which he might return. But, by the same token, if he had hurt himself or collapsed with exhaustion, the longer I left him, the more likely it was that I had condemned him.

Even as he had walked away from me, I had prepared myself to follow.

"Just let him go," thoughtful Hermes' voice spoke to me. I argued my worries over and over, but "let him go" was the only advice he gave.

"He will come back."

"How can you be sure?"

"Where else would he have to go right now?" Hermes replied with some mirth.

"But he could be hurt? He could fall ill again...?"

"Odysseus must do what Odysseus must do. As always. You, fair Kalypso, must learn to accept this."

So I waited. But not patiently. Full of fear and anxiety, as well as some selfish need. I had been alone for so long. Now I had the potential for company, perhaps even physical comfort. To feel someone's arms around me, telling me I was alive and well and wanted in the world, would have been glorious. Yet after several days of focusing my attentions on this man, he had repaid my efforts by walking away at the first opportunity. I had been spurned thus before. I must be hard-hearted, I knew, to avoid that pain again...

Emma Walker

KALYPSO'S EIGHTEENTH EPISODE

The following morning, before the sun had barely touched the horizon, I decided I must retrieve wandering Odysseus, or at least ascertain that he was well, for my own peace of mind. I would walk to the cliff that rose high above one side of the island, a point which allowed good views over at least three quarters of the land. It would be impossible to see within the thick of the woods, or down to the beach on the far side of the trees, but the available view would be enough to give me some idea of Odysseus' bearings. Planning this trip released some of my tension, so that I felt almost understanding of his decision the day before.

In the end, I did not have to look far. I noticed him from a short distance away. He was already at the very same cliffs to which I was headed, sat with his back turned to me, his eyes looking toward the sunrise splitting the sky with colour. The air was very still and calm, and I found myself creeping tentatively into the scene. He did not look around to greet my footsteps, even though the shuffling grass must have announced me. I walked to the side of him, and studied his tear-stained face. He made no sound, nor movement, even as I knelt down beside him.

"I am sorry," I whispered; sorry as much for his sadness as for having been too cowardly to tell him what I already knew he would find. In some ways, for his sake only, I had hoped he might stumble on another survivor, overlooked by my earlier search. But I'd had little doubt of the reality of his success.

We sat still, Odysseus watching the sun's gentle movements as I watched him. A bird flew out from the rocks below, flapping its wings above our heads as it disappeared into the woods. Odysseus grabbed at my waist and sobbed quietly into my chest. Once the shock of this contact had passed, I allowed myself to hold him. I tentatively stroked his hair and whispered soothing noises, as would a nurse to a tumbled child, until he slowly returned to my world.

When the sobs had subsided, I gently and silently led him by the hand, back along the beach, through trees, over rocks and into the cave.

Feeling somewhat overwhelmed, I nevertheless continued in my hostess duties, whipping together some porridge over a new fire, cautiously watching while he sat sharpening a stick, for no clear purpose, with the dagger I had loaned him. When I passed him the food, he thanked me with a faint smile.

"When does the next ship dock?"

"Next ship?" I asked.

"You have ships that pass this way? With news and supplies?"

"No ships come here," I told him truthfully. He looked at me with some disbelief and a little fear.

"But... How do you know what is happening...? How do you get news back to...?" He stumbled through unanswerable questions. "From where do you get your wine then?" he pointedly enquired as he lifted a glass.

"Oh I... sometimes make that myself," I said. He took a sip and swilled it about his mouth. He nodded as he swallowed, its taste obviously confirming my story, and turned to the porridge.

"What's in this?" he asked after a few mouthfuls.

"This," I answered, showing him some grains, "and a bit of pureed fruit."

"What fruit?"

"I don't know what it's called exactly," I admitted, handing him another of my cooking ingredients to ponder. "It's a strange looking thing, but it has a sweet enough taste."

He considered all this thoughtfully, trying to distract himself from his disappointment.

"So. A wild barley and... some kind of fig, I think," he concluded. "But you should roast the barley seeds before grinding them up," he suggested.

"Really? Well, that might explain why it never tastes the way it used to back home! I just thought it was a different type of grain."

"Doubtless it is," he agreed. "Where are your farm animals? Your crops?" he continued to interrogate me.

"Well... There are animals on the island. I could show you them tomorrow if you-"

"And you tend to them?"

"I'm not sure I understand," I stammered. Even as he ate and questioned me I could see his mind formulating something, and I was far from used to having to think so hard or explain myself. "If I need food I hunt, or fish," I explained. "Mostly fish."

"How do you fish?"

"With my net," I replied, producing this too at his unspoken request. He looked carefully over the small and tatty piece of netting I had done my best to patch up. Then, without the ridicule I had expected, he returned it to me. His actions were quite curious, nonchalant yet purposeful.

"I should like to build a small raft, with your permission? I'll need wood, of course." I stopped what I was doing. He looked at me, but did not wait for my response. "It will allow me to fish further out, catch some bigger morsels. I have no intention of offending you, gentle Kalypso, but the meal portions you serve could be larger with just a little extra work involved."

I frowned quizzically at his decision. *You're staying a while then?*

I thought but did not ask aloud.

"I do fish daily and there is plenty of edible vegetation about. And the animals tend to themselves. Mother Nature provides, you know," I said, trying to sound knowledgeable.

"Where I come from," he declared suddenly, "it is more economical to *keep* animals. To farm. How else could you be certain of enough food during the wet months?"

"Wet months?" I laughed. "There is only *one* of me. I don't have much to fear from starvation or a few drops of rain."

"But now there are two," he reminded.

"You're right! No more indulging," I mocked. "Trust me. We will survive should an icy chill one day reach this place." He looked at me intently, as though trying to decide if I were genuine; then he returned to his eating, and I sensed he felt slightly disillusioned by my lack of concern. "But," I decided, "if my lord and guest Odysseus wishes his king-size portions, he is welcome to fetch them." I steered his attention to the sea with a jocular wave of my hand. He seemed content to return my gesture with a gracious but comical bow. "So what animals do you *keep* in Ithaka?" I asked in an attempt to keep the mood light.

"Back home? I have a good-sized estate. Mostly sheep, goats, a few cows-"

"Women?" I blurted out, and was surprised by my own audacity.

"Some," he replied meekly. "But mostly goats."

"And which do you prefer?" I joked, but he merely smiled, and we said no more.

It became evident that leaving Odysseus to make plans was the best way to perk him up. I consented to listen to his further explanations on cultivating crops, herding livestock, and so on. I tried not to question the relevance of such measures on a small island with so few inhabitants, as I could see the fulfilment these schemes brought him.

As he gradually returned to full health, Odysseus spent the days acting on his ideas, always returning proudly with a large catch of fish, a good bundle of vegetation or fruits, and pots of milk. When I attempted to quell his eagerness in case we ran out of storage space, he disappeared for the day, returning with a set of wooden crates he had created from scrap wood and old tree bark. It seemed nothing could hold back resourceful Odysseus' progress.

KALYPSO'S NINETEENTH EPISODE

Ogygia. *My* island. I lived here so long that it became known so.

There's Ogygia, Kalypso's isle; there's Kalypso's cave; there's the beach on which Kalypso saved the hero Odysseus...

"So, now that you know it better, what do you think of my island?" I asked him as we waded and soaked ourselves in shallow waters. Odysseus' health was so much improved that I had forgotten already how ill he once looked. I had brought him to the lake, which graced the centre of Ogygia and where I regularly like to bathe. He seemed more confident about submerging himself than I had expected of a man so nearly drowned, but then his daily fishing exploits had already told me he was not afraid to return to water.

The lake was set within the heart of Ogygia's small forest, and gentle waterfalls decorated its rockier edges, trickling down from the cliff's heights, pushing delicately curved ripples across the waters.

Kalypso : 'Tritagonist'

Odysseus pushed himself around in circles, creating whirlpools with his hands. He stopped before me with a contented smile to his lips.

"It is beautiful," he said, and his eyes looked so deeply into mine I felt the heat rise in my cheeks. I smiled ecstatically. "Of all the places I have been to in my long travels thus far," he declared, a sincere sparkle in his eyes, "this is the closest I have come to feeling at home." He pushed himself away, floating on his back and I watched him gradually drift from my side; the word 'home' circling me like a cool breeze as he left me behind.

My island was like a pot-maker's mistake. Like a shallow bowl that had spun out of its creator's control, collapsing down helplessly to one side. Upon that lowered side lay the warm sands of the beaches, here and there decorated with tufts of rushes and shrubs, like lumps in otherwise smooth clay; out of place, yet entirely natural. The central dip of the island was studded with woods of cedar trees, groves of figs, and sporadic barren patches on which grew intermittent herbs and grasses, mixed with wild flowers and their accompanying weeds, like bittersweet companions. In the middle of it all sat the lake, filled by the occasional gracious rains. The higher ground lifted up toward the sky, so high that looking down the cliff's edge to a lower tide could produce a dizzying sickness. The rocks seemed to stretch outward, reaching across the island to one side, as if the eastern land were tugging the isle toward the sunset. Beneath this jutting arm were cut great arches into the rock face (which sometimes I fancied as the collapsed handle of this failed pot). My mother had once told me, during one of her rare moments of attentiveness, that Poseidon created these arcs as proof of his triumph over the land. Three arches of varying sizes decorated the island, but only to the west, as if proud and tempestuous Ogygia might only be penetrable as she grew weary, and by sunset could no longer fight off the sea-god's advances.

Ogygia is a small land, which was a comforting discovery. Too large an island means too many dangers. It became my very own garden – just like that beloved garden my sisters tended to and I had been forced to leave behind. I told Odysseus of my lost childhood sanctuary; he worked hard to make the island an idyllic home, improving my simple lifestyle to one of comfort once more.

Almost comfort. For the island had a life and a role of its own. It was not to be mastered by any man. As quickly as Odysseus could arrange its crops, Ogygia would grow her weeds. Odysseus would pull them up, and Ogygia would summon a gale, knocking down his vines and spewing leaves across his carefully ploughed patches of vegetation. I would watch their slow fights with some amusement.

Odysseus would one moment curse, the next jest. "I have never known a more argumentative woman!" he would shake his head and smile. "Not even your fiercest temper, Kalypso, could outdo this tormenting beast on which you live!" I would motion to him to keep quiet, lest she hear his words, and we would laugh it off, while both secretly fearing her next wrath. "You are perfect for each other," he whispered.

Days passed; Odysseus and I shared breakfasts and evening meals, but often spent the rest of our time apart, involved in our own little chores. Life had never been better for me since I left my father's house. I looked forward to meal times with great zest, not least because of the comparative feasts I could now prepare, but also because of this wonderful new company. Odysseus would entertain me with details of his work that day, peppering his tales with amusing anecdotes, making every chore sound like a great quest. Sometimes he would ask me to create something for him, often using my weaving and sewing skills. He would call on me if he needed extra hands and limbs, or if he wished to talk me through a process. Which is how I learnt the best way to keep animals, milk goats without being kicked or bitten - even shear them, which I had never considered trying by myself, preferring instead to collect that wool which had moulted or, if I could get close enough, quickly cut chunks away now and then with my sharpened knife as the goats grazed. Having considered these animals useful but hazardous in the past, I now grew to enjoy their bleating and looked on them quite fondly. Though this, too, would make Odysseus drolly roll his eyes.

Sometimes, in the evenings, Odysseus would make up stories in which Ogygia and Ithaka were not mere slabs of rock, floating upon

Poseidon's oceans, but gods, or people like us. He liked to believe that Ithaka would give Ogygia a run for her money, would try to force her to submit to his will but, just as it appeared to him that she had given in, she would turn and lash out with incredible force, leaving poor Ithaka reeling in shock. We would laugh at the irony of this small woman outdoing the bold, courageous man, with nothing but her feminine contrariness. He even composed a song about it.: "Ithaka's Ogygia would always have her way" or "win the day", or some such.

It occurred to me that Odysseus might be showing me how I to make better use of Ogygia's resources as repayment for my help on his arrival. He never said so, but each time he demonstrated an improvement to my living conditions there was gratefulness and pride to his voice. Naturally, I was a willing pupil, having seen what he could do for me. Odysseus was a patient and thorough teacher and I loved the attention. Yet all the while I was waiting for him to begin his leaving preparations and admit to such intentions. For all his talking of Ithaka and home, I was sure it was only a matter of time. The longer he withheld his decision to depart from me, the more I dreaded the day, until I began to wonder if he, too, was avoiding that final moment.

Kalypso : 'Tritagonist'
_____

KALYPSO : MONODY

Odysseus was convinced my temperamental island sat at the edge of the oceans, the furthest south than any sailor might venture and live to speak of again. Sometimes it truly seemed so. That was why the sea ghosts that haunted the path before it could not escape their watery fate, for the way beyond Ogygia was Oblivion. A dark nothingness. And no one dead, alive, or in between, wished to get caught in a current that might drag them over the unimaginable. Ships could disappear forever beneath those terrible waves. Vessels would widely skirt the island, desperate to protect their passengers and cargo, and none would go beyond its north-facing side.

Yet it was the high cliffs at the southern side of the island that both frightened and fascinated me. From there you could watch as the newly born clouds stole waters from the ocean below and flew away, like children thieving fruit from an orchard. From there they would dissolve into the blue sky above, grow and form and merge, until it was time to deliver their stolen goods on an unsuspecting world.

Emma Walker

There were days when I stood facing the Oblivion, admiring the thin shimmering line of the horizon, and well believed in the ineffable nothing. Beyond the billowing mists must surely be the end of the world, where all things begin, and beyond which nothing is visible. For what could live before birth, before the beginning of all things created?

Kalypso : 'Tritagonist'

KALYPSO'S TWENTIETH EPISODE

A contented peace began to drift about the island. The grasses wafted in the breeze. The goats munched leisurely at the ground; leaves rustled all about us; the sun beat down from above, and the noise of the waves was little more than a distant hum. Now and then, Odysseus and I collected grains together. Odysseus would hack at the roots, while I chose to run my finger tips gently over the barley heads, peeling the seeds away. He would stop and wipe his forehead, I would smile contentedly, and the he would look about him with satisfied admiration. On days like those, the whole world seemed perfect and painless.

"Argus would love this," Odysseus once mused to himself as I walked casually past his work.

"Argus?" I asked, trying not to seem too interested in the new name, though I had already begun to crave this tale. Odysseus smiled broadly.

"Argus, my dog."

"You've kept a dog in your house?"

"Ever since he was a puppy," he explained. "Argus... He had great wide eyes, with the look of an old wise man about them, but a cocky walk; a boyish wag," Odysseus described proudly.

"He was his owner's dog then?" I quipped and ducked a fistful of grass. Odysseus laughed as he watched me brush myself down from his attack.

"He was still barely a pup when I left. He just strode into the courtyard one day and relaxed down before my doorway. Various members of my household tried to get rid of him. He suffered everything, from abuse to countless bribes, but refused to move until I alone asked it of him. I made the perhaps fatal but never regretful mistake of trying to tempt him away with food. He accepted it, and hasn't left my side or my homestead since." Odysseus' eyes clouded a moment at this, and the sun momentarily dimmed in sympathy; a sharp breeze sighed through the foliage about us. As the sun's warmth began to creep back over our faces, Odysseus smiled, assuaging my look of concern.

"I named him Argus, after the giant. You know, the many-eyed giant? A great watchman. Argus was coloured in such a way - he had a tan body, black tail, white feet and belly - that if you pointed his floppy ears upward, he looked like a red fox."

"Perhaps he was?" I said.

"No. He was far too gentle, too obedient."

Odysseus pushed himself up and brushed down the grains which had stuck to his moistened skin. "It feels good to know he still protects my home," he muttered without conviction, before offering me his hand.

Emma Walker

KALYPSO : MONODY

I had not felt alone before Odysseus' arrival. Not for a long time. In the early days I was afraid to be on my own, particularly at night or during the worse of the weather. But I never had time to feel lonely, and as soon as I could indulge in such self-pity I was long past feeling it. Years of friendless play in my father's titanic house and gardens had taught me how to amuse myself when no one else was there for me. I allowed my imagination to take me on brave journeys through shadowy corridors or between menacing trees, guarded by angry black birds and spiders' webs.

I spent my days on Ogygia discovering just what Kalypso, Daughter of Atlas, was really made of, now that I had no escape from the shadows and trees. It seemed I was weaker than I'd supposed myself, yet I revelled in my own determination.

Soon after Odysseus arrived it became impossible to feel alone on the island, even with just one other person upon it. We could resign ourselves to opposite ends of the land, but while we both lived there I was sure I would never again have to be lonely.

But if he were to leave me, I would finally have to face my loneliness. How long would it take to remember who I was without him...?

KALYPSO'S TWENTY-FIRST EPISODE

In the beginning, we spoke only a little about our lives before and beyond the island. Odysseus had been consciously preoccupied, and we spent our evenings learning each other's rhythms.

One day, Odysseus appeared from the trees pushing a large wooden vat, which turned out to be two vats. He had his usual proud look on his face as he indicated to me the smaller one, lined at the base with a piece of my weaving, inside the larger, more solid specimen.

"Is it a new water container? Or a washing basin?" I enquired, with some of his infectious excitement.

"Both excellent ideas," he answered in a tone that confirmed I had not yet won the game.

"A type of bath, maybe?"

"I never thought of that," he replied, stroking his chin thoughtfully. "I expect the outer one could be used as such on another occasion. But no, my curious Kalypso, it is not a bath, nor a basin. It is a wine maker!" He watched for my reaction, and the best I could do was to raise an inquisitive eyebrow. It was a rare piece of luck if a jar of wine made it to my shores in one piece. Quite honestly, I had very little idea of the processes involved in wine making, beyond storing the large amphorae before they were rolled out at parties. My father's choice beverage had been mead, so I knew a little more about that from observing the kitchen slaves back home. Wine, if my memory served, was always opened on special occasions. On Ogygia, I and all the other creatures living here coped quite contentedly with the fresh water of our natural, central reservoir. Wine was now a minor luxury to me and any attempts to make it had resulted in meagre success - sharp tasting fruit juice at best.

"We put the fruit in the middle," he explained to my bemused silence, "then we climb in and use our feet to tread out the juice. That in turn will squeeze through your finely woven material here - which acts as a kind of sieve - and into the outer bowl. We take the central bowl out, store the extracted juice in one of the cooler caves, with a few added ingredients, and wait."

"Won't the weaving snap with the pressure from our feet?" I asked, knowing my abilities with the loom.

"Absolutely not," he assured me. "The inside bowl is fully supported by a cross of wood which rests upon the base of the outer bowl. The surface space of the material is not great enough to break. Hopefully..."

I smiled at his uncertainty, and decided to withhold all other questions for now. "You've an inventor's mind on the quiet then," I commented, admiring his ingenuity.

"I've had my moments," he replied modestly, but with a dash too much pride, so that I could tell one word from me might set him off on a trail of stories. I remained teasingly quiet, and we stood for a moment before his latest creation. Eventually I invited him to continue with his modest bragging, and he appeared to blush in my gaze. Not for the first time I felt something stir between us, some feeling I recognised and yet it felt unique to the moment. Our fingers were close to touching as we rested our hands on the vat's edge. I could feel our body heat rising and I blushed too. I glanced toward Odysseus, with a tiny movement of my head, to see if he had noticed all this. I heard his breathing, recognised the nervous, static posture he held.

"Will it work?" I croaked awkwardly, breaking the tension, my mouth feeling suddenly dry. He took a deep breath, and smiled as if I had just set him free from some difficult trial.

"Let's get the fruit and find out."

"So," I spoke while we trekked back and forth with our handfuls, emptying them into the vat, "is this really a brand new invention by the great and resourceful Odysseus?"

"Upon this island, yes," a straight-faced Odysseus answered me.

"Ah," I smiled broadly, catching the humorous glint in his eyes. "And in the rest of the world?"

Odysseus lowered his eyes sheepishly. Taking the probe in good humour, he dropped his pickings and, standing proudly before his creation, announced to an invisible audience, "I'm sorry, who else here has invented something useful today?"

"I see. This is a competition?"

"Yes it *is* a competition," he declared, "and I win."

"Another victory for skilful Odysseus," I agreed in jest, rewarding him with a crown of ripped vine.

"Do you know how long it's been since I've had one?" he asked in earnest, while gratefully fixing the crude wreath upon his head. "Too long," he answered himself. "Unruly men, unruly women, unruly seas..." he muttered as if to himself, though I knew he intended me to hear. "But considering how limited we appear to be in our choice of beverage, this, fair Kalypso, is a useful invention. In fact, I believe you will find it to be the best thing to enter your life since... beeswax candles."

"Who did invent beeswax candles?" I asked my cultured companion after giving this some thought.

"I did, two days ago!" he quickly replied, his victory crown falling pathetically to the floor as we laughed.

We gathered enough grapes to cover the base of the inner bowl, though I drew the line at picking more before we knew if his scheme would work. Odysseus sat me on the edge of the basins and wiped my feet with a piece of cloth before gamefully lifting me inside the pot. He then did the same to join me. Our feet squelched gently against the fruit and I curled my nose up in mock disgust as the slime began to fill the cracks between my toes.

"Well, go on then!" he laughed.

"What?"

"Stamp. With your feet." We padded about a few times, trying to avoid each other's toes. The barrels felt much smaller now we were both inside.

"This feels a little silly, I'm afraid," I apologised. We stopped for a moment while Odysseus thought.

"We need a distraction," Odysseus agreed, looking about us, then back at me with a strange grin. "Shall we dance?"

"I can't dance with you!" I protested instinctively.

"Why not?" he replied, and I had no ready answer. I was always taught that men and women did not dance together unless they were properly acquainted. There was no place for respectable men and women to break such unspoken rules, though I often caught sight of the kitchen slaves spinning about when they thought no one saw, rebellious to the end. Yet Odysseus' tone reminded me: we were not in my father's house. I did not even know if Ogygia was within the boundaries of the civilised world. While we were on my island, no rules of social standing need apply if we did not make them ourselves.

As I quietly disputed my ingrained rules of decency, Odysseus, impatient for an answer, took my right hand and placed it upon his left hip. His own right hand now rested on my waist, and he directed me to hold my free arm aloft as he did. I felt acutely self-conscious and awkward. But I also felt something else…

"We shall dance an epilenios," he declared quite theatrically.

"But we have no music!"

"Aha!" he replied and began humming an unrecognisable tune, turning us about, our feet stamping both fruit and each other's toes as we moved. Just as I grew suitably used to this movement, he swapped arms - directing me likewise - and span us in the opposite direction. This he repeated, to my growing amusement, increasing his speed and stamping action, at first shouting "change!" to indicate a new direction, and then, as I became used to it, "ha!" for the same reason, until I began to join in, the alternations growing chaotic in such a confined space. Eventually we were moving and stamping at such a rate I feared the whole basin might topple over completely. Throwing my head back with wild laughter, I begged him to stop. Once he consented, I realised how much we had been twirling and caught myself clinging to his arms for balance, feeling oddly aware of the curve of his muscles beneath my small palms. His skin was softer than I had expected and comfortably warm. I was embarrassed at how much I longed to caress it. He stood very still and I held on far longer than I needed to, until I worried that he might be reading my thoughts.

"I think I might be sick," I groaned, pulling slightly away.

He laughed. "And that is why women are not invited to dance at good parties. No stamina and weak stomachs." I knew that he was teasing me, but I grimaced nonetheless. If the joke had been intended to relieve the strange tension between us, it had not worked. We stood silently for a moment and whenever I caught his eye I pretended I was too dizzy to speak and he responded with a sympathetic smile, tinged with some kind of discomfort.

"What do you men do at your symposiums that women should be so excluded from seeing or hearing?" I asked, once my head had fully returned to me. We both perched ourselves carefully on opposite edges of the vat.

Odysseus smiled knowingly. "We eat, we are entertained, we talk-"

"About what?"

"The usual," he replied indifferently. "Religion, philosophy, politics. War... It's often about who has what, who wants what and who is likely to get it."

"Well, besides likely boredom, I can't see why a woman shouldn't be capable of such conversations," I decided.

"I agree," replied Odysseus. "I have been at a number of parties at which wives and daughters were present and perfectly entertaining. But they almost always made an early exit."

"Because they were bored?" I posed, and he chuckled. "I think I could manage to be entertaining all evening," I added.

"Hmm," he said, still laughing, "I expect you could, Kalypso." And now I blushed at my solecism. In kindness, Odysseus redirected his attention to the greying mush beneath us.

"Perhaps, in future, we need a beat to work to? Like oarsmen. Or a chant maybe? I do remember one that my friend Perimedes was working on." He cleared his throat, and began:

"Poseidon, Poseidon, he wants to halt our journey home; he tried to blow our ship around, until our vessel ran aground. The native women ran at us, pulled out their breasts and made us lust-"

"Hang on!" I objected.

"Oh no, it gets better! Eventually the women take control of the situation, impose their will on us and make us all see the error of our shameless male behaviour..." He laughed mischievously at my disapproval.

"Puerile nonsense!" I rolled my eyes at him. "And why do I not believe you...?"

"I'm sorry. Perhaps that's just for the men then." He laughed, feigning a coyness I could tell was a performance, and one that had graciously cleared me of my earlier embarrassment. For a moment his eyes glazed over with memories, but before he was lost to the darkness within, he interrupted himself. "*You* must know a good song to sing?"

"What makes you say that?" I asked.

"I saw that strange looking instrument you have out on display."

"You mean the pandouris?"

"That's the one," he agreed. "Bit of a battered old thing."

"I don't play it as well as I should like to," I excused myself. Something about my tone must have seemed off-putting. Odysseus relented, returning to his footwork in the vat and I joined him, our feet squelching the mush below us, pulling apologetic faces as we caught each other's toes.

"When did you start learning?" he asked as we relaxed back into the repetitive work. I could not help but smile warmly. He was as careful and precise in his interrogations as he was everything else.

"It was shortly after I arrived here," I answered. Odysseus looked up curiously.

"You found it on the island...?"

Such was the cue for *my* stories. I told Odysseus how I almost became Menelaus' wife, but was led astray by the pandouris' owner; how I dived to my death and yet was fated to live...

When I had finished he looked both amused and concerned. It didn't do to encourage such mad and uncouth behaviour in a lady, I supposed, but he certainly did not condemn my actions. Indeed, I have already recounted to you his response to my betrothal to Menelaus. In return, he told me what had happened before he was brought to the island; about the war he had fought and won in Troy, not so many years ago; a war blamed on Helen, the true wife of Menelaus. I felt a pang of resentment towards this woman. I had never met her and yet I instantly disliked her, not only for her part in the whole terrible affair, but for being the woman that so dramatically replaced me. Poor

Kalypso : 'Tritagonist'

Menelaus.

"Poor Menelaus indeed," confirmed Odysseus. "History will blame beautiful Helen for one of the heaviest conflicts in our lifetime, I'm sure... Yet if the world only knew, they would say it was all along down to the decisions of you and I..."

We stood opposite each other, the sludge of grey beneath us, contemplating each other's tales.

"Do you think it has worked?" I asked, looking down at our efforts.

"Just a little more," Odysseus replied, and stamped his foot playfully, splashing my legs. Before I could react to his challenge there was a sound reminiscent of cloth being torn and Odysseus' foot suddenly sunk somewhere below. I unsuccessfully stifled a laugh. He looked up at me, willing me to say the wrong thing.

"Is everything alright?" I asked, quickly biting my lip.

"There may have been a slight... miscalculation on the strength of your weaving. On my part." Odysseus also failed to hold back a chuckle, and we fell about arguing over whose fault it really was, trying to save what we could of the badly filtered juice.

Then Odysseus the inventor began the story of his greatest invention.

Emma Walker

KOMMOS

"But come now, change this tale. Sing of the wooden horse,

built by Epeus, aided by goddess Athene, from the clever plan of great

Odysseus,

which he delivered to the city gates of Troy, its belly filled with soldiers

eager to destroy..."

"Yes, tell us the stories of clever Odysseus," we requested fair Kalypso. "Tell us, neglected goddess, what you thought as he shared with you his tales of the Cyclops and the cannibals, the witch Circe and the moving rocks."

"Cyclops and cannibals?" She looked at our eager faces with some curiosity, but her puzzlement turned into a mysterious smirk.

"I can recite for you some of the stories - those I remember - of your clever Odysseus. The stories he told me of himself and his journeys. There were women of malice, even treacherous cliffs in some of his tales. But I am afraid you will hear nothing of a Cyclops or cannibals in my telling.

"Nevertheless, the first episode he told me I think you may know and like just the same."

She turned to the fire again, chuckling and muttering to herself, "Cyclopes and cannibals! What stories they do tell these days..."

KALYPSO'S TWENTY-SECOND EPISODE

"So, what was it then?" I asked him as we rolled and rocked the salvaged juice-filled barrel between us, taking it to its resting place in one of the caverns.

"What was what?" he replied distractedly.

"What was the invention you were going to tell me about earlier? There must have been something." He appeared to blush a little under my interest and a modest smile touched his lips. "Come on," I insisted blithely, "I can tell there was one to boast about."

"Not really," he said in a more sedate tone. "It was a good idea, but its aftermath was... less than satisfactory in my view."

"Well, tell me; what was it then? Let me decide on it." We walked back outside into the warmth of the day and rested on a sandy patch of ground, washing our feet in the surf.

"It was a horse," he answered mysteriously.

"A horse?" I laughed. " You invented the horse?"

"Not *the* horse, my silly Kalypso, *a* horse. A wooden horse to be exact."

"What was a wooden horse good for?" I asked curiously.

"Ending a war," he answered solemnly. A chill wind swept over us and I felt I could say nothing further until he did. He took a deep breath and explained:

"We were stuck in Troy, neither winning nor losing. The camps were full of disheartened men, especially after the death of great Achilles. One by one, our best warriors were falling, and he was one of the most revered, particularly amongst the common soldiers. Many of them were convinced he was immortal; he'd lived through so many battles and attempts on his life."

"Were you good friends?" I asked him.

"No," he responded very matter of fact. "Most of the kings I fought with under Tyndareus' Oath were barely acquaintances, and where I had known one or two it was often through politics. We grew close during the war, as fighting men do of necessity, but we were not all friends. Merely allies." He laughed dryly.

"Achilles, the great hero of many of those young soldiers, was little more than a mummy's boy to me. He was apparently the product of an unhappy marriage. In his youth an oracle had declared he would die in battle, so his mother panicked and did everything she could to keep him well away from men's games. And so it would always have been, but for his father taking charge and giving him up to be educated by a learned old man."

"I'm surprised, by this description, that he was trying to win *perfect* Helen's hand then?" I said, adding my sarcastic epithet to that woman's name.

"He was not," Odysseus replied.

"Then why should he be in Troy with you?"

"Oracles!" Odysseus fumed. "Damned seers. They'll tell anyone anything if they're paid and favoured enough. An oracle told Achilles' mother he would die in battle, so his mother tried to hide him from war. An oracle told Achilles' father that Troy would only fall if Achilles himself were present. That's worth a brag in any father's book - a son that will take down the great City of Troy! I'm sure I'd boast it of my son, if I didn't know better."

"So he joined you in order to defeat Troy?"

"He didn't help bring down Troy," Odysseus dismissed. "It was all a waste... But the prophecy stood, and it was too well known; how could we not want Achilles to join us? When I was sent to enlist him, his mother had him disguised as a young girl - and I'm not altogether unsure he didn't enjoy such nonsense! I would not have given him a second glance were I not under Agamemnon's command - that was Agamemnon, brother of Menelaus', and another of the lords with his own agenda," he pointed out for my benefit and sighed heavily. "This may sound more confusing than I'd hoped."

"Well, perhaps you should get back to the horse then!" I suggested and he laughed.

"Very well, impatient Kalypso, I give you the horse." He began to draw on the sand before us with a stick, describing each part as he went.

"Here we have the legs. They were four oversized and double-layered barrels, not too different in size to that splendid winemaker I've just made us." I smiled with similar appreciation as he indicated towards the cave, internally lingering over his use of "us".

"Inside the barrels would sit four of our smaller but swiftest soldiers. The outer part would be filled as much as possible with wine, so that when the Trojans came to pierce the wood, wine would flow out and they'd think it the only content." He allowed me to show my approval of this part of the scheme before continuing.

"The barrels were placed on two especially strong chariots to make it easier for us and the enemy to transport it, making it up to and - as we'd hoped - inside the city walls. Above the barrels was the large body. This we fashioned like a small upturned boat, and we added a base to it with a concealed trapdoor. We could fit a good half-dozen men within it, though I tell you now it was highly uncomfortable.

"The horse's head was created expertly, a near work of art by Epeus, and we tied to it - and to the rear of the horse - some coloured leather strips, to represent the mane and tail. There," he declared, looking down at his scribbled image, which was not nearly as clear as the image in my head.

"How on earth did you have the time, in the middle of a war, to build a giant toy?" I queried.

"Think of the manpower we had," he explained. "Six men might have taken six months over it, but we had hundreds of men sat around, desperate for a taste of long-sought victory. The possibility of a plan of attack was too much for them to dismiss, and they threw themselves at the job. Epeus was a master craftsman before the war, and he did wonderful work, endeavouring to make the object look as much like a horse as possible - that animal being so important to our enemy. We worked on the idea of the legs together; hiding men inside while offering wine - it seemed so foolproof."

"And was it foolproof?"

He paused.

"We won, Kalypso. We won because of that horse. And perhaps because the wine was drugged. Though with all the partying the enemy did when they thought we had retreated, we probably never needed it to be. The worse part was the waiting. Four men packed into the legs, looking up at the squashed men in the body. It took a great deal of hissing threats to stop my men from taking to the drink themselves. First, we needed to wait for the enemy to gain the courage to enter our abandoned camp and find the horse there. We then had to wait and see if they would accept its story. For this, we had left one of our men, Sinon, to lie about our withdrawal-"

"That sounds the more dangerous assignment," I interrupted.

"Of course! But we were all there. If we could not have saved him from their swords in time, you could be sure his death would have been avenged with alacrity."

"Oh," I said sullenly, not sure this would be comfort enough for me in his place.

"If you would rather I didn't tell you about such things-" he apologised, but I stopped him.

"No, no, I do! I just wondered... Did he survive?" Odysseus half-smiled at my concern, then became distant. I longed to acquire a stronger constitution for such narratives, for his sake. I could tell he had so many stories, and I hated to think he might hold back because I could not bear the details.

"Sinon survived the deception, though he was tortured through it. He survived long enough to follow the agreed plan - letting us out of the horse once we were inside the city walls and lighting the message beacon for our waiting troops outside. What happened after the last battle, I do not know."

"And what happened once you made it inside the city?"

"Things you would not wish to hear about," he said as he made to leave.

"I'm glad the horse was a success," I said and he responded with a grateful smile, but I could tell he was keeping a great deal inside, things he might be frightened to reveal. We were only just learning to understand each other and were still strangers in so many ways. But at least I had discovered a little more of the kind of man this Odysseus was - a war hero, a great inventor - and I was anxious to know what more...

Kalypso : 'Tritagonist'

KALYPSO'S TWENTY-THIRD EPISODE

Odysseus did not end his story of the wooden horse there. Later, as if giving me a second chance, he told me how it had not been wholly his idea. We were sat together, drinking a mead-like concoction Odysseus had instructed me in; as good as we might get to the gods' Ambrosia, he assured me, and I well believed it then. Honey was yet another treat I had only begun to enjoy on the island since Odysseus took over the food supplies. I was stung by a wasp as a child, twice on the same arm, and the memory of that pain had frightened me away from attempting to entangle myself in the lives of bees, though I knew they were far less likely to attack than their unnatural cousins. Odysseus, however, seemed to have a way with nature. He told me he knew how to scrape and tap a nest of its contents, and had plans to build a small hive. I tried not to laugh when he returned from his first honey-collecting endeavour with two smarts from unhappy drones on his arms. But I could not laugh at his success, which was impressive. Tasting the sweet and sticky liquid after so very long, I admired those stinging wounds as victory scars.

As we drank to the dusk, Odysseus spoke of a seer who had told his comrades, in the usual cryptic way, of the need to offer a horse to Athene in order to regain her favour and win the war. Odysseus' dislike of seers was always evident.

"One says Achilles will die at war, another says the war will never be won without him! Pah!" he spat. "Achilles? Great warrior Achilles? Of course he fell in battle, as so many others did beside him! His fighting skills were good, but not infallible! Any man who goes to war gambles his life, and a war as long as the one we were fighting was bound for death and casualties. Which is why I never wanted to be there..." His voice trailed. He drank a large gulp of wine as if steadying his nerves.

"Achilles was too emotional in battle. He was foolish enough to let women and love dictate his life. In the end his death had no more effect nor meaning on the war but to deflate our men yet further. It was a foolish errand to have made, bringing him to our campaign. His attitude delayed so much of our effort..." Odysseus halted again and breathed deeply. He shook his head and it hung sadly for a moment. Then, as if remembering himself, he returned to his intended story.

"It was the horse, not Achilles, that won us the war. Have I said?" I nodded calmly. Once more he sighed heavily and rubbed his brow.

"They gave so much credence to the words of old men and hysterical women," he bemoaned. "Those great and intelligent men, brave and foolish warriors all. They would give up every shred of sensibility for one word from a seer! I determined to play that old fool of a seer at his own fantastical game. The lords had been told in the past by a seer from the enemy's side that Troy would fall if we could steal the Palladium from the temple. We did so, and still Troy stood - as if the knowledge that these prophecies came from a Trojan were not enough reason for sane men to doubt them! But too many believed, and so it was done. Now our own seer told us we could only win if we dedicated a great horse to Athene in recompense for the theft of the Palladium-"

"Wait! *The* Palladium?" I interrupted.

"It's a great statue," he explained. "The image of Athene's best friend, Pallas-"

"I know," I interrupted, "but my sister - one of my sisters, Elektra," I clarified for his sake, "told me about it. I had no idea she had been to the City of Troy to see it though?"

"I don't think it was always at Troy," he assured me. "We heard the Trojans themselves stole it or were gifted it from another city at some stage, as these things often happen..."

Emma Walker

KALYPSO : MONODY

There were times, much later, when in anger I would sometimes feel as though all I ever did was listen to Odysseus' confessions, and yet he had no time for mine.

Not that I had many. Comparatively few, in fact.

In retrospect I wondered if his pauses were invitations to comment or expand on my own part of a tale. I was always too embarrassed or engrossed to take them up.

I could have told him how my sister, Elektra, had betrayed her husband with a lover; how she had run away on discovering she was heavy with child by this other man. I never knew for certain where she went, nor did I know what happened to the child, though my sisters muttered that she had abandoned it. Elektra once sat amongst us, crying about how she'd hid herself behind the Palladium statue, in fear of her life.

But I was too young to understand or sympathise with her story...

Kalypso : 'Tritagonist'
―――――――――――――――

KOMMOS

"We can tell you, shining Kalypso, the story of your sister," we announced. She looked sternly at us and a flash of ancient fear coloured her eyes.

"Are these things I wish to know?" she asked us, and we did not know at first how to answer this great lady. As we searched among us for one with a correct response, she continued: "I have asked many questions in the past whose replies have been a disappointment to me." She threw some fresh cedar chips on the fire and watched for a moment as they spat and crackled in the sudden heat. Before we could argue that perhaps our tale was not as important as her story after all, she spoke again in a distant tone.

"Oh, what care I of the truth now? He is gone and I am an old woman. You may tell me your story."

"Your great sister Elektra," we began, "was seduced away from her husband by the great god Zeus-"

"Hah!" Kalypso cried derisively, her voice cutting up our words like the strike of a sword against flesh. "Another one," she muttered as we sat in stunned silence. "Well, go on," she entreated impatiently.

"Elektra bore a son, Dardanus, whom she left in Samothrace in the care of parents whose true identities remain unknown. Some say Thuscus, or even Ilithius, was his adoptive father. Whoever it was, they raised him as a son alongside their own eldest child, Iaison. Shortly after Dardanus came of age, his elder brother was killed by Zeus for laying with Demeter-"

"Stop, stop!" Kalypso exclaimed once more. "My mind no longer hears such excuses. I have no doubt you are all instructed to continue these heroic fabrications. For all our sakes, therefore, I shall amend this story to my liking.

"We shall say," she considered before us, "that this Iaison most likely became entangled with another man's wife and was killed where caught, fornicating with his unfaithful lover. There. I am satisfied. You may go on."

We could not say we approved of great Kalypso's altering the story, but a goddess's whims must be adhered to, and so we humoured her and continued:

"After his brother's death, Dardanus' adoptive parents decided to inform him of his true identity. Armed with this knowledge he became a great leader, encouraging his people to settle at new lands in Phrygia, and later ruling over that area bequeathed him by your great father, the Titan Atlas, who was most grateful to discover Dardanus as his grandson. In turn, Dardanus' own grandson, Tros, became the leader of the people known as... The Trojans..."

Lovely haired Kalypso sat before us, unmoving, as she had done so before by our revelations. Her brow showed the signs of sad understanding. It was with a heavy heart that we concluded our tale:

"It is said that, following the destruction of Troy, your sister Elektra was deeply saddened, and her star has since faded in the sky."

After an endless pause, Kalypso sighed wearily, a great lingering sound from that elderly woman.

"My sister," she forlornly declared, "would have been long past caring."

Emma Walker

KALYPSO : MONODY

Oh, how I hoped Elektra never blamed me! How easily she could have done so, if only she had known. What a great relief it is that we mortals, living in our own small worlds, never get to see the whole picture, or hear the whole story. So much of my past, it seems, was entangled in that foolish war in Troy. Yet I knew nothing of it!

I have heard so many fantastical descriptions of myself, I am almost ashamed: 'Nymph' Kalypso. 'Goddess' Kalypso. 'Lovely-haired' and 'lustrous', 'shining among divinities'. Odysseus, it is true, would compliment my hair on occasion, and praise me in other ways with much nonsense, but I must disappoint you; I have never been a goddess or nymph. Had I been either, I would certainly have avoided so many of the tragedies I seemed to inflict.

Kalypso, inadvertent murderer of many; illicit lover of good-hearted Odysseus. Misguided woman. These are epithets the *living* at least do not yet give me...

Kalypso : 'Tritagonist'
_____

KALYPSO'S TWENTY-FOURTH EPISODE

"After the seer's prediction," continued Odysseus, "the call went out to find the strongest and best groomed horse in the army. They were to cut its throat there and then, as an offering to Athene."

"How awful," I groaned.

"Very! As if we could spare a horse! Now we were to take our best and kill it just because an old man with a dubious vision had told us to," Odyssey complained. "I wonder, had he told us we needed to kill our best *men* as an offering to Zeus to guarantee victory, would the call still have gone out? Nonsense!" He took another sip of drink. "Needless to say, I would have none of it. I requested the death sentence be postponed so that I might be allowed to consider how killing a horse would enable us to take the city."

"But you believed the story about the Palladium was true? You did think that stealing it would win you the war?"

"I had no belief that it would win us the war, but at the time I agreed it might give us an advantage," he explained. "If you lose something important in war, it is always discouraging. It seemed we'd been taking the brunt of that tactic. A challenge is always welcome at war when things are looking bleak. Challenges suggest hope. We knew it to be a good boost of morale to have a defined object for the men to aim for, something achievable. Like a standard fought over in training. The palladium was a good choice, though we suspected it might just as well be a trap. Obtaining it was certainly not straightforward.

"My problem was trying to work out how a dead horse could bring us closer to the war's end. The loss of the Palladium had failed to have an adequate impact, but the horse's death must be definitive.

"At first there was dissension - many of the men simply wanted to have the sacrifice over with so we could charge the walls, believing this bloodletting to be enough to fulfil the prophecy. Men who would have rightly thought such a course of action foolhardy suicide, had they not so tired and fraught with loss. But these were desperate times. Had I not gained the support of Nestor - wise old Nestor, whose council was so trusted by all - who agreed with my call for patience, their request might have been hastily granted. Nestor was like a father to us, and, like all sons, we did not always follow his counsel to the letter. But Nestor and I bonded over our love of storytelling. The anecdotes he told of his life and youthful battles were an inspiration to me, and he in turn admired my debating abilities. So he was the best ally I, and the entire Achaean army, could have at such a time. He calmed the nerves of Agamemnon and Menelaus and I had a night to ponder the problem of the horse.

"As I watched women work, patching wounds and washing clothes, the men pass the time waiting, so close to death and destruction, I overheard an argument between two young boys. One claimed he had hidden beneath a goat in his youth to escape penance at his neighbour's hand for stealing fruit. The argument was most amusing and neither boy was likely to win without proof. I found myself continuing it in my mind and thought on tales of men who would ride the bellies of their horses into battle, swinging onto their horses' backs at the last minute, taking their enemies by surprise."

"Is that possible?" I asked, intrigued.

"Very difficult," Odysseus agreed. "But I have seen the Amazonian women perform similar feats on horseback, so I would call nothing impossible."

The stars twinkled excitedly above us as I poured a second helping of mead. Odysseus stoked the fire gently and I moved in close to him for warmth while he continued his account.

"It occurred to me once more that a live horse would be much more advantageous than a dead one, and if we might uncover some way of sneaking a man or two inside the city gates, attached to such a horse - perhaps under the pretence of offering that horse as a treaty gift - we would have our advantage. With the help of some of my men, I stayed up all night, working with linen, skin - all varieties of material -

wrapping a horse and attempting to strap a man safely beneath it, but nothing could make a soldier look inconspicuous in that position, though it certainly cheered the men up to try. The horse would be searched and the man killed, I concluded. So it was agreed that the man would have to be concealed *within* the horse, and there was nothing more impractical. What man would volunteer to hide within the recently slain guts of a horse? Who knows what the enemy would have made of a dead and apparently pregnant stallion! It was all too ridiculous. Until, that is, I began to imagine the horse being made not of skin, but of a sturdier material, such as wood. As you have joked - a child's toy, only much bigger.

"I called to Epeus - I have told you he was a master of woodcraft? And he truly was. I mentioned my idea, and he and I sat until dawn, drawing plans and assessing our needs and timescales. The more we discussed, the more the men were encouraged by the scheme. That same morning, in assembly with the other leaders, each began to add their own thoughts to the plan until everyone saw what a merit it had been to wait and think before acting on the seer's words. The design of the horse belonged to Epeus and myself, but battle plans were organised by Agamemnon, Menelaus, Nestor and others until, by the end of the meeting, we had agreed on everything.

"As many men as we could spare from the ongoing skirmishes were set to work cutting and shaping and fixing. Precious stones were added for the eyes, but the nose holes were left open, and various

Kalypso : 'Tritagonist'

small punctures were made about the body so that those who were to hide inside would be able to breathe. When completed, it stood at a height of three tall men, and was a great source of pride I can tell you, not just to myself. While other battle plans were being arranged, Menelaus and I, and a selection of good men, would practice entering and leaving the belly. Wine was added to the exterior part of the four legs, which, though they made the horse look rather dumpy, we thought would make the gift yet more appealing. It was, after all, meant to signify the Trojan's victory and our retreat, which they would be keen to celebrate. We placed small carriage wheels at its feet to make it easier for them to roll the heavy horse into the city. We tried to think of everything from our adversary's point of view in the hope that nothing could go wrong with this plan."

"But weren't you afraid they might simply throw a torch at it? Being wood, it might be seen as a the best way to treat it, whether they approved of its offer or not?"

"Of course we were afraid of that. The plan was that only one man would remain alive beside the horse, and that was to be Sinon son of Aesimus - a cousin from my mother's family. Our entire camp was burnt and all other men set sail by boat to a point out of sight, so it might look as though they had fled. If the Trojans decided to torch the horse, as you suggest, with us inside, we would have no compensation. But at least every other man would escape with his life. The war would be lost to us. The wooden horse was our last hope.

"Inside, the wooden belly was hot and cramped, with barely a foot's length to move in. We had to wait - to breathe - in silence, though it seemed to every man as though his heart could be heard as loudly as a drumbeat. We could only take a single sword each as weaponry, and only wear the lightest of breastplates, since there was so little room, and no space for shields or long spears. We had to pray for an easy battle if it came to it, though once we were within the walls we would be able to call for the return of our allies to support us - Sinon was to light the beacon fire as a signal - but that part of the plan seemed a long time away.

"We could hear everything from within that wooden shell. Every word spoken, every thought aired by our enemy. Every victory cheer and, of course, the terrible torture of our man." Odysseus sighed heavily and I stroked his arm comfortingly. "It was one of the hardest moments I experienced in that war - and there were a great many hardships to face. But to feel so helpless... And yet to be forced to remain calm for the sake of those men about me..." His breathing grew heavier, as if he were feverish.

"You can stop this story if you don't want to tell it?" I assured him, concerned at his discomfort. For a while he sat, deep in thought, looking at the ground as if at some invisible battle being raged there in the flickering shadows.

"They never mentioned fire," he continued suddenly. "They talked of rolling us over the edge of a cliff, of destroying us with axes and swords. At one point a spear was thrown and roughly hit the side of the horse on which I rested. My heart pounded with fear, but the enemy's talk strengthened my men's resolve. We heard Sinon tell his carefully planned fiction of our weary departure, and then of the fake prophecy he was to claim had been uttered by Calchas who, despite residing on *our* side throughout the war, was a well-respected seer throughout the whole region. It was he who had foreseen Achilles' alleged invaluable role in War, and Agamemnon had been swayed to recruit him after a few happy predictions made on his behalf in the past. So there was a great deal of irony, I always thought, in that lie. An prophesy from their own soothsayer had been attributed to ours. I don't suppose either seer saw that one coming!" I laughed gently and Odysseus smiled, but there was still darkness in his eyes.

"Sinon repeated his tale over and over, and each time they treated him worse. I would not have blamed him if he had given in and confessed the truth, but not once did he do so. They hacked off his ears and nose. But he was the best of us that day, and I was never prouder of my kin. Even though some of the stories he told were slanders on me, I nearly wept to hear him cry out, insisting on their truth. There never was a better liar, and never one, in my book, that lied for a better cause. Though some of what he said about me was fair..." There was a strange turn from admiration to shame in his speech.

"Such as what?" I asked intrigued, though I should have stayed quiet. Odysseus flinched with that now recognisable pain, and I guessed any answer he gave might reveal those dark moments he wanted to hold back from me. "But it all ended well?" I quickly changed the subject.

"Not well," he argued, "but it ended. Despite protests from their own seers and prophets. There was one - a woman of their city named Kassandra, who was the most fervent and, from where we sat, terrifyingly accurate in her proclamations, so that I might almost believe in soothsayers again. But the decision, to our great relief, was made to carry the horse within the walls. Sinon, too, was eventually spared by his torturers and allowed to enter as a traitor to his own, and a new friend of the Trojans.

"We waited all night while the world outside us shouted and cheered, sang and danced, made the usual proclamations to the gods and jeered at the seeming departure of our army. I should have felt angry and bitter sat amongst those people, longing to jump from the wooden trap and take revenge on the foolish Trojans. Maybe I should have been laughing at the very thought. I suspect some of the men about did so. It would be better for them if they had, rather than finding themselves picturing the faces of those unsuspecting, innocent civilians as I did then. Fighting trained soldiers on the battlefield is one thing - we all expect to face death, and can defend ourselves accordingly. But my hands shook at the thought of leaving that confined belly and setting to the necessary task; my stomach turned each time I heard the playful scream of a child, the laughter of lovers, the relief in the voices of aged citizens, none of whom had ever wanted this war any more than I. In my imaginings, their faces became those of my own loved ones back home... I wanted to command those with me not to kill any unarmed people they came across, but I knew this would be futile."

"Why?" I asked.

"Because we were at war. We were deep within enemy territory. In such places there are no innocents. Any man, woman or child - regardless of age - could bring about your death if you gave them a chance. It is your life or theirs, Kalypso, and we were too few in number to be considerate. Besides, any order I gave could be contradicted by the headstrong Menelaus. Or completely ignored in the heat of the moment. The last thing we needed was dissent amongst our own small band of warriors. I had to trust in the integrity of those men. I *had* to..." he repeated desperately, and I could hear the regret, the need for absolution. I would dearly have loved to set him free of his apparent burden, but he did not look to me to do so. Perhaps I had been foolish to believe that the telling and sharing would be enough to clear his conscience and help him forget.

"We should sleep," I suggested, throwing the remnants of my drink onto the earth. "I could stay awake all night and listen to your stories, dear Odysseus," I reassured him, "but my eyes are growing heavy." I smiled down at him and waited for him to rise as well.

"I'll join you in a while," he decided without looking up from the fire and I reluctantly left him to his thoughts. I did not sleep well until he eventually joined me in the warmth of the cave, lying on the soft goatskins he had cut for our comfort, and then my eyes would not stay closed until I saw him drift unhappily away into dream; far, I prayed, from the horrors he had lived.

Kalypso : 'Tritagonist'

KALYPSO'S TWENTY-FIFTH EPISODE

As was to become the ritual after such a night of tales, Odysseus arose early the following morning, saying nothing to me. I watched from my resting place as he quietly picked up tools, took some food for breakfast and crept away, always mindful not wake me. I waited long enough for him to think I had not witnessed his escape; then I rose, tidied and dressed myself, and left the cave to follow after the wanderer.

I walked slowly as birds fluttered overhead. I listened to the unhurried morning waves, mulling over what I remembered of Odysseus' story and the gaps he had left within it. I thought on how close and yet how distant we had felt in the course of one day, analysing every inflection of his voice, its resonance and melody. His laugh was warming - never too loud, almost gentle. A stark contrast to those heavy, wrenching sighs. Then there was the mention of those back home, causing my body to tighten with unnamed fear. Was it jealousy? Pleasure turned to pain and I pushed it away. But I knew it still followed me, creeping at a distance, waiting to pounce when I needed it least, its claws scratching at my heart.

It preyed on us both.

I saw Odysseus sat on the cliff top: a lonely figure, resting his elbows on his knees, and holding his face in his hands. I strode toward him, wanting to wrap my arms about him, heal him with a word. I had felt his sorrow within me, each of his memories apparently invading my own. If I could only help him through this sadness, I thought, he might finally be happy within himself, and happy here.

With me.

I stopped my assent, that little voice inside pulling me back.

"Let him be," whispered guiding Hermes. And I knew his counsel to be right, though it pained me to give into it.

It was not altogether strange to find Hermes in my thoughts at difficult times. Dear Hermes, who was my nephew by blood, and yet the age difference between his mother and I made him more of a kindly young uncle. He had never failed to make time for me when visiting my father's house. I missed thoughtful Hermes' attention. Ogygia was visited by no man before Odysseus. I had thought that a blessing when I first arrived. But there were so many times when Hermes' good advice and his kind, comforting presence would have given relief and happiness.

Kalypso : 'Tritagonist'

I carried on the day, always thinking of Odysseus as I worked, always wrestling with Hermes' voice reminding me to be patient. I prepared food, making a little extra in case of Odysseus' early return; laid out the fishing nets; swept out the cave. I had risen so early that my usual chores were completed by the time the sun reached its zenith. I returned to the cliff edge but Odysseus was no longer there. Once again I heard the counsel of Hermes and forced myself to obey. Even though my guest was now in good health and more than capable of making his own way about the island, I still felt sure he needed my constant care and attention.

I returned to the cave and my loom, but my mental tension spread quickly to my spine and I tired of the effort of weaving. So I picked up the pandouris, which had been much neglected of late, and took it to the same spot on the cliff where Odysseus had sat that morning, looking out over the ocean. I strummed and plucked and hummed a few tunes to myself, while watching the distant movement of the clouds and the drifting surf. I stayed there until evening began to draw across the sky, with still no sign of the wanderer's return. So I decided to try and compose a song as something to focus my heavy thoughts.

"Hermes, advise me on how I might see him," I sang, then changed it to, "Hermes, advise me on how I might serve thee, and wait patiently for my love to..." I stopped. "No," I decided aloud.

"Why not?" asked Odysseus' from behind me. I blushed with

guilt, though I suspect he'd had no idea of my meaning. Odysseus sat down beside me. "May I?" he asked taking the pandouris in his hand.

"If you want," I allowed reluctantly. I watched him move his fingers about the strings, strum hesitantly, smile when he found a sound he liked. Something deep inside me stirred uneasily at the sight of Odysseus playing what was once Damon's.

"Can you play?" I asked him.

"I used to play the kithara," he admitted. "I had a nurse, Eurykleia - well, she was more of a second mother," he looked up and caught my eye, adding "oftentimes a first."

"You were lucky to have more than one," I said.

"You had no mother?" he asked.

"Oh, I had one," I explained, "but she grew tired of me, and was rarely there for me once my sister Maera was born. I think my parents assumed, with so many older sisters, that I had more than enough teachers of 'womanly ways'."

"Sounds like a fun household," he mocked and I screwed my face up disdainfully, while acknowledging his intended humour.

"Unfortunately my sisters were far too preoccupied to concern themselves with my education in *any* subject. I learnt what I could by observation." Odysseus smiled with sympathy. "It must have been nice to have someone looking after you."

"Eurykleia? Oh, she was good to me. She was a good nurse. Though, if I had let her be as good as she wished, I would have been no better off than Achilles and *his* womanly ways!" he laughed.

"When I was a boy, Eurykleia would play me songs to help me sleep. She had quite a gruff voice for a woman, and was not the greatest storyteller, but she made the best of it, and I learnt - as you did - a great deal from observation and listening. At times I have considered women to be the best teachers of men. It's easier to listen to what a woman's voice advising you - particularly if they have a pretty mouth."

"That's not true!" I protested.

"Oh, but it is," he laughed. "I once knew a woman who taught me some of the strongest knots I've ever learnt to tie - far better than any sailor's attempts! And I cannot deny I remember them better for watching her slender fingers at work, observing the movement of those wrist muscles, flexing and twisting."

"So she was pretty," I said petulantly.

"Compared to some," he grinned mischievously.

"Then why are you not with her now?" I asked, more petulant still, probing while he remained in good humour.

"Because she was a witch," he answered bluntly, as though I should have already known it. "She used her wits to enchant men. And underneath she was not as beautiful as she seemed. Quite cold in fact. Likely to throw any man aside for another if she thought him the more handsome or worthy of her. She was too cunning for her own good." I did not know who this woman had been, but I felt I could discount her as the reason he retained an emotional distance from me.

"Do you think Helen was too cunning?" I pried, still trying to guess at the identity of his entanglement. Odysseus scoffed at my suggestion.

"Helen was never cunning. She may have had enough intelligence to know how to get what she wanted, but she had absolutely no notion of what to do once she had."

Odysseus returned to the pandouris, strumming and singing a stunted ditty, stopping between each line to move to the right place on the instrument's slender neck, many times making do with a terrible chord and a tongue-in-cheek grin.

"*A prophecy was told of me that I would be a man,*
I was a boy and what a joy as now a man I am.
The seer was right, what a delight to my dear family,
That I should turn from boy to man for all the world to see."

I laughed and applauded the satire and he bowed in gracious imitation.

"Did you just make that up?" I asked.

"Of course!" he claimed and I deigned to believe him.

"So, what did the seers really say about the great Odysseus?" I asked.

"When I was a child, they told my mother I would die a comfortable death." He shook his head indignantly.

"That's all?" I asked him, after a silent pause. He nodded. "Well,"

Kalypso : 'Tritagonist'

I sighed, "at least that's something."

"If by 'something' you mean 'nothing'," he reproached, "then yes."

"What do you mean?"

"I mean, it means *nothing*. They told my mother what she would like to hear. What mother will pay to hear that her son will die in agony? Nonsense. Look how it affected Achilles' mother to be told he would die at war! Besides, how and when is death ever 'comfortable'?"

I thought about this for a moment.

"I think to die in your arms might be a comfortable death for me," I concluded, with a smile.

"Silly, romantic Kalypso," he dismissed me with a reflected smile.

"No, really," I protested, moving in close to him and wrapping his arms about my shoulders, resting my head on his chest. "You have exceedingly soft contours," I giggled. "This would do me quite well." I squeezed his hands between mine, but then loosened my hold, expecting him to pull away. But he didn't. I was a little startled to feel him remain there, holding me to him quite naturally, breathing gently into my hair as we watched the night sky turning.

Emma Walker

KALYPSO'S TWENTY-SIXTH EPISODE

That was the first night we slept together.

I know what you have heard of me, so you should think nothing more into those words but exactly what I have said. We slept, lying together, side by side, and that is all.

It being such a warm night, and tired from so many late discussions, we both slowly drifted to sleep where we sat; Odysseus resting against a tree, and I against him. When I woke from my light slumber, the night was full, its chilly air raising the hairs on my arms. I gently nudged Odysseus awake and we drowsily made our way inside the cave, slumped down onto his bedding and wrapped ourselves in my shawl. I cradled my head into his chest and thus we returned to our dreams.

Curiously, that very night I dreamt of an encounter with Damon. The conversation in this dream reflected one we'd had on board the ship, though my feelings toward the memory were much changed and the dream was awash with contradictions.

Kalypso : 'Tritagonist'

Damon and I had been lying inconspicuously on deck late one evening. We were wedged into our usual hiding space, behind and between great crates of unknown treasures and sailing apparatus that adorned the deck. Our knees bent and feet pushed up against the wood, we reclined together, looking up at the sky.

"It is a beautiful night," he had noted, and I murmured my agreement. "Perfectly clear stars," he added.

"They are looking quite beautiful," I admired.

"Sometimes I wish I knew more about them. What they're made of, what they are called..." he said.

"I do," I declared. He turned to look at me, disbelievingly. "It's true," I insisted. "At my father's court there were housed a good many astrologers. Did you know that the stars were once simply recorded numerically, in the order in which they appeared in the night sky? So *that*," I explained, pointing to what I hoped was bright Venus, "would be First Star. Then that, perhaps, Second. That Third," I picked my examples at random. "But the wiser men from the East soon realised that different stars appeared at differing times and so they agreed that, for clarity, they would name them as they appeared fully in the sky. And they did so, after objects and animals and ancient gods and heroes.

"My father was very interested in such things - he loved to observe the sky - and when he learned that not all the stars had yet been named, he asked to have one called after himself. But the wise men could not agree on a star that shone well enough to represent him, they said. Not a big enough one to flatter him, more like. Sometimes I'm surprised they didn't pick the sun or the moon - or even our earth - and have us know that as Atlas! But instead, they requested permission to name some of the clusters of stars after my brothers and sisters. See, *there*," I pointed again, this time with more accuracy, "those are named after my sisters by my father's first wife, Queen Pleione."

"Really?" he asked, still sounding unsure of my honesty. Enjoying the rare opportunity to teach, I swore again that it was so. The story of my sisters' stars, at least.

"That is the history, to the best of my knowledge and as told to me," I pronounced. He considered this.

"If it is so true," Damon persisted, "then which is your star? Where shines Kalypso?"

"I do not yet have one," was my true and forlorn answer.

"Oh," he replied, already losing interest. And that was an end to it.

I shared this dreamed memory with Odysseus one night, while we lay with our backs against the sand. In fact it was Odysseus who pointed out my sisters, and I accounted for them, albeit in a far less confident tone this second time around.

"It was suggested they could rename the star of Sirius, or

perhaps the star of Kynosura after my father, but there had been no agreement by the time I left for Mycenae. Still, there are my sisters and my brother Hyas, see? And there, my sisters by my father's second wife, Queen Hesperis..."

"And where should I look for Kalypso?" he asked in a strange echo of Damon's request, pointing his hand up toward the sky. I reached up for his wrist and slowly began to pull it across the sky until his arm fell upon me.

"Right here," I smiled. "There is no *star* Kalypso."

"Of course there isn't," he proclaimed. "For what star could outshine brilliant Kalypso?" I had to protest this compliment as exaggeration, thinking him to be mocking me, yet he zealously disagreed, with a little twinkle in his eye. "When I first opened my eyes on this island," he explained, propping himself on one elbow, "I cannot recall, I'm sorry now to say, your face and shape. I merely remember the light that shone down from you."

"Oh really?" I said, now the dubious one.

"Yes, really. It is the same light I see shine from you every day."

"If that is so," I argued his calm and confident words, "then what colour is this light?"

"Ahh," he intoned, "that depends on bright Kalypso's mood. When you are angry, it can turn deep red. But most of the time I see it as blue. Shimmering blue. It blinded me at first, but now I love to watch it glow. There is no star that could ever compare to it."

Oh, Odysseus had a way with words. It's hard to describe how they sounded to me. How they made me feel. I had heard such clever, confident lines before and I had fallen completely under their spell. I doubted Odysseus at times. He could say something one day, something contradictory the next. The longer this went on, the harder it was to discern the real truth of his feelings; the more I would doubt myself and him. I longed for reassurance, for clarity.

Our fingers were entwined. Only our palms were touching, but it felt as though every part of us had joined together. Even without looking, I could see him lying beside me, every rise and fall of his chest, every curve of muscle and bone, from crown to heel… I could taste his skin, feel his hair, soft and smooth… And I knew, by the tightness of his fingers against mine, that he felt what I was feeling, he shared my thoughts completely… Just for that moment…

I told myself it was enough to be with him like that. Those moments of staring up at the stars, sharing feelings, the very air tingling with anticipation, were enough to satisfy me. But they never were. I wanted to join with him completely, to know he would always be with me. The longer he hesitated, the more I wanted to hold him, to kiss him, to make the experience with Damon nothing but a childish memory next to the intensity of our connection. But Odysseus never offered himself to me, never showed that intent.

I agonised a long time over my desires and concluded that I would have to ask him outright if I ever wished to understand his feelings. I had no idea how to make such a proposal. In fact, I suspected there were no rules or methods, since this was not how it was done. It would be unseemly for a freeborn lady to offer herself to a man. But I knew, as we both did, that there were no rules of etiquette on my island. We ate and drank and washed when and how we liked, worked as we chose and rested the same. There was such a sense of freedom on Ogygia that it both thrilled and alarmed me. Before Odysseus' arrival I did not even think of it in those terms. Freedom was not a luxury, but a natural way of life. Besides, it is hard to experience freedom when you must first master survival. Only now did I have the means to test how far this liberty ran.

Once I had made my decision and grown the necessary courage, I waited until Odysseus and I were lying at ease one evening, nervously asked to speak with him on a serious subject, smiling in what I hoped to be an appropriate, attractive manner. He smiled back, friendly but with an air of caution. I ran my fingers across his crown and through his hair, I let the tips brush his lips, and he caught my hand in his, gently kissed it, and then lowered it to his chest, holding it there as if afraid of where it might go if he allowed it to escape.

"I wanted to ask you," I said, a little less confidently than I had practiced it in my mind, "if you would like... properly... to share my bed?" He did not move. He smiled, a look of confused mirth, but I could see this belied his understanding. "I mean... physically?" I clarified.

"Would you like to... make love to me?"

I was afraid at the very sound of the words, embarrassed that I had spoken them aloud. I prepared myself for his shock or disgust, for outright refusal. Even mockery. Perhaps these were all reasonable reactions to a woman who offered herself to a man? Hopefully he would forgive me once he'd calmed, and put it down to the unusual situation we found ourselves in. I was sure such a request would never have been appropriate, never heard of in the great cities we came from, although echoes of my encounter with Damon came flooding back to haunt me. Perhaps these things were simply never admitted to? I hoped Odysseus would not thereafter look at me as no better than a whore. At least, I felt sure, he was too good a man to use me that way even if he did say yes.

Odysseus looked at me intently, but not with derision or laughter. I realised the words had filled him with just as much anxiety as they did me. I thought perhaps I saw a kind of pity in his eyes, or maybe shame, but I could not tell if it was directed at me.

"Oh Kalypso," he answered mournfully, "I am so sorry... I can't..." He was apologetic, but not excusing.

I did not push him further to explain. He looked so pained and filled with regret at his response, and I was too busy acknowledging my own hurt. I felt foolish and confused. I had expected I might feel that way, but his kind reaction made it harder to bear somehow.

After this we carried on, as we always did: very aware of each

Kalypso : 'Tritagonist'

other, while trying not to show it. That night we lay together to sleep, as before, Odysseus' arms were around me, and it seemed as though he held me closer than ever, but I sobbed pitifully as he slept.

KALYPSO : MONODY

I know you have all heard how he stayed on my island for some considerable time. I neglected to record the passing of days from the moment of my arrival. We recorded it instead, while he stayed, by anecdote. But there was no sense of weeks, months or years in our small world, no marked seasonal changes to the isle. As with all such compassed relationships, I remember good times and bad; interesting conversations and ugly arguments. I would sometimes be complimented, sometimes ignored. Odysseus and I would spend wonderful evenings, talking and sharing stories; and then he would desert me for a whole day, as if trying to punish the both of us. In the end, I realised, it was only himself he wished to punish.

There were days we would walk along the sands. We would laugh and run and play like children. But while I kept running and laughing, he would lag behind, as if staying in reach of the eyes of invisible guardians, afraid to stray too far, get into trouble, become lost. And I would have to go back for him, dragging my heels, wandering why he couldn't, just once, run a little further with me, laugh a little longer. Then he'd know, there wasn't anything to be afraid of...

I didn't know about her. About his son...

"My brilliant Kalypso," he would say, spinning me about, kicking his toes through the surf, "sometimes I cannot think why I should ever want to leave this place?"

"I wish you wouldn't say such things," I would reply sadly.

"Why?"

Because I don't think you should leave at all, I would think but never say.

"Whenever you do, you always look out to the horizon in that way... As if looking for something better."

"Nonsense!" he would argue, but I could see it in his eyes. He knew it was true. "I lost many good friends to that ocean."

"I know. But that was some time ago. Each of them will have found their way to the next world by now."

"There are other friends though... I can't help wondering after them too. How many of them are still alive? My good friends-"

"Just friends?" I snapped in response to his languishing tone. "Tell me about the other women."

Odysseus sighed at my question, ominously. Reluctantly. When he answered, he did not look at me.

"There was one," he said, "called Briseis."

"Was she pretty?" I asked, pretending to myself that I could push away all the disagreeable, jealous thoughts inside.

"She was attractive enough to be fought over."

"You *fought* for her?"

"No," he laughed gently. "No, not I. Agamemnon and Achilles were-"

"Why do you tell me about her?" I interrupted curtly, and he seemed taken aback, but not altogether surprised at my tone.

There was so much I didn't know at the time. I had moments of what felt like clarity. Yet always they were shadowed by confusion, anger even, at his behaviour, his rejection of me. Rejection without reason, since I could see in his eyes that he wanted to say yes, but it always became no.

Sorry, Kalypso, no.

I could not truly understand his feelings any more than I thought he could mine.

The closer we became, the worse would be the rejection. It would be hard for me to have considered us lovers, though I could tell my attachment to him grew ever more passionate, and sometimes I knew that to be mutual. I sensed it in him, right before he would run.

I missed him in his absences, be they deliberate avoidance of me, or while we worked separately. I looked forward to those evenings we spent together, and then to lying with him as we slept.

And all that time he fought the turmoil inside him, while I thought I alone suffered...

Sometimes I would wake to find him rolled away from me, and my mind would tease my emotions with little doubts. Was it a purposeful move on his part? Did he wait until I was asleep and then push me away? Did he hate himself for being that close to me?

What was wrong with me?

I had nothing to compare his behaviour to and no one to question but Odysseus himself. How could I tell him that seeing his back turned on me when I woke left me feeling lonely and lost? I felt sure he would laugh at my childish reactions, or grow uneasy at my possessiveness. Or he might use it as an excuse to end the unspoken arrangement altogether? Any predicted outcome was enough to convince me of my own folly in the matter. Maybe I *was* childish and possessive...?

He did not mention *when* he might leave the island, he showed no signs of such preparation. And still - *still* - he had not really mentioned her...

"You asked about women. I just thought you might appreciate Briseis' story."

"I asked *you* about women," I clarified. "*Your* women, the women *you* liked, *you* took."

I was not in the mood for his coyness on the topic. Sensing this, he fidgeted in his seat, reaching for some wine. He swallowed two or three large gulps, wiped his beard and lips with his arm as he let the cup rest by his side. He continued to hold it, tilting it this way and that, picking at its rim, running his fingers over little chips and cracks. All this time I waited, impatient but still and silent. Finally, he was ready to return his attention to me and confirm my deepest fears.

"Yes," he said. "I am married."

Kalypso : 'Tritagonist'

KALYPSO'S TWENTY-SEVENTH EPISODE

Married. With a son.

I should have been surprised, but I was not. Perhaps I had always sensed it. Certainly there were signs. There had to be reasons he was holding back from me. I was relieved to know there were, and yet I felt sick to the stomach to hear them. A wife and son. I often wondered, had it just been a wife and not a child too, would things have been different then? Would he have been more open, more able to forget the past and start again with me? I never asked.

In retrospect, I know. He was ashamed of his feelings for me. Ashamed of the discomfort and unhappiness it might cause his wife if she were to ever find out. Ashamed of what his son (by then a young man and capable of all the same urges, no doubt) might think of his father's infidelities.

Would a son really care about his father's philandering? I wonder how my own brothers felt toward my father? So many marriages, and I have few illusions there were plenty more women besides. Was

Odysseus' son protective of his mother, thinking her abandoned? That was what Odysseus began to feel; he had deserted them. I didn't know the truth. I didn't know that he hadn't wanted to leave them.

But I did know he wasn't rushing home…

"Why didn't you go straight home?" I broached one evening. For it seemed the most logical question once I knew the truth. Odysseus was happy enough to indulge me with a description of his journey from Troy:

"We were weary, but roused by victory. We wanted to bask in our glory – tell everyone what we Achaeans had achieved! We had defeated the rich and powerful Troy, which was no mean feat, taking ten years and thousands of warriors to do. Victory had made us wealthy men, and still alive to enjoy it. We decided we would take the long route home, spread the news, celebrate, rest and revel. It sounds foolish, perhaps, and yet we were men who had seen nothing but the misery of war. Death. Pain. Pestilence and starvation. We had been living by our wits, our strength, our courage every day, never knowing which moment would be our last. That alone had been tiring, without the additional energy that goes into battling for your life and honour against men you know are doing the very same. And then, as night falls, and the last of the skirmishes cease against the failing light, *still* there is no rest, no sleep. Then you walk amongst dead flesh and spilled blood, strewn across the battlefield, picking up the bodies of your allies, your friends and comrades, watching as the enemy does the same. Feeling numb. Angered by the sight of birds feeding on skin, insects crawling over the torn limbs and dented breastplates of our bravest comrades. All the while hearing the heavy groans of the injured, the distant wails from women coming to terms with the fates of their husbands and sons and fathers. Even the crying of men. Brave warriors by day, Kalypso. Pitiful, weeping boys by night. Face to face with mortality and loss. I cannot begin to describe the full misery...

"So to win, to be victorious, after all that, and then to return home with nothing but wretched memories... Back to the mundanity of normal life... That seemed foolish to us! Surely we should return *happily* to our families, ready to return to our homes and work and the life we left behind so many years ago? We should be able to accept the praise of our peers, put the horrors behind us, and share our stories of courage and success without the truth of what we experienced, the nightly mourning, fear and disgust at many of our actions.

"So we took the long route home.

"In the end, what would have been the better choice? Straight home? I don't know. All I know is that everywhere we went, misfortune and disappointment seemed to follow us like a curse. Wherever we landed we seemed to have to fight for the simplest of things – food, drink, comfort – with few exceptions. We would tell them who we were, brag a little perhaps about our great deeds, yes, but then discover ourselves to be more feared and loathed than exulted. So we would have to fight yet more battles, kill more men. This we knew we could do - ten years experience told us so - and we felt certain of success. I am ashamed of it now, but we plundered many settlements on our travels after Troy, few of which deserved it. We paid a heavy price for it too, discovering the Trojans had more allies in neighbouring lands than we had ever realised. Those people relied on the wealth of their trade with the very city we had so recently ravaged. They were none to happy with us and we soon came to realise that they were as much our enemy as the Trojans themselves. But we were not as successful in our encounters this time and were lucky to escape with only half a dozen or so deaths from our exploits.

"I had begun sailing with a band of once victorious men, and now we were fleeing in defeat from a lesser enemy. To make matters worse, not far from the seas I knew to be those lying on the very watery path to my homeland, we were buffeted by storms and pushed off course, finding ourselves drifting in unrecognisable waters, low on provisions and morale.

"We eventually picked up drinking water on an unknown island whose inhabitants were thankfully disinterested in the politics of Achaea. It seemed like a blessing to have stumbled on these simple folk. They were happy to share all they had and began, I noticed, to barter with many of my men over some powdered concoction the natives enjoyed inhaling. We witnessed its use in rituals, when it caused them to dance about in a wild, energetic frenzy which, on first

Kalypso : 'Tritagonist'

sight, had made me laugh out loud. I laughed even harder when my men were invited to join in.

"It was not long after that I discovered the truth of the potency of this drug. It was, the chieftain had told me with all politeness, made from a local weed. What he neglected to reveal was its addictive qualities. It took no little time before many of my men became so addicted to it that they began to beg me to let them stay on that island rather than return to their homes and families. I began to fear they had been driven mad by some witchcraft or trickery. Those of us who had not yet partaken dragged the addicts away and back to the ships as fast as we could. They begged me to let them return, or at the very least to take on board a good quantity of this drug. The pleading and begging was more pitiful than the wailing for the dead of Troy, but I had no sympathy. I was disgusted by them and convinced this was all a clever ploy by the devious natives. I could not conceive of these men wishing to poison themselves as they did, though Eurylokhos, who had himself tried some small amount, told me it made you forget yourself more quickly than the best of wines. I knew plenty of liquors that might make a man forget his troubles, fears and pains for the night, but none that would make him choose to leave his life entirely! Sometimes I wonder if I should not have tried it. There was so much I wished to forget...

"You have nothing like that on this island, Kalypso? No potent weeds or unusual fruits?" Odysseus asked me, a strange air to his voice. He may not have tried this drug of which he spoke, but he sounded no less eager to rediscover it than one who had; desperate for something to free him from reality, dissolve his memories. I shook my head cautiously, and he sighed as if breaking from a moment of foolishness.

"I imagine I would have offered it to you already if I had some," I admitted. I must confess, on hearing his tale I knew that if I had such a drug I might well have used it, might have made him an addict sooner if it would have helped him to forget and encouraged him to stay. I knew what sort of a person that would make me. No matter how much I assured myself of my good, honest nature, that I did not think I *could* do it to him, I'll never know for sure. "All I found was the means to make this drink, after some trial and error as you know."

"Well, it is a good drink." Odysseus smiled, and drank from his cup appreciatively. It was clearly a performance, but it lacked his usual enthusiasm. This was a strange, uncomfortable side of him. He noticed me watching him, looking for clues to his thoughts, and quickly snapped back into the storyteller.

"So," he continued, "I now had drunkards, brawlers and narcotic abusers for a crew, where once I'd had brave soldiers. And I felt somehow to blame. We were heading in a direction I could only hope was homeward, since I recognised nothing and neither did any of my observant and well-travelled crew. Eurylokhos spent days on the look-out for something familiar while we sat and drifted. We stumbled upon such primitive lands, I could scarce believe such societies still existed. One island looked as though it had not been tilled or tended by man for many years. Crops and animals wildly covered the place. So we helped ourselves to the naturally available food and drink we found. We did find a settlement on this island, and came upon a man of very simple race, a great giant of a man – and though I am not the tallest of men you should ever meet, he had outgrown many of my lofty companions. He was wide with it, around the gut and arms and legs. His neck was almost as large as his head. He had one bad eye so that, to see you while he spoke, he needed to look from a particular angle.

"He was incapable of understanding much of our language and took an instant dislike to us, as I must say we did to him, though at first we remained friendly and tried to coax him into offering us something of worth. A show of his good faith and friendship to the Achaean's - not that we clearly meant anything to him. I soon discovered he fought with the strength of ten men, and lost yet more of my companions in needless violence with this fool. We only got away through trickery and concealment. I had to rely on deceiving that rotten eye of his so that my men could creep away beside his flock of goats and sheep…

"Oh, I did some foolish things, Kalypso," Odysseus sighed.

"And yet you make it all sound so exciting," I exclaimed, yet yawned dreamily, and he laughed at the irony and my meek apology. "It *is* interesting. I know plenty of bards who could not compose better entertainment, and you have it all first hand! All that travel and the strange people and giants and powder eaters..." But it was late, and although I felt terrible about it, my yawns grew infectious as I spoke.

"I wish it *had* been that inspiring, and not quite so senseless," Odysseus sighed again.

"Well, *I* think it was inspiring. You should tell me the rest tomorrow..."

Kalypso : 'Tritagonist'

KALYPSO'S TWENTY-EIGHTH EPISODE

But tomorrow would always begin with disappointment; an evening of close confidence resulting in a morning of cold rejection. And one day Hermes voice could not be heard above the tumult of my impatience. Each night I indulgently listened while Odysseus may or may not answer my questions with his long tales; each morning I bore his abandonment. I began to feel like a slave girl, carrying more and more of his pain for him, while he marched ahead of me with ease, not seeing nor caring how I struggled. I waited and waited for him to notice me, to offer me his support. It was only a matter of time before I collapsed without it.

"After all I've done for you!" I shouted at him.

"Done for me?" he interrupted with contempt. "What have you done?"

Oh, how easily he could dismiss me! The woman who salvaged his life!

"You were shipwrecked on this island - *my* island - with nothing to your name but a set of soggy clothes and a plank of wood. I cared for you when other islanders might have eaten you for breakfast or tossed you back in the water."

"Other islanders?" he yelled, swinging his arms about him at desolate Ogygia.

"On another island!" I clarified, thinking angrily how it was *he* in the first instance that had told me such silly stories. "I looked after you-"

"And you were not unrewarded," came his bitter retort.

"Meaning what?" I could not help but feel shocked as he spat his words at me. I was used to his occasional swings of temper, but to have one so squarely thrown at me...

"I know the day you found me you first filled your shawl with the collected remnants of my ship, my crew, my friends! Locking them up in your little chest of... of damaged and destroyed lives-"

"Oh, what should I do then? What should I have done? Left it all to litter the sands? Perhaps one day stab through my foot with a rusting dagger?"

"But why keep those things?" he implored. "Why not give them away?"

Why keep old relics? Why indeed, thought I. *And why hold on to a past that is so far away?*

"To whom should I give them? Perhaps you would have me

exchange them at the local market? Oh yes, of course - I live here alone, Odysseus! There is no one else. You think I keep them for pleasure or greed? What purpose would there be in that? If you want them, take them. Return them to their owners. Take them and go."

We both stood, breathing heavily, hearts beating rapidly, as we accused each other, until I could no longer be in his presence. I turned and left him. I marched angrily to the shore and began to pull in the shallow fishing nets, my cheeks burning with rage, half wishing at that moment he *would* go somewhere else, find another island on which to take out his anger. But with each tug of the netting I felt more helpless and annoyed with myself. I didn't want him to go. I just wanted him to want to stay.

After a while, he joined me at the sea front. He did not offer help, and I did not acknowledge him. We inhabited our own stubborn worlds for a moment or two longer. I concentrated on the work while he, in his usual distant way, looked out to sea.

"You could build a sailing vessel? Sail to the next island and trade there for things you need?" he suggested calmly, as though this had never been a disagreement, but simply a problem to be solved.

"What do I need?" I asked, standing proudly above the day's meagre catch as if it were good enough proof. "My island provides me with everything I should want. And since you have been here, helping me and improving things, I have more than ever."

"This island is nothing but a prison on which you eke away at survival!" For a moment I wished to say the same of the life he would be returning to, but I bit my tongue this time.

"Well, if that is what you think then why don't you take your own advice? Build a ship, take the 'stolen' loot and get away from here as fast as you can."

"Don't tempt me!" he threatened, and now it was his turn to stomp away, back to his preferred place of melancholy; that little rock formation overlooking the sea he liked to claim as his own thinking space. His point of contemplation. Above his pool of tears.

Kalypso : 'Tritagonist'

KALYPSO'S TWENTY-NINTH EPISODE

So it was that as regularly as I would bleed, Odysseus would disappear inside himself and fill the air with a sombre mood. He would sit on the cliff edge and watch the world below, from sunrise to moonrise. I saw him weeping and wanted to comfort him, but I said nothing. Over time, I learnt to leave him there, to let him work through his moods in his own way. Later he would return to me with implied apologies that would turn to pleasantries until we were laughing and playing again. And I conveniently forgot the melancholy he would make me feel. The rejection. I would be there, waiting to cheer him up on his return. No better than his pet dog, I realised bitterly. Giving that unconditional love and attention until being kicked away when no longer needed. Even when he admitted to me how wrong his behaviour was I would still reassure him all was well, and he would still refuse me.

"Oh Kalypso... Tell me to go?" he would beg of me.

"Why should I ever do that?" I would answer, thinking to comfort him while my heart sank lower, never knowing if his pleas were meant to incite my compassion or raise my anger. Surely if he wished to leave, he could leave? How could I stop him? No matter how much I might want to.

On and on we would talk about him. Then he would disappear, only to return to unburden himself again. In retrospect, I must concede, I sometimes thought he used me. Though never maliciously. Insensitively, perhaps. But he was right, I did not go entirely unrewarded, though my rewards were not as he thought; not those material relics of *his* past.

Of course, for all my bitter complaints, I know I would not have changed that time for all the world. I would live it again and again just to have him here with me.

After that particular argument, when he alluded to my collection of "spoils", washed ashore from many a sorrowful shipwreck, I realised I could never stop the past from intruding between us. Odysseus left the cave to be with his own thoughts, far from me. I could not recall for sure if he had returned the night before, though I had imagined him next to me as I slept.

Something I would do a long while hence.

Hermes no longer needed to guide my patience. Time and habit helped to prepare me. I let his absences become a part of our island living, always relying on past experience that he would eventually return. Where else could he go? I might fret over his whereabouts if I needed him, or his comfort if the weather turned, but no longer with enough regard to distract me from my day. Odysseus was his own man.

Without him present, I rose in my own good time, and chose to tidy my hair using some pearl combs, sliding them hard against my crown to pin back the locks that would regularly fall across my face. I always felt a strange comfort in noting the length my hair had grown since I arrived. There were few other ways to tell how much time had passed. I left the cave, planning to make my way to the nearest waterfall to bathe, when to my surprise I came face to face with Odysseus.

"I thought you had gone?" I said, a little too curtly no doubt, though he ignored any offence.

"You've changed your hair," he remarked. "It looks nice like that." My tension lessened with his unexpected interest and I blushed a little, both from the compliment and all the harsh feelings I had been storing.

"I remembered these combs this morning," I pointed them out. "I've not used them for sometime." He noted them briefly, then began to converse with me, as casually as ever, while he laid his tools about him.

"You brought a great deal of personal belongings with you to the island?" he probed.

"Not really. Just a pouch and a flask. You've seen those. Oh, and the pandouris, of course."

"And the combs were within the pouch?"

"These? Oh no. These were from..." I stopped myself, realising where this was leading. "I found these when I arrived."

"In this cave?"

"Yes," I lied, and he inconveniently caught my eye at just that moment, causing me to look away nervously.

"I see," he responded with a trace of suspicion. Then, when I said no more, he added, "I wonder who lived here before you?"

It always felt strange to lie to Odysseus. Not least because his eyes searched mine in such a way, as if to encourage a confession from me.

"I found various items, about the entire island," I half confessed. His cool reactions hinted that he had always guessed at the truth of my possessions. "I keep anything I find in the back of the cave."

"Oh," he said again and the ugly sound crawled over me. He must have sensed my unease as his tone suddenly shifted. "I didn't mean to accuse you of anything last night. It was wrong of me. I have no excuse. I don't know why I said any it."

"I *was* going to show you the items," I continued feebly, "when I thought you might be... interested."

"Why would I not be interested?" he asked. I realised his absent-minded behaviour was a game. Perhaps he had already found the

Kalypso : 'Tritagonist'

collection and thought ill of me for it? I used the only excuse I had left.

"Some of the items I found... after you arrived. I did not wish to upset you more than you had been when you realised..." *about your mssing companions*, I thought, but still found myself protecting him with silence. Or perhaps protecting me. It was true that I had hoped to show him those objects one day. One day when I knew they would seem like irrelevant relics of his past. In the meantime, I hid what I could, wrapped within and beneath old ragging, in a dark crevice of the cave, amid a collection of other treasures from numerous hunts over the years. Unimportant artefacts that I had hoped would attract no attention, and waited.

He seemed indifferent to my excuse, but some kind of intuition was nagging at me.

"Would you like to see them now...?" I asked, half-heartedly motioning towards the cave. There was a pause as he stood for a moment, uncertain, then nodded his agreement and followed me back inside.

A small fire spat gently on the central hearth and Odysseus sat patiently as I sought out the objects, crawling on my hands and knees through the low dark tunnel, stretching my arm to the furthest point possible. They seemed so much farther back than I remembered. The cold surface of the crevice made me shudder uncomfortably. I worried the objects may have been ruined by damp and dust, or tiny winged invaders. They remained wrapped in the same shawl I had used to collect them on that first day. The shock of finding a man amongst the wreckage, and then the altered pace of life that followed, had disrupted my usual routine so that some things had been completely forgotten over time. I suddenly felt a fondness for this shawl, as if it were a long lost friend I was glad to have remembered at last.

I placed the bundle down between us and allowed Odysseus to open it himself and scour the objects. He did so tentatively, as if, now confronted with the opportunity, he was afraid of what he might find. He picked up many of the items, looking over them as if they were as unfamiliar to him as they were strange to me, and I wondered if I had been mistaken in thinking them as his. But each momentary confusion would be followed by various sounds of recognition. He would place each one back down in its own area of the ground before us, in an order known only to him, until each piece sat on display, waiting to be named. Finally, when he seemed satisfied with the pattern before him, he explained it to me.

"This," he said holding up a green gem, "I am sure was one of the eyes of the horse."

"The wooden horse you made?"

"The very same. At least... It looks that way. Though it has suffered a battering and lost some of its shine... some of its glint. I had taken it when all was done in Troy - I took one and Epeus took the other."

Kalypso : 'Tritagonist'

"Like a reward?" I suggested, but he did not answer me. His attention had already moved on.

"What made you think to keep this?" he asked, holding up some dirty brown sacking. Indeed, on first sight, it had seemed rather innocuous. I had assumed it might once have been a bag or sack, though it was too tattered when I found it to be certain.

"It was because of this," I then explained, going through the scraps he had left behind on the shawl and extracting a piece of cord, which I remembered to have been about the sacking when I found it. "I noticed the strands - they appear to be metallic, possibly gold or copper, so I was unsure if this might have been a valuable sack...?" Odysseus smiled then, with a look that suggested he was pleased at my foresight, pleased to see the scrap again, and perhaps a little surprised at himself for not recognising its value.

"It was important once," he agreed, "though it was never so much the bag as its contents that were thought important. On my journey from Troy, my crew and I stopped at the island of aged King Aeolus. Like me he had a great inventive mind, so we discovered, and he and I liked each other right away. He gave us hospitality and showed us about his kingdom - an island, he explained, often plagued by great gales. Indeed, the coastal breezes which beset it were unlike any I had encountered on other islands. They seemed to waft in great cyclones, circling about the entire place, first in one direction, then another. Only when they rested was it safe to pull anchor to leave or enter the harbour, and then it must be done as swiftly as possible to avoid being caught in the next recurrence. It was a better wall of protection from unwanted visitors than the bricks and mortar of Troy - even better than your undead sea monsters, Kalypso! More terrifying, you might say, in its unpredictability.

"Because of this, Aeolus worked tirelessly to discover ways to tame nature. He had a great many instruments for predicting the winds, and many more concepts for controlling it - though few, I would say, were fully proven successful. I told him of the difficulties we had suffered in trying to return home to Ithaka, the storms and sudden changes in weather, and he sympathised. Indeed, he knew all about such occurrences. In his youth, he had been quite the sailor and he recounted to us during our stay a great number of fascinating stories. Visits to lands peopled by men the colour of blue, great artistic giants, strange uncultured populations of all shades and sizes... Most of it seemed barely probable, yet his tales made me yearn to be young and carefree again, so that I might sail as far as the seas would take me and find such places - and others besides - for myself."

"But you are still young," I nudged him. "Why don't you go now?"

"Because I'm not young," he sighed gently. "Even if I am considered young of age next to those old kings Nestor and Aeolus, I feel too old inside with the life I've lived. And carefree I am most definitely not these days."

"That seems sad," I said, "that you should feel too old and

trapped by your life to be able to do just what you want, to explore the world..."

"I did not say trapped," he dismissed, then paused playfully from his stern tone and added, "unless this is your way of asking me to leave, fair Kalypso?"

"No, no!" I protested a little too eagerly. "I would not have you go. Not unless," I added, fearing *I* might become the trap, "you would promise to come back with all your stories of discovery." He smiled and drifted into thought for a moment, but I could see the truth of it in his eyes. He could never keep such a promise, no matter how much he might mean to on making it.

"So, what was in the bag?" I asked, drawing him back to his story and saving me from my disillusion.

"One of King Aeolus' great inventions! What else, for a parting gift to his visitors? We'd waited on that island for Aeolus to determine the best wind on which we could sail homeward. When it began to blow, Aeolus gave me an incredible object - like a giant mouth attached to a bellows. Not a small-spouted one such as you might see being used on a craftsman's fire. This invention of his was gilded and jewel-studded - he told us his daughters had completed the gaudy decoration. It had two great long handles, attached to two giant panels, between which sat a sealed and tightly woven canvas bag. At the mouth of the bag, where the palettes were jointed on either side, was a gap that let in the air. You quickly parted the palettes, using the handles, and the air filled the pleated bag. Then you squashed the bag down between the palettes to fan the captured gust back out. See?" Odysseus attempted to demonstrate with his hands.

"I think so," I said. "Just a giant bellows?"

"Exactly," He confirmed. "It stood almost as tall as you and perhaps twice as wide."

"So this was once a giant sack then?" I asked, running my fingers over the small ragged remnants.

"The biggest bag imaginable!" he proclaimed. "Aeolus claimed it had come to him from the land of giants, where it was considered no more than a small sack. It took three strong men to carry the bag and its contents to our ship, and a great deal of manoeuvring and reorganisation to make space for it onboard."

"But why would he give you such an odd and inconvenient gift?" I wondered aloud.

"Aeolus honestly believed, with his 'wind machine', that a sailing crew might be able to blow their ship in any direction they chose - even against the natural push of the wind."

"By the gods, that *is* invaluable!" I exclaimed.

"Hmmm," came Odysseus' less than enthusiastic reply.

"You don't agree?"

"Oh, I agree that it *would* be invaluable, Kalypso. But I think old age may have withered Aeolus' once excellent mind a little if he truly believed it could work. It would have taken too great an effort simply to

Kalypso : 'Tritagonist'

emit a good gust from the bellows against a still sea air. Perhaps a small fishing vessel, were it able to take the extra weight (though it weighed much less than you'd think) and give up its space, might make use of it in gentle weather, but against the sails of a mighty warship such as ours, it had next to no chance of success. In a storm it had less chance than that! It was impractical but beautiful and I could not refuse the gift or the old man's intentions. To my shame, much as I had grown fond of Aeolus, I was most grateful when he hid the wind-maker, as he called it, in this bag. He had presented it to me in the privacy of his rooms, out of sight of all others. I had just refused his eldest daughter's hand in marriage with politely feigned reluctance. I thought it likely my men would only laugh at the old king's naivety and I did not want to cause offence. So I commanded them not to open the bag without my say so and never hinted at what lay inside. That was the gravest mistake on my part."

"Why?" I asked.

"Curiosity, Kalypso. As it does us all, it got the better of my men, and while I rested, they tore open the bag and found the strange contraption inside."

"And did they laugh at it?"

"Worse," he sighed. "They did not understand its significance. They thought the bellows might be some kind of unusual container for holding treasure. My own men - brave soldiers and experienced sailors that had stood beside me through thick and thin for so many years -

believed that I was now hiding something from them. It was the spirit and curse of Thersites in them all," he muttered.

"Thersites?"

"A troublesome man, Thersites, though some would say not without reason. There are those who can bring a whole company down with malicious gossip and negative thoughts." I nodded my agreement, thinking for a moment of Melaina, Ligys and poor misguided Eudokia. "If that were a good trait in a man, Thersites would be considered gifted."

"He was one of the lords in charge with you?" I asked.

"No, just a common soldier. He commanded a small section, it is true, and he'd had his glories in the past - such as they were - to warrant that command, but he had no real power, nor was he ever likely to have considering he lacked natural prowess. It did not, however, stop him from envying our superior roles, questioning our judgements before our loyal men, and accusing us of greed and inadequacy at times when morale was already low."

"Sounds like a terrible man to have as an ally," I agreed. "Perhaps it would have been better of he were the enemy?" But Odysseus sighed heavily.

"I've made many mistakes, Kalypso," he grieved. "From start to finish, they're all mine. I publicly beat Thersites, for his insolence. I struck him down before the assembly."

"Did you kill him?"

Kalypso : 'Tritagonist'
───────────────

"No. No, not him. Although I as good as did. He had mocked us, and I had despised him for it, but in truth he merely voiced the common soldier's darker and not *un*common thoughts. If oration were his skill, he might have been a genuine enemy within our camp. Thankfully all he knew to speak was spite, which can be easily beaten down. Vocally and, I'm sad to say now, physically. I made a laughing stock of that man, as he had tried to do to us lords, but when I looked around at the soldiers who watched his fall, I saw Thersites' face in everyone. I saw the lords and their quarrelsome nonsense, their pride and possessiveness, for exactly what it was. It was hard to know at whom the crowd should really have laughed.

"That day on my ship, when I woke to find my men tearing kind old Aeolus' gift to shreds in search of gold and jewels, Thersites' face was all I saw about me again. His disgrace came back to haunt me. I had not respected my men enough to trust them with this unusual gift. Not one of them. I had no respect for their opinions, their ability to be reasonable and indulgent to an old man's whims, or at least to maintain dignity until we had left the king's lands. I had made it seem as though I was withholding prized possessions for my sole benefit. My men, those under my command, now mocked my decisions, disobeyed my rulings, and looked on me just as Thersites had demanded the Achaean army look on Agamemnon. He told the soldiers they should leave him, with all his prizes, gold and women, and see how much they meant to him without an army. Had I not stepped in, he might have convinced them. In truth, you can trust no man, friend or foe. Nor any woman, for that matter.

"When I woke from a long needed sleep, I found my men sheepishly avoiding eye contact with me, trying to hide the remains of the massacred bag and bellows. I was dismayed at their destructive actions. They had turned from grown men to pitiful animals over mere possessions. I explained to them, in all seriousness, what they had pulled apart and broken beyond repair. Yet again, superstition got the better of my crew who, without listening to my protestations, reversed course for a return to Aeolus' island to beg for a replacement. It was a most humiliating mission; not least in having to face that poor old man and see his sad expression as I showed him the ruinous job my men had performed on his invention. He informed us all that it was a prototype. There was to be no replacement. I could not bear to stay long in case he wept. We left that same evening with no entertainment or gifts, my men hanging their heads in disgrace, demoralised and blaming themselves while my own shame increased. In their penance, they began to equate that broken bellows with their only hope of getting home..."

"So what happened?" I asked after a reflective pause.

"What happened, dear Kalypso, is that I ended up here, and they... They were left behind, swimming to Hades."

Without warning, he hurled the remaining pieces of bag on to the small fire, which crackled and spluttered under the weight, and then burst alive again before us, turning the deep brown material to charred black ash, dispersing it casually about the flames. I watched uncomfortably, dividing my attention between Odysseus' hard, downward glare and the newly angered fire. No more words were said. Odysseus walked mournfully away, back out into the daylight, and I slowly packed the remaining objects into the shawl, returning them to their alcove, though not so far back as to be hidden this time. When he was ready, I reasoned, Odysseus might bring them out again, to mourn or eulogise as he saw fit.

KALYPSO'S THIRTIETH EPISODE

When I saw him next, he was sat wearing nothing but one of my shawls about his waist. I could not help but smirk at the sight. My weaving had improved a good deal with practice, but this piece was not nearly enough to cover his masculine shape.

"I thought it was Achilles who preferred to wear women's clothing?" I joked as I joined him.

"Turns out it is surprisingly comfortable," he winked.

"So you and Achilles finally see eye to eye on something?" I smiled. Odysseus did not respond. He seemed neither cheered nor saddened by my jest, so I nestled into his arms, feeling his warmed body against my back. He felt relaxed and looked content, but always there remained a pensive tension to his manner. His breathing was tight and uneven; stilted inhalations, slow, thoughtful exhalations.

"You said you never saw any reason for his being involved in the war, didn't you?" I urged.

"I never saw the point in any of us being in the war," he

Kalypso : 'Tritagonist'

complained, then sighed in his usual heavy way. "Achilles and I had far more in common than I may have admitted. He was a young, impetuous liability, yes, but he had no more inclination to be there than I did. In truth, I felt sorry for him. I know how it was for me when I was called to join the war - and I had far more reason to be there. *I went to the house of Tyndareus to win Helen for my own; I had the idea for the oath.* All of which happened long before Achilles was barely old enough to lift a sword. I simply never thought I - or anyone else, for that matter - would be called upon to honour it."

"Why would you make such an oath then?" I asked confused. I felt his body tense beneath me slightly.

"It's a long story," Odysseus replied stiffly.

"Isn't it always with you!" I laughed kindly.

And yet unusually it was not forthcoming, not easy for him to begin. I looked at him inquisitively, but his face was sad. He was holding back a greater load.

"I have been unfair, Kalypso," he said, and now my heart quickened with uneasy anticipation. "I have maligned Achilles too often, when I am no better a man than he." I found myself breathing out a great sigh of relief at these words. I'd had such a fear of what he might have said to me this time. That one topic we had so carefully avoided. I knew we were not far from its mention.

"Achilles was barely a man when I was sent to call him to war. Only fifteen or so. Still like a child, by all accounts. My own son would be of a similar age now, and the thought of him having to face the bloodshed we saw in one year alone makes my stomach turn. I can sympathise with Achilles' mother, desperately trying to keep him away from it all." Odysseus' eyes glazed. I saw in him then something he had never shown me before. He was not simply obliged by the laws of society to return to his family. It was not merely shame. He was frightened for them.

"I am afraid for my son," he confirmed my thoughts, the weakness being pushed, with some effort, from his voice.

"Why?" I asked, surprised. "The war is over, is it not?"

"That war is, yes."

"You think there is another war?"

"Who would know, trapped here on this island, with no news...?" Mid outburst, Odysseus stopped, remembering himself. His apparent anger gave way to a distant, helpless gaze. "It may not only be wars he needs to fight."

"But every man - every *boy*," I corrected, "has to do his military service in Achaea, doesn't he? All men have to prove their strength and prowess somehow? Especially the son of a king - how else could he prove himself worthy to follow in his father's stead?" Odysseus sighed another heavy sigh, which for once was not an accusation of my feminine ignorance. "I'm sure it's only natural you should be afraid that your son might get hurt-"

"A man does not get hurt! He either fights or he dies, and that is

Kalypso : 'Tritagonist'

all." Odysseus' interruption was stern and rehearsed. As soon as he was finished, he turned to me with an exhaustive look of sorrow. "I'm sorry, Kalypso. It's nonsense, what I just said. Isn't it? Nonsense... An ingrained response. As a soldier, you patch over wounds, you push any pain from your mind. These are weaknesses, and nothing should distract you from the job at hand, lest you fail and pay for that failure with your life. This we are reminded of every fighting day by our superiors. This I have told my own troops as they struggled back onto the battlefield, weary and downtrodden, soaked in their own blood as well as that of their comrades and enemies. Their kinsmen and friends... And all for a conceited whore and a man's damaged pride. I have seen men turned cold as stone by pride, so much so that they would kill their own child to ensure them victory." He shuddered at an unspoken memory.

Before I could ask him to explain, we were both startled by a peel of thunder high above us. Seconds later the heavy droplets of rain began to fall. Odysseus grabbed a splint of wood and stole a flame from our fire, before the rain might put it out, protectively hurrying it into the dry hearth within the cave. Meanwhile, I collected up all I could carry of the pots of drink and food, and soon followed him inside. We set about, for the next few minutes, pulling the fishing raft to higher ground, tethering it to the roots that grew beside the cave, collecting up those items left outdoors - drying clothes and Odysseus' tools and contraptions. All the while the sky grew steadily darker, thick with a cloud that seemed to be trying to engulf us. The rain fell in sheets, and the flashes of lightening made my heart jump and race. Birds swooped and squawked about the trees as if they too felt my sudden fear.

"What about the goats?" I suddenly shouted to Odysseus through the rain, now falling in a torrent, as we ran towards the cave with the last of it. I instantly realised how odd that sounded. I had never considered their well being during past storms; I had never previously felt responsible for them.

"They will find their own shelter," he called back, helping me inside the dry cavern. Then he smirked at me, but not unkindly. "Gentle Kalypso," he said, running his wide hand over my now sopping wet hair, "animals do know what to do. They're much closer to nature than us." I knew this. And yet it did not alter my concern. This storm had a mysterious timing to it, a fierce anger. I was afraid for everything.

Kalypso : 'Tritagonist'

KALYPSO'S THIRTY-FIRST EPISODE

Storms always begin the same way. First, there is a long dry spell that eventually begins to stifle and oppress. When I lived alone on the island, I could avoid these uncomfortable heats by crawling into my cool cave and sleeping. But all the while I shared the land with Odysseus, I felt compelled to continue despite them. On some occasions, we might go for a swim in the lake, or a gentle walk in the shade of the trees. On others, we simply continued with our chores and activities as if nothing was happening, fully aware that something was from the discomforting headaches, incorrigible sweating and the aching tiredness of our muscles and bones.

Like the granting of a prayer, there would come a sudden short breeze, briefly touching everything along its path, until each leaf, each blade of grass and grain of sand had shivered with excited anticipation. Then our eyes would be drawn instinctively to the sky. The clear blue would be invaded with colossal, low-flying clouds, darkening and vibrating with a strange aura, jostling against each other as they rushed forward, desperate to cover every inch of blue, as if competing to be the last cloud to do so. Meanwhile, beneath them, birds would fly precariously, plummeting down towards rocky crevices and leafy shelters. In the grasslands, the laborious chewing of the goats would momentarily cease as they lumbered and scurried towards trees, or simply dropped down to the ground and waited (a sight I always found disconcerting). Odysseus and I would begin to pack up, sometimes with excited gusto and chatter, to cover up the natural fear throbbing at the nape of our necks; sometimes in thoughtful silence, fully attuned to each other's desire to move on to somewhere safe.

It was never so much the rain nor winds, and not even the lightening strikes from which we felt compelled to hide. It was the sea. Ogygia was a small and gentle island, but its shorelines displayed their unmistakeable battle scars, suffered from the ocean's temper, and we had both noted cuts and bruises in the vegetation some considerable way in from the coast, which we put down to the same adversary. A usual, pleasant tide would merely lap at our cave's doorstep. But if the tide rose too high, reaching the cave would involve a perilous trek through unpredictable currents.

As the warning rumbles hollered from somewhere above our heavy heads, Odysseus and I would make our way into the dry. The sky would change to a dark blue-grey and a wall of rain would sweep across the land. The stronger winds would start to encourage the waves to bulge and thrash, drenching the rocks from below.

Kalypso : 'Tritagonist'

I would weave while Odysseus would carve. I would cook and he would talk. It could be the best of times, particularly if the day's chores had been keeping us apart. Good, long storms - which were not so frequent as you might think, despite the hot and changeable weather - would offer plenty of time to reflect on events, develop ideas together, or probe at issues and stories we'd had little time or inclination to previously bring up.

For the same reasons, thunderstorms could also bring with them much personal and emotional danger...

The cave may well have provided us with the best protection against the elements, but it did undesirably amplify the booming and crackling sounds of the thunder. It was unnerving. Rumbles would continue to growl through the darkness long after they had ceased outside.

The day of that strange storm, I had not noticed the usual discomforts, although in retrospect I noted the lethargy and heat. But this one had crept up on us both. I was uneasy, yet I felt strangely safe with Odysseus being there. We had started a good fire and begun to reheat our victuals. I even brought out the pandouris and we both took turns in strumming and singing. All about us, the cave gently hummed from the incessant drumming of heavy rain, a noise only interrupted by the misshapen rumbles. The fire danced about itself, lifted by the occasional gusts that reached our sanctuary. For a while this seemed pleasant enough. When the pandouris became tiresome we rested on skin blankets before the fire and talked some more.

"It is strange," I said, staring at the shadowy patterns on the arcs above me, "that you now know so much of my past, and ask me very little about my daily activities, while I always hear about your day but barely know a thing about your life before you came here."

"I think you know quite a lot," he argued.

"I know a lot about the war, yes," I countered. "I know about Achilles, and how the war ended. I know your best friend was Eurylokhos, whom you regret falling out with." Odysseus was so silent I could not even hear his breathing. I spun onto my stomach to look at him. "I'm sure he feels the same," I said, letting my fingers stroke against his comfortingly. "Good friends don't hold grudges." Odysseus forced a smile and let his fingers catch at the tips of mine as they passed, holding them gently before letting go, sending spasms of warmth tingling through me. I wondered if he was aware of my feeling this way, and I blushed at the thought. "You can tell me anything, Odysseus," I assured him, as well as myself. "If you want to. I do want you to."

I waited for Odysseus to begin one of his usual stories, but he did not. In the flurry of our escape I had forgotten what we were discussing outside. All I remembered was that pang of fear I had felt when I thought he might mention her. *Why should I care if he does?* I reasoned with myself. *They are far away and I am here. What harm can it do?* Lying there in Odysseus' silence, I convinced myself that now was a good time to confront my fears.

"What was she like?" I asked with a false nonchalance that did no better at disguising my real feelings than a thin veil.

"Who?" He looked at me, shuffling uncomfortably. "You mean my wife? Penelope?" I raised my eyebrows sardonically at the name. "Why do you ask things you do not really wish to know? Do you wish to know?"

"You're right," I agreed. "In truth I don't want to know. I want to go back to that time before you admitted to a wife and child. When it was just you and me. I wish you could make a choice about who you want to be with, where you want to be. I wish you could be happy and say what you mean!"

"But I could never be yours, Kalypso. You know that. And you know why. Not while my wife-"

"So you've never been with another woman? In all your life, all your travels...?"

He sighed gloomily and the answer was clear. "Not one that counts, no. Not like that. There have been other women, yes. But it is different."

"How?" I demanded angrily.

"I love Penelope. I have always loved and respected Penelope and probably always will."

"Probably? Hah!" I revelled in any weakness he showed, though my own heart cracked with suspicion that it was merely kindness in the face of my distress.

"But she is not here. And I am."

"Yes. You are." He sighed. "There have been women, Kalypso, besides my wife. But I have never loved them. I've been bewitched, I may have taken the spoils of war, but I'd never before-"

"Spoils of war? So you do own some women?"

"Not really. Truthfully, I never touch them. I've seen the trouble foreign women cause among soldiers."

We sat in silence, both contemplating our own unhappiness. I had no interest in more stories of his war. I just wanted my own troubles to end.

"I know I asked you before," I said, "and you refused to answer me, but why the oath?"

"Do you really want to know?" Odysseus replied quite seriously.

"Why should I not?" I asked, still a little perturbed.

"I do like the way things are between us," he replied after a time.

"So do I," I smiled.

"There are some things, I know, that we have always avoided discussing." We were both lying on our sides, looking at the fire, avoiding eye contact. I knew what he meant; I could continue to refuse to hear the subject. Part of me did not want to encourage him to discuss his wife. It sent daggers through my heart to think that he still preferred her to me. Yet how could I hate her, when she knew nothing of this? And how could I refuse Odysseus, the man I loved and my greatest companion in life, the chance to open himself completely to me? I had to face my own envies. I plopped down on to my back, resignedly.

Odysseus invited me to lie by his side. I shuffled to a space between the fire and his warmed body and he propped himself up on an elbow, looking down at me.

"You promise not to be upset?" he asked.

"I promise to try not to be," I reasoned, since I had no idea what might come. He waited a moment, as if trying to decide that this compromise was enough. Then he began.

"I made the oath for my wife." He paused again, expecting me to protest perhaps. To change my mind. For my part, I felt my inside tighten a little, but took a deep breath and tried not to show my feelings on my face, so he felt it safe to continue.

"We - that is, most of the eligible bachelors, and some not so, of the time - were all competing for the hand of beautiful Helen. Unfortunately, she truly was as radiant to look on as the bards had told, and not a man at that competition would have refused to lay down his life for her," he sighed. "Ironically, in the end, many of them did.

Whilst the games continued, the house of Tyndareus (Helen's father) was filled with strong men, buoyed by their own self-importance, all thinking themselves the worthy winner, and so it was that many a day was spent trying to stop these men from killing each other in argument. As much as I, too, adored Helen from the outset, I had little interest in dying before I even stood a chance of winning her. I had hoped, if I could only get an opportunity to talk with her, I might be able to convince her of my suit and win her over without the need for blood nor sport. Not that I doubted my abilities, you understand. I just knew the odds of winning fairly were not in my favour. Helen was such a prosperous possession - not just for economical purposes, but also... well, for male pride. Any man seen to be her husband would be the envy of all others, so trickery was rife amongst the contestants. I myself broke the rules by sending requests to Helen, via trusted and well compensated servants, to ask for a private audience. At first she seemed to refuse - such is the game women play. But persistence was *my* game, and eventually she agreed to meet with me in secret if I allowed her to attend with a chaperone. I agreed of course. I had no intention of damaging the lady's reputation - not that I think, in Helen's case, anything ever could. No one seemed to make much of her past abduction, an event which any other woman might suffer from.

"Early one evening, while the other men were feasting and training and bragging amongst themselves as usual, I met with the beautiful Helen, in a secluded part of the gardens, accompanied by her cousin, Penelope. Both women were modestly veiled, but there was little doubting it truly was Helen and no impostor. She asked me some questions on my parentage, where I came from, what Ithaka was like, and so on. I felt I did the best job I could at making it sound like the

Kalypso : 'Tritagonist'

most perfect island in the Ionian Sea. To me, Ithaka is a jewel, but I know it to have been described as rugged and harsh by those who do not know and love it as I. I believed myself to be eloquent and persuasive. Surely a women, a gentler creature after all, would be more interested in a man who could talk to her than one who could merely throw a spear a good distance? I was far from being incapable of protecting a woman, but what good is strength in front of a peaceful home fire?

"When her enquiries dried up, I tried to question her in return on what she would want from marriage, what sort of a person she thought herself to be, what she liked to do. As the conversation progressed, my boyish infatuation with her beauty simply waned. She showed no emotional interest in my words and gave only bland answers to my queries. The effort was tiresome. The conversation came to an awkward end. I remember how we three sat in silence for an eternal moment, each waiting for the other to speak, and I can still hear the uncomfortable sounds of the rippling fountain, the crickets in the grasses, the birds fluttering about.

"And then, just as I thought they might make to leave, Penelope spoke. She asked me to clarify something I had earlier explained about Ithaka - to do with the great port, I seem to recall. She spoke with a clear and steady voice, yet I could feel the tension between the two ladies. Helen had obviously been intending to excuse herself with her cousin's help. I answered, since it would only have been polite to, though I felt no need to continue the conversation either. But Penelope asked another question. Then another, and another, until I realised this was a game. A game in which Penelope and I would see how long it took for Helen - always so used to being centre of attention - to break with frustration at the inconvenience.

"Penelope told me some time afterwards how much she had enjoyed this. Helen, she said, had been quite spiteful about meeting me, whom she considered to be no better than a goat farmer. Indeed she had a derogatory description for each of her suitors and felt none of them truly deserved her.

"She did eventually snap at our continuing conversation, annoyed at being present yet unacknowledged, I suspect. She informed Penelope in no uncertain terms that it was time they left. As they did, I saw Penelope lift her veil and smile conspiratorially at me. Many people accused me of settling for Penelope as the consolation prize. Indeed, I think even she suspected it might be so. But I did fall for her, that very night. Compared to Helen, I knew she was the better choice of a wife for me.

"I returned to Tyndareus' halls that night to find our host in absolute disarray. There had, as ever, been fighting amongst the contestants, but this time, intoxicated and tired with it, a stabbing - thankfully not fatal - had ensued. It was then that I suggested to Tyndareus a way to bring all the men together in a common pact - something they might all honour. We ran through various ideas on regular sacrifices to gods to keep them focused, or perhaps rules and harsh punishments to hold them all in check, until finally I suggested he bind them to an oath. Something simple, but which any man who wished to continue in the competition must swear to, or else he forfeit his place. The oath would state that all suitors of Helen would support each other's rights to compete for her hand, and the eventual winner would accept the troth of all other men bound to the oath to protect his right to claim Helen as his wife, fairly won. If anyone broke or later contested the oath, he would not only have to fight the husband, but the rest of us too. And no man wants to have to best more than twenty strong warriors by himself for the sake of a difference of opinion. It was taken on so successfully that a grateful Tyndareus even offered to arrange for me to win Helen by stealth. Instead, I asked that he allow me to compete for the hand of his niece, Penelope, and guarantee me a win. This he did."

"But if you had married Helen," I interrupted, "do you think you would have held all those men to the oath the way Menelaus did?"

"In retrospect I might say no, but how could I be sure? There was something quite powerful about that beauty of hers, even if it was a veneer."

"So you got your wife," I returned him to the story.

"Yes," he said. "I created and swore to what I thought would be an uneventful oath at a grand ceremony, so designed to have the right effect on the men swearing with me. Tyndareus sacrificed a horse, we all took the oath, then we drank a good deal and fell into bed. There were still fights and disagreements, but under quite a different atmosphere, since we were now all in it together. Tyndareus, however, was not content to hand over his daughter to any old barbarian, and again took me into his confidence, asking me whom I thought to be the most suitable husband for Helen. I chose Menelaus."

"Why?" I asked sceptically. "How could you possibly make such a decision?"

"It wasn't too hard. I now felt I had a little insight into perfect Helen. I knew that Tyndareus would want a strong son-in-law, someone who could rule his estates well on his death. Menelaus may have been a quiet, stocky and stern looking sort, but our interactions had shown him to be sensible enough and I believed him to have an honest heart. He was unlikely to dishonour Tyndareus or Helen, for that matter. He was also unlikely to care about Helen's lack of conversation skills, since he did not strike me as someone looking for comfort in stories and discussions.

"Tyndareus agreed with my assessment, and persuaded Helen to choose him from amongst the suitors (though how he did so remains a mystery to me). He then helped me to win Penelope, despite her own father's objections. It took a fair time for me to persuade my new wife to leave the disturbing attentions of her father behind and return with me to Ithaka."

"She didn't want to leave?"

Kalypso : 'Tritagonist'

"*He* didn't want *her* to leave. She felt guilty at causing so much disagreement between the two men she was bound to honour. In the end I gave her an ultimatum, and she chose me. Perhaps I was wrong to have done so, but she seemed to accept her new life in Ithaka soon enough. Within the year we had a son, Telemachus. The moment he was born I felt my life was finally complete. Everything was perfect. Until, shortly before my son's first birthday, I received the first of three messages from Agamemnon, the brother of Menelaus. I heard of Helen's apparent abduction by Prince Paris of Troy. I was being called to honour the Oath of Tyndareus, which I had sworn almost two years previous. I wrote back explaining that the oath had been created to avoid conflict at the time of the competition, but there was nothing in it to state that it remained in place indefinitely. I was sorry for Menelaus, but I saw no reason to start a war over Helen's actions, which I'm sad to say hardly came as a surprise to myself nor my wife.

"Less than a month later came the second summons. As the author of the oath, I was being held fully accountable for its consequences. A list was provided of those men who had already agreed to join Menelaus and Agamemnon in admonishing Paris and all those who harboured him; a list which included many names I had not heard for a good while. Penelope noted it with some concern, but I was still happy to reassure her. I wrote again, this time to say that I was pleased so many men had agreed to stand by Menelaus and, were it not for the fact that I was needed at home, I am sure I would be among their number. However, it seemed to me there were plenty of good men and brave warriors already signed up to the quest, and I am sure they would not mind excusing me at this time. I had not long been a father and I wished to stay in Ithaka and support my wife and son. I felt sure he would understand, though I now know I had underestimated Agamemnon's familiarity with good fathering.

"We heard nothing for a few months, except by way of news brought to us from the harbour. The armies of Sparta and Mycenae were amassing and heading for Hellespont. Penelope worried endlessly, cursing Helen's name and saying she had always known her cousin would eventually bring ruin to the men of the Aegean. The third and final message was less of a request and more of a warning. It was immediately followed by a visitor - one of Agamemnon's own men, by the name of Palamedes. His purpose was to collect me to honour my pact, or hold me accountable as a coward and an oath-breaker. The punishment for which could be anything he decided - even death. Penelope's worry turned to terror. She disliked conflict in any form. She wrote to Agamemnon, telling him I had recently had a fall and gone mad from the injuries. I was not in my right mind and could not be trusted to fight, let alone lead an army.

"Although Penelope had written without my knowledge, I was happy to encourage her plan. I had no intention of leaving Ithaka and my family for some ridiculous dispute over a woman. Who knew at that time the extent to which the dispute would grow? I was convinced the

Kalypso : 'Tritagonist'

armies of the two brothers and their cohorts would reach Troy and either agree a ransom or storm the city, taking Helen back by force. Paris would come to his senses and release her or face Menelaus in a fair contest. It seemed unjust of them to revoke the oath regarding Paris - a man who had not sworn to it. Making him fight all those other suitors who had done so could be seen as a crime in itself, and so once more I considered myself unneeded. Troy would not go to war over one woman, no matter how beautiful she might be. Penelope reminded me how strong my own infatuation had been when I had come to compete for her cousin. Perhaps I had forgotten this, but I refused to let Penelope's fears overwhelm us, and demanded that we carry on with our lives as before. This in itself was a challenge. I doubt you want to hear about such things, but my wife had been strangely affected by Telemachus' birth. She did not seem happy in her role as mother and her moods were at best erratic, at worse permanently doleful. My own nurse, Eurykleia, took charge of my son and I thought this would please Penelope, give her time to rest after the birth. On reflection, perhaps I should have spoken to her more about her feelings, tried to understand why she was so unhappy. By the time of the final request to join the men at Troy, I had grown used to her withdrawn attitude. Things were not unhappy between us, from what I could tell. They were simply not the same as they had been before Telemachus' birth.

"Penelope heard of Palamedes arrival from one of her maids. He had arrived in port, along with Nestor and Menelaus, all asking after me, and Palamedes was preparing to make his way to my house for talks. I was working the fields with my father when my wife came running toward us, tears streaming down her face, frantic and incomprehensible. I sent her back to the house and told her to continue in her story that I was mad. Hopefully we would convince this envoy to leave me behind. We had not reckoned on Palamedes methods of persuasion.

"I consider myself a clever man, Kalypso, but Palamedes was more than my equal. What he did not have in good manners or speech he made up for in strength and guile. Worse still, he seemed to have no compunction towards other lives. Some might see this as an excellent quality in a soldier, but it is still deplorable in a man. Penelope invited him into our home and at his request informed him of my whereabouts. I thought we put on a convincing play: I stood in the field throwing salt about at the crops and pretending to plough my fields with a horse and ox attached to the one plough. My father meanwhile stood about, wringing his hands and lamenting to the gods at how he had been cursed with a senseless son who would bring ruin and damnation on the family. All the while Palamedes watched. He would ask me nothing by blunt questions, completely ignoring my display.

""Why have you not joined Agamemnon's party as requested?"

""Is he having a party?" I responded, "What a wonderful idea!" And I danced about with boyish excitement, throwing grasses about the place and asking what foods I should bring with me, what I should

Kalypso : 'Tritagonist'

wear, and what guests would be there. That cold man showed not a hint of emotion, which in itself was unnerving, and it took all my strength to stay in character for as long as I did.

""You do not fool me, Odysseus," was his straight reply. "I have heard of your artful behaviour and I have no time for trickery. You will not fool me."

""How can a fool fool?" I laughed vacuously.

""You will join Menelaus' coalition by nightfall," he ordered me, and began to return to my house. As he walked away, I was amazed to see him draw his sword and hold it in his fist as if he meant to use it. I caught my father's concerned look too, and quickly chased after him, still trying to stay in my mad character, dancing about him, talking as much nonsense as I could muster, but always watching the sword. His hand never once twitched in my direction, but his eyes showed a well-formed, determined plan was in his head.

"When he reached my home, Penelope was sat by the table, weaving. Telemachus was playing on the floor with my nurse, crawling about the rug, while my young pup of a dog, Argus, bounced about him. It was such a beautiful scene, a perfect, blissful, family moment that I welled with admiration. I saw Penelope raise her head, but not look at me. She fixed Palamedes with a look of sheer panic. She told me, before I left, that there seemed to be something intrinsically evil about him. It is hard for me to think that of any man - we are all, I liked to believe, complicated enough to be made of both good and bad.

A good orator relies on this. But it seemed all the good in Palamedes had, for some reason, been washed away.

""Do you still insist in playing the moron with me, Odysseus?" he demanded. "Will you not accept your part at Menelaus' side, in accordance with the oath you swore to him?"

""I have never sworn Menelaus was an oaf," I jested, though no one laughed. Not even the hint of a smile brushed the lips of any there; the mood amongst the adults in the room remained apprehensive. Each tried to look anywhere but at our confrontation. And then, without warning, sword still in hand, he marched across the room, kicking my poor dog out of the way, and grabbed Telemachus about the waist..."

Odysseus paused in his tale. His breathing had quickened at the memory and his eyes filled with a fearful anger. I quickly refilled our wine cups before asking him:

"What did you do?" Odysseus took his cup gratefully, and the movement seemed to return him to the safety of the present, away from his traumatic recollections.

"One moment my son is capering about the floor, carefree and innocent as a child should be, the next he is being dangled at the waist by a man ten times his size, while a sharp sword, so huge next to his tiny frame, rests against his throat. It's strange that I can so clearly recall the glint of the blade's edge against his skin. It all happened so fast. The women barely had time to protest. I felt completely powerless. All the while Palamedes remained as expressionless as he had been since his arrival.

""Well, mad Odysseus," he said, "if it be so, you must make amends for dishonouring your vow to Menelaus. Your son's life would seem to me to be a fair bargain, since you yourself are in no fit state."

"I was struck dumb, Kalypso. There was not a hint of deceit about him. I kept trying to catch my son's eyes, trying to reassure him with a look that everything would be well, that he could trust me. All I could see was uncertainty staring back at me. Telemachus could sense something was wrong, but he was too young to process its relevance. I was amazed, and slightly proud that he did not cry or struggle. He just watched me as I did him, shifting my attention now and then to his neck where, if I had seen even a droplet of blood...

"My wife shook and wept silently, and everyone present seemed rooted to the ground, fearful that any movement would be matched by the blade. The only noise came from Argus, who barked and growled angrily at the outrage - an animal being the only one of us unafraid, able to see the scene for what it was; and for that I rebuked him roundly. I shouted his name harshly as a warning. I thought his noise might cause Palamedes to act hastily and, if not hurt my son, then turn his aggression on my dog. I would never forgive myself if any member of my household were lost that day - not for my sake.

""Palamedes had won, and he knew it. I would rather leave my living son and go to war than see him dead at the hands of a brute for my foolishness. At that time, I would have done anything Palamedes asked of me to guarantee my son's safety. If I noticed even a moment's hesitation - if he dropped the sword or looked away - I knew nothing could stop me from killing that man with my bare hands. With anything I could grab hold of. How dare he use my son...?"

I have tried to imagine how I would have coped in such a scene. Would I have been able to just stand there and let Odysseus deal with this impossible decision alone? I have played the scenario out in my head, becoming quite the pro-active heroine at times. I would not sit weeping while my husband and child were in peril!

"Did you kill him?" I asked.

"I did nothing that day," was Odysseus' enigmatic answer.

Before I could ask more, a loud clap of thunder rumbled about us, accompanied by a noise akin to the crack and split of a great rock. When the noise finally abated, there was a stillness to the air. The previously incessant buzz of the rain had paused for this king of thunderbolts. Even with the fire blazing and spitting before us, it felt suddenly darker. We both sat up and looked about us, as if making sure it truly wasn't a stone-shattering storm. Perhaps it was the presence of Odysseus, or mere common sense, but within moments I remembered myself and my surroundings and allowed myself to feel safe. So it came as some surprise to me to look into Odysseus' eyes and see fear. Very strong fear. As if he could see Zeus himself standing above him, great thunderbolt in hand, ready to punish his crimes and put an end to his miserable life. But it was not Zeus he thought of in his

Kalypso : 'Tritagonist'

terror.

He began to edge slowly back towards the bedding, like a frightened child. His actions vexed me, and when the mutterings began I grew alarmed.

"He has found me," he whispered and stuttered over and over. I wondered if it was the drink, or fatigue. I edged tentatively towards him, crouched beside him and tried to sooth his fears.

"Who? Who has found you?" I cooed calmly.

"Poseidon," he answered, at all times keeping careful watch of the corridor leading to the cave's mouth, as if waiting for some great evil to approach him.

"No, no," I laughed uneasily, my own eyes being unavoidably drawn to his invisible danger. "Poseidon will not come here. No one knows you are here but me. And besides, dear Odysseus, what could Poseidon possibly want from you?"

"The gods will destroy me in the end. All of them. They just play with me, dragging out my destruction"

"Well that could be true of any of us," I interrupted. "And yet I am not afraid in here. There is nothing to be afraid of in here." Still the thunder outside rolled about us. Odysseus clenched tightly against me and I was afraid to move away lest that scare him further.

"I have killed a man," he mumbled his confession into my chest, too ashamed to look me in the eyes.

"You were in a war, Odysseus. Of course you had to kill men. The gods will forgive you - they will understand."

"I killed him in cold blood, Kalypso. We were not at war. But I killed him."

"You mean Palamedes?" I asked. Odysseus was deathly quiet for a moment.

"Him too," he finally agreed. I worried, but said nothing.

"Why did you kill him?"

"My son..."

"You were protecting your son," I acknowledged.

"He threatened my son." Odysseus made a noise like a sob, but no tears appeared.

"I know he did. You told me-"

"I would kill any man - any number of men - who threaten to harm my son. My only son. My heir. My beautiful boy, Telemachus..."

"The gods will forgive you. They would surely do the same?"

"I had him stoned to death."

I sat back, wondering how he had managed such a deed, but afraid to ask. "I'm sure it was deserved?"

"But I should not have done it! I am a bad person, Kalypso. You should tell me to leave. You should throw me back to the pitiless sea."

"The sea has already shown you mercy. It spared us both! And you are not bad, Odysseus. We have all done regretful things. My own journey to this island was marred by my bad behaviour and foolish mistakes-"

"I watched an innocent woman being raped by shameful soldiers. I blinded a man in a drunken fight - *not at war*! I drove a man to suicide... These were not foolish mistakes, not bad behaviour! My soul is blackened by such deeds and I cannot escape their torments. I wake in the middle of the night with the torturous remains of the same nightmare on my brow. Their faces... Their cries..."

"So much time has passed now, Odysseus," I reassured him, feeling older as I spoke.

"If you were not lying there beside me, Kalypso... There are times, in the dark, when I imagine myself running at the cliff edge, running without stopping, still running upon the air as Poseidon drags my body beneath the waves..."

"It must be years by now," I interrupted, trying to discourage these suicidal thoughts by ignoring them.

"I never properly grieved, Kalypso. Never. Oh, I cry at times. But always, I had to focus on the living. I had to keep my men in order. I had to get back home... And now I have to know *you* will be happy. I do not have time to grieve for those gone forever. Swathes of men destroyed because of the actions of one woman... Because of me... How can I begin to grieve?"

"I am here for you," I said, realising how little that helped, groping for the right thing to say and grasping at empty words. We sat in silence for a while, as I thought of all the lost people from my youth. Men of rank, acknowledged by my father, who died of war or disease or age. There were always certain rituals, I realised. Rituals for the living. Poking and pushing at a dead man's carcass with a stick until it floated away was not a part of those rituals, and still hung heavily on my mind as well.

"Why don't we do it properly?" I decided. "We'll sacrifice the best of our sheep - well," I interceded myself, thinking of the unfortunate deaths of those poor, unsuspecting creatures, "*you* can, and I'll join in with the preparation and prayers. And then we will hold some funeral games."

Odysseus, his head still resting upon my chest, gazed up curiously at me. "Funeral games? And how will we do that, dear Kalypso? Am I to compete with myself?"

"No, of course not! You'll compete against me." A soft smile spread across his face. "Why not?" I insisted. "We'll throw rocks and see whose goes further. We'll run laps. We'll throw spears at a distant point. Once I have won," and he chortled appropriately at my false hubris, "we'll eat and toast your friends as you tell me of their great deeds. Then we shall drink until our eyes fail us and we stumble into a dreamless sleep. What say you?" He smiled thoughtfully. "It is a start, at least?" I persisted. I had visions of healing his soul, as I had once cared for his body. How could he refuse me?

Kalypso : 'Tritagonist'

KALYPSO'S THIRTY-SECOND EPISODE

After further friendly cajoling, Odysseus agreed to humour me (as I believed I was doing him) and we set about our preparation. We took some time discussing possible events, which caused a great deal of mirth and was so pleasant a distraction that I was disappointed when we finally concluded the details.

Odysseus agreed to pick out and kill two of our best rams (out of sight of me) as offerings and a good feast of a meal afterward. Meantime I chose two long spears of wood, and two large rocks, though one was a good deal lighter than the other. Already Odysseus mused at my cunning. He sharpened the ends of my spear-sticks into points and began to rack together a second fishing raft. It was exciting.

We woke early in the morning. Odysseus allowed me to join him in his stretches. Ever since he had regained his strength, he'd worked tirelessly on developing the perfect early morning routine.

Occasionally I would mimic him. From a distance at first, but he soon spied me doing so. I thought he might be annoyed, think that I was mocking him, but he simply laughed, then worked extra hard, spinning and stretching. It became a game - a challenge - as he deliberately moved faster and stretched further to see how long it would take me to give up the imitation. I confess I did give up long before him. He complained later that day that one of his thighs ached much more than usual, much to my amusement.

"Why do you do it?" I had asked him while I relaxed against a boulder and watched his repetitive show. He was never embarrassed to let me watch, and I believe he secretly enjoyed my attention. Any embarrassment was all mine.

"It's a great way to wake up," he answered, panting. "Keeps your body healthy... Strong... Focused..." He stopped, bent over to rest with his hands on his knees, waiting for his breath to naturalise. He caught my look of concern and added, "Feels good." The sweat was glistening against his forehead, arms and chest; his cheeks were flushed. I wasn't entirely sure how this could feel good. I felt that a brisk walk and a day's work were enough. Maybe a swim in the lake... But not for Odysseus.

"Is this a military thing?" I asked.

"What do you mean?"

"Are you still thinking back to your time as a soldier? Exercising in preparation for battle?"

He scoffed. "Exercising during war is not a priority. We try and do a good drill each morning. Put the men through their paces. But there is no free time in war. Only preparation for the next battle. Minor attempts at rest. Cleaning weapons and armour, checking horses, chariots, men's health and spirits. Meetings organising the next assault, planning a counteraction, considering all possibilities. We try, but... No. It isn't because of those days. I don't choose to do anything of those days any more...

"I have done this since I was a young child. I joined in with my father's exercises for as long as I can remember. I stretched before heading out to the fields, before hunting, before organising the house... Yes, I suppose it did become routine during military service... I don't know, Kalypso, it's just a part of my life, the way I am."

I worried that my questions might have confused or shamed him, but he resumed his routine after this conversation, and so it continued every day, with no hard feelings toward me or my imprudent queries.

On the morning of the games he was particularly benevolent, stretching and moving slowly enough to talk me through it all.

"No reason to cause ourselves injury before we begin," he explained like an educator, an enthusiastic twinkle in his eye.

"Not before wrestling at least," I smiled.

So we exercised, we took breakfast, and both dressed in short tunics. Then we began in earnest.

Our first challenge, in my opinion, was the most disconcerting. Odysseus had built two small rafts from two or three short planks roped together, with accompanying oars. Our original plan had been to sail around the entire island as a race. This was not a traditional event, but since in any competition we held Odysseus would doubtless be at an advantage, it seemed to make sense to come up with some alternate ideas. Nevertheless, many of Odysseus' compromises needed a good deal of tempering. I could never tell if he was hoping to win by a fair fight, or if he meant to give me the opportunity to beat him. He gave nothing away. Still, I limited the round island race to a far shorter length alongside the beach - from one rocky peak of land to another (we were lucky that Ogygia had such useful start and finish points in her features) - lest we spend the entire day at sea and have no time for anything else.

It had always amazed me how quickly Odysseus made it back to the sea after his ordeal and deliverance. Perhaps all men are like that - undeterred by the pitfalls nature throws their way. When thrown from a horse, do not the instincts of the brave tell them to return to the horse and ride it again until the fear subsides? Even while recovering from uncomfortable pain, they must prove the fall was a fluke, an accident. It seemed from the stories he shared with me that each time he put to sea some terrible episode befell Odysseus. Poseidon did not favour him, and yet one of his earliest decisions on Ogygia (once his health had returned) was to build us a better fishing vessel! For sailing further out from shore and throwing the nets deeper, he had said. Odysseus had jumped back on the waves.

Kalypso : 'Tritagonist'

Sometimes he might disappear for an entire day, floating about by the darker waters, those waves that washed over the crowns of the undead, the hull-piercing rocks. Yet there would be Odysseus, ignoring his phobias, bobbing precariously about these undersea perils, seemingly fearless. On such calm days the water would shimmer and sparkle, huffing against the shore. I would be the nervous one, sat on the beach, watching as I weaved or cleaned or did any number of chores and activities, always absently distracted by this man, always listening to the waves' complaint. He was invading their world. He shouldn't be allowed. So many times they had expelled him but he would not stay away, this determined sailor. My heart would skip if ever I saw him dive into the waters and my breath would stick to my lips until I saw him appear with a gush of watery sighs and clamber back into the boat. One day they would take him from me. That they made clear. Yet there was nothing as he fished and dived and swam to suggest any danger. He looked bold and certain. Drowned Odysseus, the shipwrecked sailor... It was nothing more than a far-flung dream. For hadn't he always been here, just as he was now? Courageous, clever Odysseus of Ogygia...

And so our first event was this shoreline race, which latterly seemed apt for the occasion, though neither of us ever said so. Odysseus had offered me a head start, but I declined. Instead we agreed that I would row on the inside, closest to the island. We began at the rocks nearest my cave, and ended at the great triumphal arches beneath the cliff he knew so well, his favourite point of contemplation. It was shallow water most of the way, this being a relief since the rafts were quite small and flat, and felt likely to turn over with a single shove.

We each balanced ourselves precariously, oars at the ready, and repeated the rules to each other. It quickly became evident that we were not agreeing on who should start the race or how. After some disagreement on counts and words, we decided to leave it to nature. The next bird to fly close by would signal the start. It was quite absurd. For what felt like an eternity we both unwaveringly watched the space before us. Just as we began to notice each other's steely expressions and laugh at our ridiculous plan, a gull did indeed soar past our starting line. I was first to notice it and quickly set off, Odysseus cursing just behind me, accusing me once again of conspiring with the island.

It was not a very smooth or dignified race. Our rowing was accompanied by shrieks, splashes and curses. I wondered if all the frivolity was contrary to what should perhaps be a serious, solemn competition, but Odysseus made no complaints and I was torn between enjoying myself too much, enjoying the sight of Odysseus laughing, and reminding myself to win the challenge, to beat my opponent. Odysseus, I could see, was just as torn, since one moment I would catch an aggressive determination in his eyes, and the next he would be laughing so hard he could barely keep his balance.

We had decided there should be no rules on how the finishing line could be reached, leaving it all to personal invention, except that both body, boat *and* oar must cross the line. I had adopted a seated position on my raft, knees aloft. I thought it might allow me better balance, though I felt certain it hindered my speed. Odysseus chose to stand, making him appear not unlike a temple statue on its plinth, with his glistening bronze skin and bearded face, eyes widely purveying the stretch ahead, holding his oar like a sceptre.

I soon regretted our racing. It was such a beautiful warm morning, and I had never before joined Odysseus when fishing. We had even stopped bathing regularly together in the lake.

How nice it would be, I thought, *if we could take a few relaxing trips now and then, just float together, leave the island without leaving my home; free from daily distractions, with only nature to amuse us. A chance for us to spend some time alone...*

A woman's cackling laughter echoed about me.

"A *last* chance...?" came a teasing female voice inside. It stilled me.

"Last chance before he leaves," it crowed.

"No more chances left."

I recognised its piercing tones and yet I could not place it. "And he *will* leave you..."

The water hit me square in the face.

I blinked the heavy droplets from my lashes, but by the time I had a dry view, Odysseus was ahead of me, smiling over his shoulder. Already triumphant.

"Wake up," he joked, a broad and cocky smile across his face. I recovered my senses and the race began in earnest. He was stood, proud and erect, with his back turned to me, deliberately positioning his raft in front of mine, so that I would have to make a great effort to get round and ahead of him. This was a dirty trick in need of a counterattack. I waited until his balance seemed at its most precarious, then used my oar to knock inconstantly against the back corners of his raft. All this was bad sportsmanship, we both well knew, but as we had no rules, we were not breaking any. Odysseus yelled back at me, protesting in good humour to cease or accept the penalty, his raft rocking about turbulently as I persisted with my assault, watching with amusement as he struggled to retain his composure. I was now kneeling and stretching to reach his raft, which he attempted to move a small distance away from me. I could tell he was not trying hard to defeat me, not pushing himself forward with any great speed - doubtless for my benefit. I felt sure he could have finished the race long ago if he were taking it seriously, and certainly he could have got away from my incursion. Instead, he remained just far enough in front of me so that I might come at him.

Very little actual rowing was taking place, and our rafts were already drifting with the current towards the beach. Odysseus was

Kalypso : 'Tritagonist'

floating away from me, but he had begun a new plan of attack. Turning slowly about atop his raft, I could see the mischief in his eyes and was excited with guessing his next move.

Which was, without warning, to plunge into the waves between our drifting craft, dissolving beneath. I looked down with alarm. I knew he couldn't win by swimming, but I already feared that was not his intent. I watched his empty raft, oar resting aloft, bobbing gently, repetitively. Everything was silent. Odysseus had not reappeared.

Before I had time to consider what he could be doing and where, he erupted at my side in a froth and flurry of water. As he began to sink back down, he used all his remaining strength to lift up my raft and turn it over. He roared with the thrust and I shrieked. The noise was tremendous, like many children at play. My lower body slipped into the sea, my fingers gripping hopelessly to the wooden slats, nails scraping against rope and damp splinters, my oar having disappeared somewhere beneath me. Odysseus was not so cruel as to tip the raft all the way and have it land on top of me, but he was determined to shake me off. I knew I could not win the race without my oar (our rules stating so), and I would therefore have to dive for it before it floated away. I could still feel it knocking against my knees as it slowly drifted down to the seabed. At which moment, an idea occurred.

Following Odysseus' example, I left him alone on the water's surface, still attempting to dislodge me, and dived beneath, grabbing at the fallen oar, swimming forward with erratic kicks of my feet. I could not tell where Odysseus was by this point and only hoped that he was still attacking my vessel. I could not let him notice my trajectory until it was too late. I swam beneath his raft, and pulled myself up at its bow, with as slow a movement as I could control. The less attention I drew to myself, the longer I knew I would have to execute my plan. It proved to be virtually impossible to clamber onto Odysseus vessel, whilst hauling up my oar and keeping his raft and oar steady, without his being aware of me. Nonetheless, he appeared to happily play along, taking his time to react and relinquish his hold on my vessel, so that I was almost aboard his when he began to chase after me.

But he quickly noted his failure. I had not only played the game, I had potentially won the contest. Excitedly, I began the tricky job of rowing with effort, speed and my extra cargo, thoroughly exhausted but buoyed by the excitement. Meanwhile, Odysseus returned to my abandoned vessel and, lying prone across the slates, the ends of his limbs sticking out into the water, he was frantically paddling with his hands and feet. We were both wildly off the straight course we had planned due to our antics and the tide, but we had floated over halfway towards the finishing line. Odysseus would only be able to defeat me if he could retrieve his oar, and I was determined not to let that happen. For the first time the race became quite real and competitive, just as I'd hoped it would, though the feeling in the pit of my stomach was almost unbearable. Much as I wanted to win, I worried at what that might do to Odysseus' pride. This was, after all, in memory of his friends, his past... Was it not proper that he should be victorious...? He certainly worked very hard to catch me up.

The rocks marking the finishing line were fast approaching as I pondered the rights and wrongs of our childish games. Only feet away from being champion, I looked back to see Odysseus still close behind me, but trailing from the weariness of having to use his own inadequate limbs to propel him. I suspected he now wished he'd made the rafts smaller. Still, he was battling bravely, and smiled when he saw me watching. I was suddenly overwhelmed with shame. I yelled back to him to catch and threw him an oar. He caught it as it fell to the water, a smile of warm appreciation on his face. He rowed himself up behind me, so that our rafts floated as one in length, and we both sat, without effort, without speaking, and waited for the waves to coast us over the finish line.

Although technically I won, and Odysseus did so proclaim me the winner with formidable admiration, I never felt it as a glorious victory. The amusement had overtaken the competition from the start. We pulled in our sodden rafts, leaving them to rest against the rocks, and walked along to a soft, sandy patch of ground, collapsing with fatigue, both smiling up at the clouds above. Now and then we would both look to each other and chuckle, content with our achievement, before returning to gaze at the floating white patterns above. It took some time before my head cleared, breath calmed, and the ground beneath me grew still once more. My arms and legs began to ache from the abrupt stillness I imposed on them, but I suspected Odysseus was the more exhausted of the two of us and refused to feel sorry for my state.

Once sufficiently rested, I propped myself up on my elbows and watched the tide approaching the island, enveloping the land, and pushing its way teasingly up to our toes. Odysseus' eyes were closed to the warming sun. We lay uncannily close to where I had first discovered him and the image made me tense. I looked across at the rocks, grey and brown boulders, barriers to the foaming waves. Those rocks that had only a short while ago meant so much more to us. Triumph. We had looked to them excitedly and fought to reach them as if they were the most precious part of this land. Now they were just protrusions, lumps in the landscape, splattered with seawater and decorated with seaweed. A resting place for our one-use rafts. Odysseus' point of sorrow.

"What shall we do with them now?" I said aloud. Odysseus' eyes opened. I had not intended to disturb him, but he followed my gaze and quietly contemplated the scene for a moment. Sitting himself up, he slapped his hands against each other, brushing away the excess sand, a determined look about his face.

"Leave them for now," he decided. "I'll come back and collect them later. I have an idea how we can use them again. But for now, I suggest we head back and toast your victory!" I blushed coyly at this, but allowed him to help me to my feet and joined him in the gentle return trek to the cave, pestering him to no avail on this "idea" of his.

Kalypso : 'Tritagonist'

He intended it to be a surprise, and a resolute Odysseus was a hard man to break.

After the morning's exertions, and with the sun nearly at its zenith, we both agreed a break for food and drink was in order before we continued. We ate a good deal of flatbread and honey, some sprinkled with seeds, some topped with fruits. We had never taken so much time nor feasted very long at that time of day before. Odysseus disappeared briefly, returning with some wine from those great vats of his, that first invention, which he had since improved upon. He handed me a poured cup with personal pride, as he often did. The wine we made was never the same twice, and Odysseus had sketched many notes about the cavern in which it was stored to try and explain these peculiarities. On the day of the funeral games, however, it seemed to taste just right - not to sour, nor too sweet. Perhaps it was because of the fruits and honey we were eating at the same time; or perhaps it was just appropriately so, a gift for our special efforts.

"To our first champion, fair Kalypso of Ogygia, daughter of Atlas!" Odysseus raised his glass at me and drank. I smiled and joined him, but a discomfort would not let me go.

"Odysseus, is it right," I asked, "that we should be... well, enjoying ourselves during these games?"

"Dear, soft-hearted Kalypso," he smiled broadly as he poured himself another cup. "Sometimes I forget you would never have been to such games before. We do our grieving at the pyre. We make our sad speeches then, in honour of the deaths of our lost and loved friends. But the games we use to honour their lives. It is good for them to be a time of celebration. If the friends we honour were here with us now, they would be merry too. In fact, I have no doubt they would be roaring with laughter at my recent defeat. I think you may be the first person to beat me in a race using my own methods!"

"Certainly the first woman!"

"Quite so," he agreed. "Which would give no end to their mirth!"

"So, does that mean you are the fastest of your people?"

"Me?" Odysseus laughed jovially. "Not in the least. Let us just say I am blessed with a strange good luck at such times. At one of the last funeral games I took part in, I competed in a footrace with two very fast men, Ajax the younger, whose father was my equal at boxing that day, and Antilochus, son of my good friend Nestor. Both were younger men than I, known for their swift feet, and only rivalled in this by Achilles. Both felt they had a far greater chance than an old man like me. Hah! Antilochus, the more admirable of the two in my eyes, I left far behind me, but Ajax was determined to win no matter how close I got to him. We were far closer than you and I got today! And the crowd was behind me, the underdog, which spurred my feet the more. Ajax was so intent on beating me that he was focused only on the prize, and not at his path. So it came as more of a surprise to him than anyone else when he tripped over something (though no one could see quite what) only moments from the finish, and fell all too unfortunately onto

Kalypso : 'Tritagonist'

a pile of steaming dung. And I won first prize. The spectators found the whole event hilarious and Antilochus took it all in good humour. But little Ajax was so enraged at his misfortune, he accused me of conspiring with the gods and winning only by divine intervention." Odysseus smiled at me, shaking his head in amazement. "Today, I think I know how he must have felt. It is rare to meet a person who can outwit you at a game you thought to be yours alone."

We spent the afternoon at play, throwing rocks and spears, and measuring distances. We'd spent the days of preparation looking for two of the roundest boulders on the island. Despite Nature's love of curves, this proved to be an arduous task, and our final two choices were rather lumpy in shape, though beautifully smooth to touch. Odysseus' rock was a pure deep grey colour all over, while mine had speckles of brown and lines of white decorating its surface. Mine was also three quarters the size, which we had both considered a fair handicap; though it would not have mattered if it had been attached to wings, I could in no way beat Odysseus in any throwing competition. Once this became obvious, we took to seeing if Odysseus could better his own efforts, and then comparing these throws of the weighty rock with throws of a lighter spear, the latter predictably doing him more justice. We had some fun rolling the rocks along the ground to see if that made it more of a contest for me and, indeed, I proved a little more adept at this, giving Odysseus and his great lumbering boulder a good run. Nevertheless, and despite his morning's exertions, it was clear he had the better arm strength, and we were neither of us too surprised or disappointed by this.

So, in wit and tactic I had proved champion; in strength Odysseus was the unmistakable winner. We next played for accuracy with a brief archery competition. We had only the one bow between us - an item that had washed ashore a long time ago and which Odysseus had gone to some pains to restore, restringing and cleaning it, whilst regaling me with tales of his personal collection of weaponry. He had undertaken this task with reverent gusto. He took it away one morning, looking like a bent and battered stick, but returned that evening with a barely recognisable and quite beautiful piece. He had cleansed the sea's effects from the wood to bring out some decorative carvings and faded gilt work. We both pondered over who might have once owned the weapon and how it ended its days so far from its owner. It was inspiring to have the use of this mysterious relic, to watch it come back to life for this celebration of all things lost.

We chose for our target a large tree, with a good clear piece of trunk. Again, Odysseus proved himself the more skilled, though neither of us were better practiced. I might have called for an unfair advantage had it been the case that he used the bow and arrow a good deal during his recent war, but he assured me it was never once used. Spears and swords, he said, but never bows. Not by him. His favourite remained at home in Ithaka.

Kalypso : 'Tritagonist'

After more than my fair share of practice shots, I found my way to hitting the bark, but never as accurately as those swift lines made by Odysseus. I found myself rubbing the scarred tree as if to apologise and help soothe its wounds, though none of our arrows did more than chip away at the surface, and most of mine failed even there.

Finally, we settled for a wrestling match with a suitable twist for fairness. We tied our own ankles together, helped each other to stand and agreed that the contest was to be one of balance, the aim being to make your opponent fall and to keep him on the ground long enough for you to be declared winner. I was very grateful that we were holding this event on the softer sands, as I proved just as capable of making myself fall over as I was adept at tumbling by Odysseus' hands. We soon realised this was not only a test of balance but also of stamina, with all the jumping about to try and avoid the advance of an opponent whilst gaining the advantage on them. In truth, the competition amounted to who would tire out first, which, I was surprised to discover, was Odysseus! The exertions of the day having finally got the better of him, he tried to declare me the winner. Since I had spent most of the event on the ground, with Odysseus trying to pin me down with his hands while not being toppled by my wriggling and thrashing to get free, and since the contest had only ended due to his being too tired to continue, I called instead for a draw. He smiled absent-mindedly at this but said nothing. I put his reaction down to exhaustion and hopped and jumped away, to his amusement, to fetch us some refreshments.

The games were declared over by late afternoon. That evening, we began a proper ceremony of mourning. We built a large fire and Odysseus disappeared toward the fields, returning in due course with a hacked goat's carcass that I made much effort to disassociate with the bleating fellows that graced the grasses, saying a quiet prayer of thanks and forgiveness for the poor animal that had given its life, while Odysseus conversed on the usual events at a funeral pyre - how sometimes whole horses, cattle, even slaves or prisoners could be added as sacrifices. I wondered at the necessity to honour death with yet more carnage, but decided it would be an inappropriate question at this time. Our single carcass was added to the already roaring flames, followed by the fluid offering of the sacrificed animal's blood, which he poured from a small pot.

Odysseus also produced a curiously filled bag. The bag itself I recognised, for I had made it, at Odysseus' request, using scraps of collected cloth. It was a fair sized bag, being the height and width of two hand spans, and was drawn at the top with some fine woollen thread. My curiosity was piqued by what its contents could be.

Odysseus and I stood quietly, watching the fire devour its offerings, the sun setting ahead of us, the tide now in decline, lapping against the beach below. It was a quiet, still night, so much in contrast with our energetic day. A mysterious feeling of reverence for our makeshift ceremony overcame me and I felt for Odysseus' hand, hooking my fingers gently against his for reassurance, though I could not explain my need for this. For a brief moment I worried uncomfortably that this might be contrary to his desires, disrespectful to his mood. But my gentle touch was instantly rewarded by a clasp, and we stood, arms entwined, leaning in close for comfort.

Darkness slowly crawled across the sky from behind us, creeping low and cool. Though I felt overwhelmed, I was sure it was the smoke and not sentiment that made my eyes begin to water. Odysseus handed me the patchwork bag and bravely stepped in closer to the fire to free a part of the well-cooked goat. We moved a little further away from the heat and shared the flaky leg meat with herbs, leaves and bread for accompaniment, and more warmed mead than necessary to wash it all down.

We shared fewer words than we had earlier in the day. The mood was sombre. I worried that this was a bad sign, since I had hoped our day's events might help alleviate Odysseus' unhappiness, not add further to it.

His day, however, was far from over. Unbeknown to me, he had spent some time considering how best he might commemorate and grieve for his lost friends. Now I was to learn of his decision. He bid me drain the last of the mead from my cup, and once I had obliged him, he refilled it with a deep red liquid that I took for being the remainder of the goat's blood. I had never tasted blood, though I had heard tales of my father bragging that he had done so, or knew men who had done so, and some stories told to me by older siblings had been filled with warriors desirous to drink the blood of their victims. This idea both appalled and thrilled me, and so my initial, silent discomfort at Odysseus' offering, turned to a strange reverence at the request to join him in this act.

"To lost comrades and departed friends," Odysseus toasted aloud, and we drank. I cannot recall if I was the more disappointed or relieved to discover that I was mistaken; the red liquor was nothing more than wine, the darkness and flickering light before us having played tricks with my perception. Odysseus threw the contents of a third cup into the fire and then asked me for the bag of mysterious objects. I wondered if we should have invoked the gods at this stage, perhaps thanked them for sparing us and bringing us together; something told me, like a whisper in the ear by my dear Hermes, that such a suggestion would not be welcome. Odysseus' view of the great overlords of Olympus had often been derogatory in view of the nightmare of Troy and everything after, and I had never shown him a keenness to indulge them.

Those ancients and their unfathomable ways were never of much interest to me, and those newly added to the list of the revered were often men and women once known to my family, whose true stories and virtues I had full knowledge of (or at very least second hand knowledge) long before the bards glorifying venerations began. It is perhaps not known to you how peculiar it is to hear of your own

Kalypso : 'Tritagonist'

ancestors proclaimed as gods for their roles as leaders in battles and events, or simply because they were born into grand families and expected to achieve such status.

Surely Odysseus should be added to the list? The god of cunning, the great tactician? All those warrior friends and comrades of his with their strange quirks and various abilities are no better than the great ancestors with their powers and play.

But Odysseus was not born of a great family like I. His mother and father were of a mortal line of sailors and thieves - a lower class; while I was born of a Titan and an Oceanid - both ancient families of renown prestige. There is nothing about me that qualifies me as a goddess but heritage. Yet Odysseus valued kingship over godliness.

I laugh to think of dear Ogygia with her great population of one goddess, one king and their many hoofed and winged subjects. What use did she have of kings and goddesses? Foolish ancient terms. Odysseus and I were simply a man and woman, free from social roles. While he remained on the island, we were god and goddess of our world, king and queen of our land, and could remain so forever.

From the bag he pulled out a collection of strips of wood, at which moment I recalled an incident days before. He had asked after the planks of wood on which he had arrived on the island. Of course, I still had them. Even now I find it very hard to throw anything of sentimental value away, no matter how small the sentiment is. Look through my chest of oddities and you will find fish bones from the first morsel I ever caught, shells that I found pretty and any number of relics - some known and some not - found on the shore lines or scattered about the island. Odysseus' first day is recorded many times over in possessions, and those planks were hidden away in storage for no good reason than that I could not bring myself to destroy them.

So I was somewhat taken aback when, on handing them back to their original owner, Odysseus immediately took an axe to them and began to chop them into shards. I had to turn away and felt slightly annoyed at his sudden destructive temper. He disappeared with the ruins to his usual place of contemplation, and returned very late in a morose state. He had not seemed in a particularly angry mood that morning, so I could not say at the time what had come over him.

Now I saw the answer. On each of those hacked shards Odysseus had etched a name. The name of a lost companion. The ceremony at the pyre became a roll call.

"Achilles," he read aloud. "For fighting in a war he should never have been a part of, were it not for me. A brave man and leader, who died too young." And with the declaration spoken, the name was thrown into the flames, flashing and crackling, sparks rushing up to the heavens.

So it continued: "Eurylokhos, kinsman to my wife, my second in command. For all his faults and arguments, he saved us from debauchery and bad judgment on many an occasion. He desired to one day lead, and in time might have made the best of commanders. We had our arguments. His questioning of me served a good purpose. All differences aside, he was a good strong and knowledgeable man...

"Elpenor, the youngest of us, died because I was not looking out for my men the way Eurylokhos demanded! Fell to his death from the roof of a whorehouse, drunk and tired. I failed him...

"Baius, my helmsman...

"Macar, my good companion...

"Friend Misenus...

"And Polites, so very dear to me..."

After each name called, each set ablaze, Odysseus would drink and I would tentatively join him. His voice burned with emotion and my head swam with a giddy mixture of the heat and constant swigs of the strong wine. So many of the names he mentioned, the descriptions he attributed were lost in a haze.

I had seen Odysseus broken before, tears in his eyes for his past and his grief and his losses. But there was something quite different about that night. His grief was evident, yet so was his pride, and those two opposing efforts were veiling him in an unnatural darkness... It is difficult to describe. He was Odysseus in person, but I swear his soul was so apparent I barely recognised the man. And what a wretched soul I saw that night. He looked older. Aged. Usually Odysseus looked the same to me, day by day, no matter what his mood. If I thought back to the first moment I saw him, he would appear in my mind as unchanged, as identical to the man lying next to me each morning.

Not that night. Even with the flames brilliantly lighting us, his face and eyes were darkly shadowed. He seemed smaller than usual, even next to my comparatively fragile frame. I was desperate to hold him, but terrified to touch him. My awareness was slowly ebbing away. My senses only returned more sharply at the mention of his mother.

"Your mother?" I exclaimed, though I hadn't meant to speak quite so loudly, and then was unsure if I had. His hands and the bag were now empty. His mother had been honoured as the final place in the procession and was gently turning to ash.

Perhaps it was the drink, but the constant noise and heat of the fire was becoming tiresome. I longed to rest. I slumped indelicately on to the ground. Nothing more was said until Odysseus joined me, squeezing at his eyes with his fingers. He might have been sad, or he might have been adjusting them from the brightness of the flames, wiping away the smoke... I placed a hand on his knee which I hoped would seem comforting, and he took hold of it in a gentle grip.

"I heard about my mother... the death of my mother... Both she and Agamemnon - you remember, Menelaus brother?"

"The one who started it all?" I slurred.

"I visited a seer's house... On recommendation..."

"Whose?" My voice was now sounding irritating even to me in its inaccurate pronunciations, and the fact that it kept speaking even when I had told my brain to keep it quiet.

"A... lady we met. I mentioned her, I think? The house of ladies who could not be classed whores - were far better than such? Beautiful, clever..."

I snorted at his explanation, another unexpected noise, but he took it to mean that he had explained enough; I understood.

"The seer Tiresias lived in a forsaken place. The ground was like nothing I had ever witnessed before - black as charred wood, though cold and hard. It appeared as though it had only that morning flowed onto the land. There were solid ripples like those made by water, and slivers of craters all about. The air was rancid and misty. It was the most inhospitable place to live, which is why, I was told, Tiresias lived there. He had no care for beauty, being blind since a young man, and simply wished to be left alone. But he was an infamous seer-"

"You don't like seers!" I exclaimed, my words sounding more childish by the moment. I felt silly and embarrassed but totally lacking self-control.

"No I don't," he agreed in good humour, "but I was not alone on this voyage. When my men and I were told that Tiresias might be able to aid our return to Ithaka, I was sceptical. He was meant to know the ways of the sea, meant to know how we could return home, how soon we would get there. How could a blind man, who had spent countless years living on a remote part of land and shut away from all, know the best way for us to return home? I doubt he'd know any better than you."

"It's that way," I slurred, throwing my hand in the general direction behind us. "Just around the corner." Odysseus smiled.

"But I had men with me who believed - or at least wanted to believe in something. So I went. Alone, because I had been told he would not wish to be disturbed and would take against a crowd (his hearing apparently still being perfect)." Odysseus sighed and I felt dozy. "It was an awful place and a fruitless journey. Instead of learning of routes and time, he told me tales of death and murder. I had never before that day considered what kind of welcome I might receive on returning home. Only that it would hopefully be warm and sympathetic. Now, by Tiresias, I was told of the death of Agamemnon, at the hands of his own neglected wife, Clytaemnestra. She had never seemed anything like Penelope. But she was my wife's kin - her cousin; sister to Helen. What a family! Agamemnon had done his wife great wrongs, and they were a curious couple. There was never love between them, merely strife.

"But it did make me wonder. A woman left alone all those years must harbour a great many grudges and suspicions towards her husband, and it would be easy for her to find another lover. Even more so if it was thought her husband had died...

"As if that were not enough, Tiresias had much worse news for me, in telling me of the passing of my own dear mother. Two agonies I had not asked for! He said she died from the heartache of longing for my return. So I worried even more for my wife. My mother always

Kalypso : 'Tritagonist'

seemed of a far stronger countenance, and yet my absence had weakened *her* to such a degree... What if my wife was suffering the same? I left Tiresias in a state of utter confusion with nothing good to tell my men but that we were cursed by Poseidon and hunted by death. Tiresias had news that many men sought the hand of my wife in my place, and after hearing of Agamemnon's bloody misfortunes... Who knows in what vein my wife may greet me?"

"If she's even still waiting," I yawned noisily, again without meaning to. There was I, almost completely fallen onto Odysseus, my back against his side, my head lolling against his chest, speaking quite unsympathetically and out of place, incapable of stopping myself from doing so! Still, perhaps Odysseus was tired too, and perhaps he was almost as inebriated as I. Either way, he did not react angrily to my drunken outbursts. He looked down and chuckled.

"I think it is past your bedtime," he announced. The last thing I remember was his lifting me up in his arms and stumbling with me along the short distance back to our bed.

KOMMOS

"It occurs to me," she said, "that I might be mistaken about some of this." Kalypso registered our confusion and continued:

"Memories are funny things. They come and go as unpredictable visions, creating their own version of the story as they pass and repass. It may not all have happened in the order in which I have told you." For a moment she appeared to have confused *herself*. We murmured amongst ourselves, but Hermes drew us all back to the moment and Kalypso again stirred the fire before us.

"The games... they might have come sooner. Yet they might not... All I can say is that they happened. I know I felt terrible the next morning, particularly in remembering the foolish things I had said. And worse still much later, when I realised how far my plan to help Odysseus had backfired on me. I helped him, only to lose him.

"Each time I share a moment with you, I find I question its reality. I wish I could remember better. For myself as well. It is a grave misfortune that time and age rid us of our own realities. And too soon!

Kalypso : 'Tritagonist'

So many lost conversations. Doubtless they would mean nothing to you as you grasp about for another moment of heroism, something grand and proud to remember Odysseus by. I know; it is the stories you yearn to hear. You wish me to tell the tale of Odysseus, great orator, great inventor, great warrior. I can only tell you the stories he told and shared with me. One of you, perhaps, will sing it well someday. Then Odysseus will become a hero of his time and to you all.

"But he was my love. It is enough of my story that you simply know Odysseus was my great love. And I believed I was his.

"Meantime, he and I would talk about birds, insects and plants, cooking utensils and tools, cleanliness, fantasies, childhood stories and memories... And sometimes death, war, loss, anger...

"And fear... Far too much of that.

"I do remember wonderful nights spent lying together on the grasses of the high cliff, drinking warmed wine and watching the moon and stars travel across the sky; or lying on the sands of the beach through a sunset. Days spent playing through the forest, trying to catch a stray goat or search for an herb or fruit or vegetable. All those carefree moments you miss and long for once they are gone.

"I remember, too, and just as plainly, the moments of fear and dread and hurt, as Odysseus' thoughts would turn to his home, his land. The anger at his indecision, at his telling me how much he longed to stay with me, yet still refusing to do so.

"So... No, I cannot tell you of all the moments that passed

between great Odysseus and I, through the many years we were together here. That it would take as long a time as we have on this earth is quite reason enough. That I can still tell you as much as I can is a miracle! As I sit and think on my memories of conversations, arguments and silences - both good and bad - I wonder how much of my musing is real and how much is what I wished had happen. If I could only recall every word with true accuracy, if I could paint an honest picture of the complicated man and our complicated relationship...

"Ah, but the memory fades too soon. We hope the dead remember us; but why should they when the living forget so quickly...?"

Kalypso : 'Tritagonist'

KALYPSO : MONODY

I remember one day, before Odysseus left, I woke and looked about me. I had slept on a wooden-framed bed, four tall poles in each corner, linen curtains decorating each end, like sails tied at the waist, vines decorating the woodwork. The base of this bed was made from those two rafts from the funeral games. Odysseus had engraved our names on the wooden slats of each raft, one raft saying "ODYSSEUS", the other: "KALYPSO : TRIUMPHANT". I felt more honoured when he presented me with this heart-felt present than when he had proclaimed me winner after the race!

To one side of my bedchamber was a large wooden chest, within which lay all my worldly goods. On the other side sat my water basin, now carefully balanced upon the upper V of the X-shaped stand Odysseus had cleverly made from two planks of wood and some intricate slot work. I had slept beneath a blanket of goats' wool, dyed a yellow-green shade, and upon a bedding of wool cuts, feathers and skins. Wrapped in the arms of the man I loved. On the floor were scattered those multicoloured rugs which were made from the results of various wool-dying experiments. The cave carried the sweet aroma of those flowers - violets and other blossoms - threaded between the vines that wrapped about the bedposts, mixed with the smell of recently burned cedar wood chips.

I had candles of beeswax and oil burning lamps. Two large wooden vats, for straining and fermenting fruits for wine making, took pride of place inside a deeper cavern. Their contents could be collected from the carefully cultivated vines and orchards, which grew beside the untamed part of the forest. Alongside these woodlands, the livestock were carefully penned within enclosures, while barley and root vegetables grew in perfect patches about them. Just beyond the cave's mouth rested a wooden raft and its long oar, adorned casually with a large fishing net.

I doubted that day, if I had married a great lord like Menelaus, or tarried behind a popular bard in his travels, that I would ever have found myself waking in more comfort and luxury, feeling any more content than I did now. It seemed impossible.

Yet another thought also crossed my mind. All this time I had believed Odysseus' inventing was a pleasant distraction from the sadness he was regularly wont to feel. Now I saw these same constructions and inspirations as simple delays.

"I shall make you a proper bed before I leave, dear heart," Odysseus would say. "Kalypso, I will teach you how to catch the bigger fish," or "Let me show you how to tie up vines... trim the goats without

Kalypso : 'Tritagonist'

feeling their kicks... tap for honey and roll beeswax into candles..." To all this, he would add, "before I leave", until I forgot to hear those final three words. It had been too long for them to matter.

"Before I leave..." It was always said so gently. Sometimes apologetically. Never determined. Why would he ever want to leave?

If I look back with unhappy thoughts, I can see too many instances when he tried to leave, or should have left. I know now that those unusually long fishing trips and swimming excursions I often witnessed were in fact his way of learning about the local sea and its mysterious perils. That Hermes has safely guided you here to learn of my story must mean that someone learnt the secret of my island's defences. Natural or supernatural. Someone who then told my dear Hermes, who has come looking for me at an age when he should be resting. I do not regret that it is you and not Odysseus who visits me. For I feel sure that Odysseus will find me again when the time is right. He will remember me.

Emma Walker

KALYPSO'S THIRTY-THIRD EPISODE

It was a dark day that truly heralded the end. Odysseus had disappeared alone, while I battled an unusually ferocious wind. Weather is generally clement on Ogygia, even through storms and rainfalls, but these gales had a cold bite to them. It took no soothsayer to convince me that they were a bad omen. Past nightmares and ill tempers were about to be blown away.

The tide was approaching and looked to be high. I busied myself with cleaning the shoreline, checking that nothing valuable was left to be washed away, and that I had plenty of dry kindling in the cave, since I rightly predicted rain would soon follow.

As the first few drops began to splash about me, I looked for Odysseus and could just make out his distant silhouette on the cliff. He was standing. He seemed to be waving, something large gripped between his fluttering fingers. Thinking that he was seeking my attention, I made my way up shore to higher ground and began to walk towards him. I was a little put out by such an inopportune moment to be ushered to the cliff, the heavy cold rain splattering loudly as I walked, though as yet it was still not falling hard. But Odysseus was quite animated, and that being so unusual I was compelled to find out why.

Before I had reached the cliff something struck me about the scene. Odysseus' back was turned to me. He was not trying to attract me at all. And the higher I climbed, the more I could see the truth of it.

I froze.

I shivered as something brushed past my soul and turned me to stone.

Neither reaction was due to the cold change in the air. Indeed, even as the rain began to pelt against the grass at my feet, promptly covering them in mud, I felt and heard nothing. All my senses had been drawn to the distant black object floating against the horizon. It could be nothing else but a foreign ship.

I blinked away sticky raindrops like tears and felt a heavy sickness in my belly.

"Can you see it?" Odysseus voice came abruptly from beside me, startling me back from my senses. We were both soaked through.

"See what?" I asked frostily, deliberately refusing to accept it.

"There! The ship!" he cried excitedly. But by now our vision was blurred by the weather and though I still knew where to look to see it, I was glad that it had disappeared through a shroud of mist.

"I see nothing," I responded cruelly, deliberately disappointing him.

"You must have seen it!" he exclaimed, taking my arms and shaking me. I thought at any moment he might make me join him in a dance, and my annoyance grew. Then he opened up the cloth he had been holding in his hand. It was cream, bordered with dark red squares, and in its centre two green warriors fought, spears crossed, one - the larger - holding a great round shield on which was a bird or flying insect of some kind.

"See?" Odysseus flapped the tapestry before me like a prize. "It was Menelaus ship!" For the second time my heart stopped. "He sent me his standard, wrapped on wood, floating toward me with the tide, I fished it out, it's his, and now he'll come back, he'll take me home!" Odysseus barely took a breath as he spoke, such was his excitement. A great gulf of misunderstanding emerged between us.

"Not now he won't," I argued sullenly. I did not need to explain. The weather had steadily worsened as we stood talking and I determined to return to the warmth and safety of the cave. I turned on my heels. Odysseus did not follow straight away. I suspect he was straining to keep the ship in vision for as long as he could. Half way through my journey I heard him skipping up from behind, the standard beating angrily against the breeze.

"Soon, though," he said as he rushed past me like a child running home to a feast.

Kalypso : 'Tritagonist'

KALYPSO'S THIRTY-FOURTH EPISODE

Of all the people that might come to find him, even merely visit, Menelaus was the worse choice. How could Odysseus not see that? He remembered his good friend, Menelaus, the careful, considerate man Menelaus, the warlike warrior Menelaus... I remembered the jilted Menelaus. A man I had wronged without ever meeting. Did he know I had survived to live here? If he had seen Odysseus, had he also seen me? I wondered if Helen the whore had joined her husband aboard the ship. Or maybe Odysseus' own family? It could be a rescue mission... But then who knew he was here? All those years passed and we had neither of us noticed a ship sailing so closely by before...

Odysseus was too excited at the prospect of leaving me. The cave suddenly shrunk in size as he jumped about, discussing preparations for greeting the lord and his crew, how he might introduce me...

When he eventually remembered my past relationship, he suggested changing my name. Now I could definitely return with him, he said. I could join them on the last of his adventures. Menelaus wouldn't mind - he was sure it would all be long forgotten by now...

He was not thinking straight. I said nothing - there was no need for me to. I waited as Odysseus slowly tired himself out. I felt unwell. The cold and damp were not diminished as I tried to warm myself by the fire. My head and nose ached. I took off my wet clothes, wrapped myself in a warm blanket, and crawled onto the bed. Odysseus, oblivious, still talked, laying the tapestry out on the ground to dry. I had wanted to rip it from his hands and throw it back out to sea. Now, as I lay curled and shivering, I imagined it burning, providing the perfect amount of heat to make the cave a cosy, comfortable place once more. In time, as Odysseus fussed and hummed about the place, I fell into a disagreeable slumber.

Kalypso : 'Tritagonist'

KALYPSO'S THIRTY-FIFTH EPISODE

I had a dream. I was sat in my cave, though not alone. He was there, as equal to me as I am to you now. But it was not Odysseus who sat with me. It was dear, guiding Hermes. I was weaving, and he sat drinking and eating before me. I had barely thought of him, I realised, for quite some time. His early, invaluable guidance after Odysseus' arrival was now nothing more than ritual knowledge to me: "Leave him be and he will come back to you." Something about Hermes was different this time. He wanted to help me, but he was not here to do so. I felt nervous in his presence and my weaving became inconsistent. Mistakes appeared...

My fingers were picking at the threads now, and my shuttle was nowhere in sight. Eventually, as my frustration grew too hard to bear, he spoke, not unkindly but with great authority behind the words.

"It is done," he said. This was a dream, and so, in the way dreams often work, I knew exactly what he meant and yet remained confused.

"It isn't fair," I cried, my fingers covered in threads, still picking hopelessly at the incomplete shroud. "I can't get it to work properly, but I must, I have to..." I was panicking over my weaving. I had to finish it, make it perfect before Hermes departed. Yet still my mind knew what he meant.

"It is done," he said again, and taking the end of one thread, he pulled at my hard work, and I watched how quickly he made it unravel. I tugged back in desperation, but the effort awoke me with a jolt.

The cave was in semi-darkness. There were gentle spits from the embers of the fire, slowly burning itself out. The waves were splashing close by outside, so I knew the tide was high. I had not heard the waves in my dream, I recalled, though everything else had felt as real as it had on waking. I saw the body of Odysseus sleeping heavily beside me, his face etched with the aging frown I found so endearing. Even in sleep his thoughts were still heavy.

It had all been a dream, I thought to myself. A strange and foolish dream, and I would not be giving him up. Nothing could make me do so.

I settled back down again, this time determined to control my mind, imagining myself to be back in my father's house. But now it was not King Atlas' court, but King Odysseus and Queen Kalypso's. There were our children, playful and clever, making Odysseus laugh heartily, the way I had always longed for, as I smiled with perfect contentment. As sleep gripped me, dream fought against my imagination. I clung to these images as long as I could, watching as they slowly slipped away from me. I felt Hermes whisper in my ear, though I could not remember the words when I awoke. I just recalled the uncomfortable feeling they provoked. A feeling only outdone by the sight of three women walking into my fantasy. Eudokia and Ligys were playing amongst my brood of children. Ligys I scowled at, though she failed to see it, but for Eudokia I felt a painful and compelling need to clasp about the knees. I wanted to beg for her forgiveness and friendship. I wanted to confide in her all that had happened to me since we last parted. I thought she might show a willing interest, but I could not catch her gaze either. Even as I made my way toward her, it was something else that caught her attention. As I turned to follow her smiling gaze, I saw my Odysseus, draped in the arms of Melaina.

This time I awoke, panting and hot, to find Odysseus gone. It was morning, and I was thankful for that, though my stomach felt empty and nauseous. Hunger pains would have been easier to satiate. This was something else, something I had only felt once before, and I could not believe it possible that it had found me here...

Emma Walker

KALYPSO'S THIRTY-SIXTH EPISODE

The day following the sighting of Menelaus' ship, the day after, the day after that, and so on with a routine, full of spirit and enthusiasm, Odysseus made his way to the cliff, carrying Menelaus' banner, watching and waiting, preparing for his escape. All enthusiasm for inventing had ceased. I no longer waited for his return in the evenings, but took his meals to him; meals which soon returned to the small portions he had once complained about.

"It is strange to think that when I first arrived here I was such a sullen wreck, with the weight of a world - and Hades - on my shoulders," he commented as I passed him some bread and wine on one increasingly rare occasion when he had returned to join me. "So many lives... So many deaths!"

"A heavy load indeed," I agreed nonchalantly.

"And you, my beautiful goddess Kalypso, whom I admire and respect above all women - perhaps even all people! You, my best friend, have brought me back to life, you have listened to my woes and supported me, even when the little you asked for in return - and deserved - was never properly given you."

I remained unsure as to where all these compliments were headed. They usually ended in some form of guilt-ridden oration, designed to make me feel a greater strength of obligation to his needs. That day, I was simply not in the mood to be invoked.

"I have come to the conclusion," Odysseus confided, as much to the world as to me, "that I did it all for one reason alone. My love for Penelope. And it is you, fair Kalypso, who has made me realise that. You have returned me to myself."

The words punctured my chest like a blunt sword. Their truth was irrelevant. It was the fact that he should make such a declaration in my presence, when he must know how hurtful that would be to me. I found I could say nothing. I worked at my loom with my face turned away from him, fighting back the urge to shed tears of rage and the desire to point out his inconsiderate scorn in the most violent of terms.

"I have killed greater and lesser men than I in war, for which I blamed Helen and Paris of Troy. I blamed myself, of course, for creating that ridiculous oath. While it avoided all the quarrelling, it provided far greater bloodshed. It was by reason of the quarrels, you see, that I believed I had entertained the idea; but no. In truth, it was for Penelope. I reluctantly agreed to join with those lords in going to war against Troy, not just to protect my son's life, but also my wife. If I had been the cause of our son's death, through cowardice or stupidity... She would rightly never forgive me. It was never Helen at all..."

I had heard enough. I dropped my weaving shuttle to the ground, the sound of which clattered about us and brought our eyes into direct contact. I did not reach to retrieve it, but rather sat there and held his surprised stare for a moment, my cheeks burning, my mind swilling over with insults, injustices. It was as though he had been appealing to no one but himself, as if he didn't care that I was present and suffering his words. I took a deep breath and could see him wince, visibly preparing for the worse, like a prey cornered by its hunter. I took another deep breath to wash away the sympathy and, with all the self-control I could muster, I announced it.

"I think you should go." I shook with every word. Fear and regret mingled against each other. But it was said. Although he mistook my ultimate intention, he did not wait for further instruction. Carefully and nervously, he made his way from the cave and out into the soft rains, still falling. So often he had abandoned me of his own will, but now I felt a strange sense of power, that I could successfully command him so. I had, of course, in my anger, meant for him to leave the island altogether, but now that I sat alone in my very empty cave, tears still teasing the corners of my eyes, I wondered how far I might be happy to go along with this new and painful desire.

I left it a while - this time for my own needs rather than his - before following him up to where I knew he would be. He was

Kalypso : 'Tritagonist'

repentant and weeping. I knew I felt sorry for him and was at war within myself to hide it. He had come to a breakthrough in his mind, which, despite the pain it caused me, was a huge relief to him, and I had trampled that relief with my own rejected feelings on the matter. He looked up at me with eyes that intoned he knew he had said the wrong thing. No matter the truth what he felt, he should have been more respectful of my feelings. I knew all this, though he said not a word of it, as this was an old excuse, a repeat performance. I pitied him as I always did. Such a clever man was great Odysseus, in all things but the emotions of women. There are many things a man should and should not say to a woman. Truth should be economical and, if it does not favour its audience, it should not be spoken at all. These rules did not occur until far too late to Odysseus, so skilled in his ability to argue with other men, yet lacking the sensitivity needed for the opposite sex...

And yet, why should they occur with me? Did I not love him enough to allow him the freedom to say whatever he chose to? I wanted him to be well, to be himself. But I also wanted him to love me as much as I did him...

He was an insensitive moron, though I knew this was never his intention. Hence I pitied him. Often I would forgive him, sometimes explaining his errors, other times just forgetting the whole thing.

This time I pitied him, yes. But I found, as I watched his tearful face and apologetic eyes, that I could neither forgive nor forget. He no longer needed me. He had realised the truth of it, and the truth was he loved his wife more that me. He stayed on this island only to clear his mind and empty his heart of all the bad, so that he could return to his wife and child as the perfect, loving husband and father. He did not need me anymore. I could have attempted to convince him otherwise, as I had often tried to in the past. I, too, had skills in manipulating with language, so I had learnt. Feminine wiles, he called them, which he claimed were natural in all the powerful women he had met. A "goddess" like me was bound to have many. I had no wiles for him that day. I smarted still from the insulting rejection, and my hope that he could heal that wound, as he had done so many others, faded the moment I saw him. I knew he was afraid of my temper and wished to appease me for the sake of peace, rather than love. I knew, as I had known before but chosen to ignore, that he wished to be with his wife more than me. I knew there was no comforting either of us.

"It seems to me, unhappy Odysseus, that there is no reason for you to stay here and waste away your days in my company any longer." He began to protest that this was not so, but I made a superior wave of my hand to stop him. Goddess I had been called, so goddess-like I would act, and with surprising results, as he instantly withdrew and waited on me. "I wish for you to leave. Pick up your tools," I smiled half-heartedly, "and set to work on a new raft. A boat. Something that has a better chance of carrying you past the rocks and on home. I'm happy to help you in any way I can," I lied. "I'll arrange some

Kalypso : 'Tritagonist'

provisions and better clothing. As soon as the raft is built and the winds and gods are behind you, you can be on your way."

"Why do you say these things to me?" Odysseus sobbed. "Do you mean to trick me into staying by making me feel so bad that I will not have the strength to leave you? Do you hate me now? Tell me, Kalypso; I want to make things right by you, I long to. If I could only find a way... I hate that I can't... that you might hate me... But if it is what you must do..."

"I wish I could hate you, Odysseus. I do wish I could; it would make it that much easier to let you go. I have wanted nothing more than for you to love me as I love you; that we could live here freely for the rest of our days together, with no ties, no bonds, no rigid protocols and entrapments. I wanted you to believe my friendship was genuine and good, and yet I cannot believe, if the situation were reversed, that you would continue to keep me here against my will. And that is what I am doing, isn't it? Keeping you here where you no longer wish to be. You cannot leave for fear of hurting me, and I do not want you to leave because I love you. But if I were trapped on an island, trying to return to you, Odysseus, and my companion would not let me go... How could I love someone who keeps me from what I most desire? I see that now. You must go."

I am not sure how sincere I sounded, but the words were enough. The tears fell properly from his eyes. He took hold of my hand and held it to his cheek, his lips, grasping it so tightly I felt every shudder of his body seeping through the bones of his fingers and into mine. I moved nearer to him, still standing as he crouched before me and allowed him to weep against my belly, stroking his hair. I was caught between so many emotions that none would make themselves known. I was at a loss what to feel, relying on some superhuman strength to contain me.

"How will I know?" his muffled voice mumbled sadly from below, making my heart flutter with pain. "How will I know that you are well, if I am not here?" any contemptuous pity I had held for him before now dissipated completely to the love I knew to be true. As it always did. I let my tears, somehow withheld all this time, finally race down my cheeks.

"I don't know," I confessed. "You will just have to have faith that I am."

I knew I could not weaken my resolve. His love for me, no matter how tender and heartfelt, would forever be forfeit to that for his wife. At least until he saw her again. I had convinced myself for so long that it was only his son he wished to return to. His heir. Only the family unit as a concept. He had made it impossible for me to think that way any longer.

Nothing happened. Menelaus' ship had disappeared over the horizon almost as quickly as it had appeared, and it never returned. Odysseus' enthusiasm for escape waned. His spirit slowly ebbed. Soon he showed signs of moodiness overwhelming him again. He had not been rescued, and now even I had begun to push him away. I had given him the chance to leave, as he had wished to, yet he did nothing to make this happen. I grew weary with humouring him, from so much recent turbulence, and instead I berated him for it.

"How, after all this time, can you still sit there and mope like a child?" I demanded.

"What can you possibly know of my grief?" he yelled. "I had only just begun my life with Penelope. I've been trying to get back to her for almost twenty years. How quickly do you expect me to accept the loss? How soon should I forget?"

"There is no timescale-"

"Well, there you are then!"

"No! This is merely another excuse. It always has been and always will be."

"An excuse for what?"

"To refuse me and yet do nothing to leave. To spare your conscience from the guilt of betraying a wife you left nearly twenty years ago, refused to return to when you had the chance, and clearly, from your inactions, no longer love! If you ever did."

He turned white with rage and walked away from me. I found I did not care, my own anger was so intense. He could have confirmed my accusation or called me a liar. Neither version mattered anymore. His convenient rejection had chipped so much of my passion away I no longer knew if I wanted his love anymore.

I heard him later return to the cave, pick up his hunting spear and some rags and disappear through the woods.

His patience, too, had ended. He would wait with me no more.

Kalypso : 'Tritagonist'

KALYPSO'S THIRTY-SEVENTH EPISODE

Now and then I heard him through the trees, hunting - far too often for my liking. I heard the occasional tree fall and kept a mental account of these moments. But for the most part I ignored the inconvenience and returned to my life, some semblance of my routine before he had arrived on my shores. I fished. I collected vegetation and fruits. I cooked and cleaned, composed new songs to the moon and the stars and the gods. I felt sure he could hear me and I did not try to avoid this. Though we barely came in contact I was always aware of his lingering presence. And as my anger slowly abated and my bitterness ceased to burden me, this became a comfort of sorts. I did not know what sort of relationship we might forge together now, but we could not remain on bad terms forever. Not on such a small island.

When he did not return as soon as I had expected, I scornfully thought that perhaps he had finally found the courage to leave. I crept slowly about the sand ways, and all his usual haunts, finally spotting him beside a camp fire, polishing the spearhead of his hunting tool, holding it aloft every now and then as if returning to some long forgotten memory. I could have gone to him then; held him in my arms perhaps, or passed a joke to lighten the mood. Then we might have woken together the next morning and carried on as before.

Carried on until the next time, I thought, as my anger outgrew my compassion. I walked back to the cave, cutting a path through the trees, and left him to his musings.

And there it was.

I froze in my tracks at the sight of it, a mixture of pain, betrayal, sadness, fear, anger...

I returned to the cave, slumped against its cold wall and sobbed.

Kalypso : 'Tritagonist'

KALYPSO'S THIRTY-EIGHTH EPISODE

The following morning, I snuck up from behind him as he ate breakfast. I was exhausted from lack of sleep and the skin about my eyes and cheeks stung from a night of crying. I had woken with a determination. I was frightened but I had to know. I stood by a tree near to his makeshift camp and watched while he prepared and cooked some bird meat. I could not tell if he had sensed me or otherwise; he showed no obvious signs.

"When are you planning on leaving?" I challenged him.

"What?" Odysseus was not startled to hear my voice and he pretended to be absent-minded as he chewed.

"I found the boat, Odysseus. Last night. I just wondered when you were planning your escape?"

"What boat?"

"The one you have hidden in the trees."

He looked up at me with dark eyes and I felt my pulses vibrate with a terrifying energy. *I must keep my calm, I must stay in control,* I thought. I wanted to run away; I wanted to grab hold of him; I wanted to kiss him and beat him, and neither one more than the other. "You know, you'll never get it to sail from this side of the island. The waves are too unpredictable."

He smashed his food plate to the floor. My heart jumped and body froze at the sound. His nostrils were flaring and I felt the air around us hit my skin so suddenly, like an escape route, like a hand trying to pull me away from danger. But I stood firm.

"This is what you do with your days now, Kalypso?" he growled. "You insult me, then follow me around and spy on me? You were the one who told me to go!" I tried to say no, I formed the shape with my mouth, but the sound would not escape. I have reflected that perhaps a lie cannot escape against so fierce an anger.

But I had not been spying. Or at least, that's what I told myself.

I was concerned for him...

It was an accident...

I had not meant to find it...

And what if I hadn't? Was he really planning to just leave? Not to say goodbye? This man who once needed me and loved me, whom I nursed back to health and cared for, would set sail without a further thought for me? I squeezed back the bitter tears.

"So when?" I demanded as he stamped out the small fire, kicking the ash about, mixing it into the sand.

"It is a fishing boat. Don't worry," he span and looked sharply at me, "you have me well and truly trapped here."

"You already have a fishing boat - a perfectly good fishing boat tied up by the cave!"

"This is better," he mumbled, picking up the two pieces of his broken dinner plate. He turned them over in his hands a few times. I shuddered at how much he made them look like weapons. My feet were too rooted to the ground to move away.

"Too much better," I agreed. He grimaced angrily at my accusation. "What is this all about?" I pleaded.

"This is what you do, Kalypso," he snapped with frustration. "All this time... How many years have I been here? I don't even know! You've kept me here... All this time I can't say how I really feel because I'm scared."

"Of what?"

"Of you! Of hurting you... I love my wife, Kalypso. I love my wife and my child. They are my world... And that is why I can't say what you want me to."

"Fine. You just keep reminding yourself of that every day and eventually it might come true," I dismissed him sarcastically.

"How dare you?" he snapped and I winced at the coldness in his voice. "How dare you suggest that I'm lying about my feelings for my wife, my child?"

"How do you expect me to think otherwise?" I countered, trying to hold back any guilty unease he was making me feel. "All this time you've stayed here, all the time it took for you to even admit their existence..."

"You didn't want me to talk about these things!"

"When did I ever say that? When did I ever stop you from talking about anything you wanted?"

"I see how you react when I mention her name; I see what it does to you! And all those objects you found from my ship? At least the ones you told me about. The ones you hid away in your dark little cave..."

"What? This again? I thought we had been through this? Can you hear yourself? I thought we'd settled this?" I shouted, genuinely baffled. "You talked of how disappointed you were when your men questioned your own greedy intentions - and you had more need of possessions than I ever will! Yet still you don't trust me, still you accuse me!"

"I learnt the perils of hiding the truth from those I needed to trust me," he argued angrily. "You should have told me about your 'collection' from the start."

"Why should I? I told you my reasons for keeping it secret and I honestly believed my own integrity in the matter. Much like you did, I am sure, when caught out by your men."

"No, Kalypso. They thought I was hiding well-earned treasures from them and not wanting to share out the wealth. You did not want me to see those objects, and not from greed. I see now, I was wrong to imply that. You simply wish to add me to your collection, Kalypso. You want to keep me from any memories of my past, anything that might remind me of my desire to return home-"

"Your desire to return home?" I scoffed. "The desire that's so strong that you still returned to me every day, and only now do I see the first attempt to change that!" I spoke harshly and yet, on the inside, as I told him this obvious truth, I panicked at the reality of my words. "I don't know how long you've been here - I don't know how long *I've* been here! And for you to dare to talk about trust and openness with me, when all the while you were hiding your escape boat in the bushes and just waiting for me to give you an excuse to leave in anger, to justify abandoning me... Which I won't do!"

"You won't keep me here forever," he snarled, still focusing on the two pieces of pottery.

"I know," I yelled, and my voice broke with a sadness I suddenly couldn't control.

His face changed. I saw him try to look my way. His shoulders slumped with remorse. He tried to fit the two pieces of plate together and for a moment the crack between them disappeared. I saw him shake and felt every part of me reach out to comfort him. My eyes misted over with tears and through the blur I saw him walk away, disappear into his solitude again.

It took sometime before we calmed down from this argument.

Longer still because we both knew we were wrong - we were hypocrites - and neither of us wished to admit it. I realised then how similar we were in pride and temperament and could not help but soften at this knowledge. All those things I had thought disagreeable in myself I loved so much when I saw them reflected back to me. It was only pride that continued to keep us apart.

As I pulled in my tattered old fishing net late one afternoon I saw him walk toward me along the shoreline, allowing the rising tide to lap at his bare feet. I wish I could describe that sight and my feelings, but no words could ever do it justice. There are no words for the way the heart both soars with joy and lurches with fear at the return of a loved one.

What was he coming to tell me?

My heart beat a rapid rhythm, but I continued my work, keeping a sideward glance towards his approach. He stopped a few feet away. The dying sun made him glow like a new statue, and I knew I loved and feared him more than any deity in existence. He alone would decide my fate now. His eyes did not look menacing, but still I trembled.

"Would you like some help?" he asked, without moving. I shook my head and finished hauling in the day's small catch. I thought he might again lecture me on all the ways he had taught me to improve this. Instead he suddenly fell to his knees before me and clasped me around the legs.

"Kalypso, I have wronged you. I beg you to forgive me," he wept into my dress. My hands were filled with netting and fish. I was unable to move as he had both my legs clasped together. I looked down on him quizzically.

"Please let me go," I said as gently but firmly as I could. Slowly he moved his hands away and slumped to the side, never once catching my eye.

I thought about walking back to the cave, starting supper, composing another song before settling down beside the fire and resting until morning. I thought how perfectly simple that all sounded. Would he be there, or would I be alone? My heart still stirred for him. But something felt very different now. I put down my catch and slumped on the sand next to him.

"You were right," I admitted sulkily, "I do want to keep you here. But I never meant for you to stay against your will, you must believe me! You just didn't leave, so I thought… If I did or said anything to make you feel trapped, I am sorry. I can only excuse myself by telling you I did so because… I fell in love with you. I didn't mean to. I wish I hadn't… I am sure to you that sounds quite foolish."

"It doesn't," he replied softly.

"How have you wronged me?" I asked, remembering his previous plea.

"I have never shown you the love you deserved."

"You never felt it-"

"I wish that were true. If I had only met you at another time…

But I have obligations. I can't ignore those."

"You've ignored them *this* long."

"I did want to believe that... maybe I could let go. I loved you since the first day, Kalypso. You are beautiful, wise, heroic... You make me laugh. You inspire me. I have felt a childish freedom in your presence and all of these things have been wondrous to me. But-"

"You still love your wife."

"I cannot change that," he sighed.

"More than me?"

"It's different. My days here are filled with you, dear Kalypso. I wake up beside you, smell your hair, your skin. You move and I cannot help noticing every rustle of your clothes, every wisp of your curls. You talk and laugh and I forget that there was ever any bad in this world, or that I was ever part of it. You fill my senses completely. Then the wrenching guilt attacks me over what it is I've forgotten. You can't know how terrible that feels. How could I forget such an immense responsibility?

"Penelope is the mother of my child. I long to see my son again. I want him to know his father is a good man. I want him to learn by my example and not from my shame. I don't expect you to understand that."

"Good," I said miserably, and immediately regretted it. I did not mean to be unfeeling; I wanted to understand. "We could have had sons?"

"You would make a wonderful mother."

"Just not to *your* children?"

"Why don't we leave here together?" He brightened. "I'll take you to Ithaka where men will fight over you..."

"Take me to Ithaka as what? Your mistress? A friend? The spoils of war? A slave, perhaps? So I can watch you play happy families, far away from *my* home, my freedom *here*? And I suppose you will not care then that other men will try and make me their wife?"

"I can't deny that I will feel some jealousy. But I do want you to be happy."

"I want you to be happy, too."

"I know," he said. "In some ways, I think ours is the truest love I have ever known, despite all the pain we've caused each other."

"But how can anyone ever be happy, living a lie? You may have found a way to convince yourself it's possible, but it's not for me."

"Please, Kalypso! You must believe me, I am not living a lie-"

"You have trapped yourself in a prison you made," I ignored him. "You live only to make money to feed and clothe your family and household. Everything you own goes to them. You wake when you have to, sleep where you're told, make friends and enemies as dictated to you by need and greed. You make war because you can no longer hunt; you farm; everything is provided for you by your slaves and yet still you have no time for yourself because that time is always demanded of by others. Until you came here, you thought of yourself as a king, a soldier, and a husband. A father. On this island you have had the chance to become who you really are."

"Then that must be who I really am. A king, soldier, husband and father. I know you want to believe I am different here, but I cannot deny all those things within me. I have tried, Kalypso. All day I let myself be distracted by this beautiful island, and by you, dear heart. But I close my eyes for sleep and I cannot ignore those other things. Sometimes I wish for your sake I could... But I have to go home."

A chilled breeze blew across us as he spoke. The tip of the sun was about to disappear and stars were getting ready to shine. We neither moved nor spoke. Then one solitary tear fell from my eye and splashed on to the sand and, as if a tidal wave were about to break above us, he grabbed hold of me tightly and we cried together, sobbing into each other's hair, cheeks, necks...

That night he retuned to the cave and held me closer than ever before.

Kalypso : 'Tritagonist'

KALYPSO'S THIRTY-NINTH EPISODE

It was as you might expect. I tried to stay out of the physical preparations for his departure, but could not stop myself from helping in my own small way. I hated what he was doing, but I did want him to be happy. I secretly hoped and prayed to the gods that he might change his mind, or that our parting would only be temporary. That he would return home to find his wife had remarried a man she loved and whom Odysseus would have to respect as her new husband; his son would be fine and healthy - possibly married himself, or at least well enough for Odysseus to feel confident about leaving him behind. Then he would return to me and we would be free to love for the rest of our lives and then through death...

I started to weave a shawl for him. I wanted him to have something to remember me by. A shawl seemed personal and practical. He would be warm overnight and dry in bad weather while sailing in that little vessel of his. I collected together those finds he had recognised from his original ship. I was nervous about handing these over as I did not know what reaction they would receive after so long and the foolish arguments we had shared. But when I laid them out for him he smiled. A sad smile, but not an angry one.

"Keep them for me," was his response. "I will know where they are when I need them returned."

It is amazing how easily women sacrifice their true feelings at times like this, letting the man do whatever he pleases, encouraging him in his endeavours, all the while falling apart on the inside. I only had one fear left now.

"What will you tell them about me when you get there?" I asked. He seemed to understand my meaning and smiled apologetically.

"I wish, dear heart, I could tell the whole world about you. How beautiful you are, Kalypso, and how much you have made me feel. If I could stand atop great Mount Neritos and proclaim it, I would. If I could live my life again, perhaps, my fair goddess...

"But it cannot be so. In truth, I will say as little about you as I can; not because I do not want the world to know, but because I cannot tell them. I do not wish to cause any further pain...

"I fear, the more I speak about you, the harder it will be for me to conceal the full story and my true feelings. So you must forgive me if, by some chance, you ever hear too short an account of our love, and know that it in no way reflects how I feel and how much I could say."

"I understand," I reassured him. "Too much might send them all here looking for the 'brilliant goddess' you describe, which I could never live up to, and then where would my sanctuary be?"

"I do love you, Kalypso. I will probably always love you. I hate having to leave," he said, taking my face in his hands.

"Then don't," I suggested coolly as he tenderly kissed my forehead. He looked sombrely at our feet and sighed gently. Then he pulled me close to him and whispered into the air about us.

"In some ways, I never will."

The night before he left, we sat together, drinking beneath the stars as we had done so many times. I was terrified, trying to retain everything that happened, never taking my eyes from Odysseus, wanting to remember every moment, every word, but constantly being dragged towards the fear of tomorrow. Odysseus tried to make merry. We were to stay up all night, confessing all those things we had never managed to before.

"Do you believe in omens?" he had asked.

"Of course," I said, hoping he'd tell me of all those dreams he'd had of me. But instead he told me he saw his wife, blaming herself for his absence, his child waking fearfully from nightmares. I knew then he would never forgive me for hurting them. There was nothing more I could say or do. No easy answer, no compromise had arrived from the gods, from the sea... From inside me. He could never rest until he knew his family were safe. He would never let *me* rest.

"Why did you never want to make love to me?" I asked with sad curiosity. Such a forward question, I knew, and I thought back to the young girl, so afraid of asking for his affection, being overly forward in the past. I felt suddenly old in the face of this new, reckless courage and impending desertion. His expression, however, echoed that of his past self, the first time I had asked. Still an obscure mix of repentance and pain.

"In the beginning, I couldn't. I mean I physically couldn't." He paused with a little embarrassment. "I was exhausted and emotionally broken. I had no idea who or what you were. I thought of all the mistakes I had made, the wrongs I'd done to others. I saw your kind and gentle face and, once I felt I could trust you, I wanted to hold you so tightly. Make you as happy as I could. You saved my life and let me stay here with you. And I couldn't imagine how lonely you must have been." I shuddered slightly at this. I had never considered myself as lonely, but now he said the words I felt them, unexpectedly, eating inside me, reminding me... What would this feel like tomorrow...?

"But nothing happened," he continued. "And I thought of my wife. Of how many betrayals I had already committed, in so many ways. I was not the man she knew me to be any more; not the man she had thought I was when we married. I began to wonder what man that was. I owed her some kind of honesty... And I was so tired. I didn't want to add another mistake, another betrayal to the list.

"Then I began to realise your affection for me had grown, and I

Kalypso : 'Tritagonist'

couldn't escape feeling the same way. I don't know how or why; I had never expected such a thing to occur. Love had always seemed like a docile, simple feeling. It grew between two people as they grew together. It took years to nurture. I had heard the stories of people and gods being brought to their knees by passion, protecting their loves even to their own death. I heard of it, but never expected those intense feelings. They lay in fiction and other people's remembrances. I am a logical man, Kalypso. I was a happy enough man without that kind of all-encompassing, often tragic love.

"When I saw you, I was struck with something I could not explain, but instantly knew. You make me feel... Whole. I should not say these things to you, I know. It is wrong to say it all now. But I want you to know this is how I feel. You are loved. And I fear that love. It was agony, Kalypso. But how could I make love to you when I knew, one day, I would have to return to my family and leave you behind?

"And there was that other fear, gnawing at me always, that if I made love to you... I would not be *able* to leave. My marriage would be over, my child abandoned. If I gave into that last little piece..." Odysseus rested his forehead in his hands and took a few deep breaths, closing his eyes to the world, as if nothing he had yet suffered had been more exhausting to him than this confession. I could only watch helplessly as he struggled inside himself.

"I never knew I'd be here so long," he concluded. "Maybe if I had known... but once I had made the decision - what I thought to be the right decision at the time - not to, for both our sakes... For everyone's sake... Any day could have been my last..." I rubbed his arm comfortingly and we fell into an embrace.

"I'm sorry," I whispered as I felt my eyes grow heavy with tears striving for freedom.

"No," he soothed, "you've nothing to be sorry for. I just wish... that's all..."

When the morning finally came, I watched him take the boat out and check how watertight it was. I busied myself, packing a small box of food and drink. He said nothing on my actions, though he noticed them. I laid the shawl I had made him on top of the provisions and he loaded his small cargo.

At first we said nothing to each other. I sat and watched, holding on to my knees for comfort, the wind seeming to blow more ferociously than usual. He took this as a good omen. Finally, he knelt beside me, took my cheeks in both hands and kissed me on the lips, over and over, murmuring to me how I should remember these kisses. Kisses to last a lifetime, he insisted. Then I could not hold back the tears again - it was almost cruelty.

"I promise I won't forget you for as long as I live," he whispered.

"I'll be right here," I mumbled between sobs. "I'll wait for you right here. When you are ready, come and find me. You will always be able to. I will always be here waiting. Until then, say nothing more to me."

He looked at me and I sensed he implored me to let him speak one last time, but I could not. Just to hear his voice would destroy my resolve. I needed to hear him say only that he loved me and would stay with me for all eternity. That he would never try and leave me again. That he could trust his past to take care of itself and would live instead, happily, in our future. But those were words he would never say, and words I could never in good conscience ask of him. "You have my heart," I concluded. "I will be better off without it." I felt the tears try to escape and looked away. I knew, if I looked back, the same would be mirrored in his eyes. "Take good care of your own first," I mustered as he walked to his boat. After a few moments, he was riding the waves, and slowly he began to slip away.

I walked away. I walked to the cliff edge. I sat and I waited. I hoped above all hopes, even now, that he would realise he wanted me more. I had dreaded the sight of that boat on the water. Yet I watched it, tears streaming from my eyes, blinding my view countless times, I watched it sail away. It moved so slowly, I thought it would never disappear from my view. I hoped it would never go. I knew it had to. And when it was no longer a distant speck on the horizon, the world stopped once more.

I sat there long after he had faded. The tide didn't bring him back. He didn't regret his decision. At first I believed I could swim after him, pull him back maybe, or join him on his journey. But still I sat on the grass, unable to move, just watching. Finally the noise of the waves awoke my conscience. And then it all became like a dream. A wonderful, tortuous dream. I was here, on my island, as I had always been. Nothing had changed except me.

KALYPSO'S FORTIETH EPISODE

The first thing I noticed was the stillness. The peace.

I heard a bird squawking above me, my ears witness to the beat of its wings against the quiet air. Nothing there, nothing visible, yet something was making that sound. So it was with my heart.

I felt sad. Yet calm. Determined again. My mind emptied. I laid down on the grass. For a long time I did not move. Eventually I slept, and when I awoke, all was as still as I have told you. Every noise could be heard clearly: the leaves and grass moving against an invisible breeze, that bird's wings beating against nothing. Nothing has a sound, I thought. Loneliness is not so quiet as I had imagined. The vacuous space within my breast felt heavy. I stood up. I began to make plans for the day…

KALYPSO : MONODY

So near to the end of my tale, I should again point out one fundamental and oft forgotten point: He came to me.

There was no coercing by me, no craft involved. He landed on my shores; his appearance there a complete surprise. As a drowning man, he needed my help and I saved him, because I could. Because only I, the mistress, knew how. Only I could see how much he needed, when not even he was aware of it. I was the mirror, and for a moment he saw himself in someone else.

For some time after he left I found myself walking. In angry meditation. First one direction, then back over my footsteps, across from one side to the other. I told myself not to think about it, but it stole into every footstep until I would shout at the sky with anger, kick at the sand, the lazy tree roots; scream at the gods for favouring one life over another. But to no avail on all counts. I would not let myself cry. I would not. I must not. He had said he loved me. That he would always love me. He lied.

Did he lie?

All that time, energy, affection - wasted. This is the lot of the mistress. To give everything to that man in need, and then have him, once repaired to the man he wants to be, walk away and return to his wife. As if *she* can maintain this side of him as well as I! As if she even knows him now.

To make me the bad person for being angry at his decision; for being rightly angry! Have I been so bad as to deserve this? Without so much as a consultation, but for him to go behind my back and have the gods demand his release? He could not even face me himself with this request - this brave warrior of Troy! I walked every inch of my pain through the paths and across the beaches, all the while hoping… maybe… when I turn this corner, he could be there? He could have changed his mind? Maybe he will repair *me* this time?

This then is the lot of the mistress. To be abandoned for faithful Penelope. Loving, understanding Penelope. The woman who could not know him as well in her entire lifetime as I have in seven years. All those secrets, dreams and wishes… All those dark confessions.

No, Odysseus sails away and doesn't look back. The man who should have been *my* love leaves me, a lone figure in the sands, convinced he does the right thing because he does the right thing by his imprisoned conscience. Giving no thought to *my* needs, *my* demise.

Returning to that small circle he drew about his marriage so many years ago, long since washed away by the rain.

These are thoughts separated from him; and now so am I with each crashing wave. Because he could not love me the way I needed him to.

I simply saved him from drowning. Nothing more.

Kalypso : 'Tritagonist'

KALYPSO : EXODUS

The Chorus have faded into the darkness and left me here.

Alone.

For the last time I feel. Sat on this stone stage in the role I have created for myself. Alone in the cold comfort of my cave. I can hear the waves pounding the shore outside. They sound like an audience's applause. I have not given into Hades – I have lived every day of my life, borne every regret and pain.

Waited...

Time and age change the way we view our lives and those people with whom we shared our moments. I have reflected so much these past few days, I have barely lived in the present. Damon took advantage of me. He abused my adolescent trust. But I cannot deny that I chose to let him do those things. After all, he gave me the chance to walk away... Virginity is just a rite of passage, and I can't say I wasn't glad to be done with the experience. If it had not been Damon, doubtless it would have been Menelaus who forced himself upon me, which could have been better, might have been worse. I sometimes wonder how Helen fared with such a ritual. Odysseus led me to believe that there was more than one rumour she was anything but a virgin on her marriage bed. For any other woman that might have been a scandal, but not, it seems for beautiful Helen the whore...

And if I hadn't chosen Damon, might I too have fallen for Paris? I had no notion of how he or Menelaus looked, but poor Menelaus did always come off the worse in my imaginings.

Would my elopement have driven so many men to war? There would have been no Oath of Tyndareus, so I imagined Odysseus would have stayed at home, with his perfect wife and perfect family. The horse would never have been built, and Troy would probably have survived such a comparatively small-scale attack, if an attack was ever made. Odysseus would never have floated onto my island and no one would ever have known of my continued existence...

Sometimes I imagine being married to Menelaus, and entertaining with him. In those daydreams it would not be Paris that caught my eye, but a visiting Odysseus. Would he have brought his family with him, or come alone? Would I have seemed quite so beautiful to him if compared there to his wife? Would we still have fallen in love if he had seen me as another man's wife in a crowded household...? Would we ever have met if I had chosen differently...?

Klotho is far more creative than we often give her credit.

Kalypso : 'Tritagonist'

They say I died of a broken heart, alone, on my "depressing" island of Ogygia. If only it were possible to die of such a tender sorrow. But hearts keep on beating long after they are broken. No, in truth, I have lived plenty more years since Odysseus left me, as you now see. I watched the remains and spoils of a good deal more ships float across this coastline, but no one chose to wash upon my shores again. I did wait for Odysseus to return. I suppose, in all that time, there were moments when I felt sorry for his wife. She waited twenty years the same way.

So, Odysseus didn't tarry long with his wife, you say. No sooner had he returned than he longed to sail away again on some new adventure. You see how he loved his women! For all the pain he put me through to return to his wife, he wasted no time in leaving her again. We women are merely useful pauses in his story. Strange I should find myself empathising with the woman I once thought of as my greatest foe.

Penelope was entirely too indulged.

Though I cannot blame her. For by history and Odysseus was she so, while the mistress is left to the bards and the gossips...

Sing to me of the woman, Muse, the woman who loved that hero of Troy, who set him free and waits a thousand lives for his return...

GLOSSARY

Amphora - A large, two-handled jar, narrow at the neck, used for storing wine or oil.

Chitara/Kithara - A five-stringed harp-like musical instrument, bigger in size than a lyre.

Clepsydra - A water clock.

Deuteragonist - The second actor on stage; the second most important character in a story.

Echo and Narcissus - Echo was a nymph who was cursed to speak only the repeated last words of another. She fell in love with Narcissus, who rejected her (and all other offers of love). He was cursed to fall in love with his own reflection.

Epilenios - A dance celebrating the gathering of grapes, often performed at agricultural festivals.

Hades - In Ancient Greece, the underworld and domain of the dead.

Hetaerae - High-class concubines.

Klotho / Fates - One of the three Fates (or Moirae), she spins the thread of a life on her spindle. The other two Fates - Lachesis and Atropos - measure out the thread and cut it, respectively.

KOMMOS - A theatrical conversation between actor and chorus.

Lyre - A stringed musical instrument, similar to a small harp.

MONODY - A solo song, usually a lament.

Palladium - a statue or image on which the entire safety of a city depends, such as that mentioned of the goddess Athena.

Pandouris - Also known as a tri-chord, it is similar to a guitar, having frets but only three strings.

PARABASIS - A pause in the action (usually in the middle of a play, during which the chorus leader would speak to the audience).

Pederasty [pederastic] - Relationships between two men, one of whom is an elder and one an adolescent. Some, but not all, are of a sexual nature.

Skyphos - a two-handled wine cup.

Symposium - a drinking party.

Tritagonist - The third actor on stage in an Ancient Greek theatre; the third person in a story.

ACKNOWLEDGEMENTS

With thanks for their inspiration and input: Tim Elsenburg (and for additional editing); Kunu Gordon; Pete Basham; Trevor Lawn; Liam Elliott; Daniel Cundy (for introducing me to Joseph Campbell and a whole new world of personal mythology); the Open University (in particular, the course: *A295 Homer - Poetry and Society*, and its companion and recommended readings, including the Richmond Lattimore translation of *The Odyssey*); and my family.

OTHER TITLES BY THIS AUTHOR

Death by Chocolate (paperback, M Publications 2008)
ISBN-13: 978-0955978807 Available from **Lulu.com** and **Amazon**
Morana is an Angel of Death, Alter a Demon of Death. Sharing a flat (for convenience), while working on opposite sides of the same business, they are suddenly forced to work together to solve the ultimate question: Why have they both been sent to collect the soul of Wilfred Bailey Jr - famous actor, womaniser and socialite - who's still very much alive...?

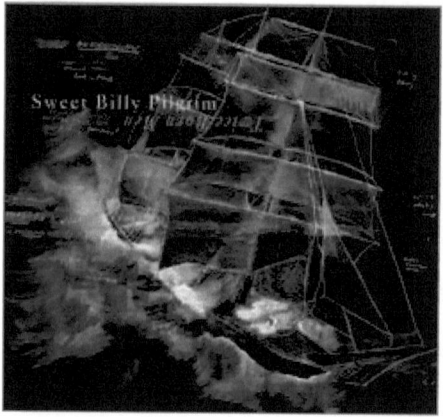

'Are there no heroes or gods anymore...?'

SWEET BILLY PILGRIM: Twice Born Men (CD)

2009, Samadhisound

includes the beautiful and inspired song *Kalypso*

www.sweetbillypilgrim.com

www.ingramcontent.com/pod-product-compliance
Ingram Content Group UK Ltd.
Pitfield, Milton Keynes, MK11 3LW, UK
UKHW041258180426
11947UKWH00008B/553